APOCALYPSE
NEXT
TUESDAY

APOCALYPSE
NEXT
TUESDAY

DAVID SAFIER

Translated

by Hilary Parnfors

nova

Published by Hesperus Nova
Hesperus Press Limited
28 Mortimer Street, London W1W 7RD
www.hesperuspress.com

Originally published under the title
JESUS LIEBT MICH by David Safier
Copyright © 2008 by Rowohlt Verlag GmbH,
Reinbek bei Hamburg

English translation © Hilary Parnfors, 2014

This edition first published by Hesperus Press Limited, 2014

The translation of this work was supported by a
grant from the Goethe-Institut which is funded by the
German Ministry of Foreign Affairs.

Typeset by Madeline Meckiffe
Printed in Denmark by Nørhaven, Viborg

ISBN 978-1-84391-508-9

For Marion, Ben and Daniel
… I love you

CHAPTER ONE

There's no way that Jesus can have looked like that, I thought to myself as I sat in the parish office staring at the painting of the Last Supper. He was a Levantine Jew, wasn't he? So why did he look like a Bee Gee in most of the pictures?

Before I could get any further in my thoughts, the Reverend Gabriel stepped into the room. He was an elderly gentleman with a beard, piercing eyes and deep frown lines. But then most people would probably get wrinkles like that after more than thirty years of shepherding.

Without any form of greeting, he asked me: 'Do you love him, Marie?'

'Yes... erm... of course I love Jesus... great guy...' I replied.

'I mean the man whom you want to marry in my church.'

'Oh.'

The Reverend Gabriel always asked very indiscreet questions. Most people who lived in our little town of Malente tended to think that it was because he had a genuine interest in his congregation. I, on the other hand, thought that he was just incredibly nosy.

'Yes.' I replied. 'Of course I love him.'

My Sven was indeed a very lovable man. A gentle man. A man who made me feel safe. He was a man who did not mind in the slightest that he was with a woman whose BMI called for plaintive prayers. And most important of all, I could be sure that Sven would not cheat on me with an air hostess – unlike my ex Marc, who I can only hope will end up burning in hell under the watchful eye of particularly creative demons.

'Sit down, Marie,' Gabriel said, pulling an armchair to his desk. I sunk down into the dark leather, as he sat down opposite me, at his desk. I had to look up at him and realised immediately that this was the angle he was aiming for.

'So, you want to get married in church?' Gabriel asked.

'No, in a chicken run,' is what would have loved to have answered. Instead I did my best to sound pleasant. 'Yes, that's what I wanted to talk to you about.'

'I just have one question for you, Marie.'

'And what would that be?'

'Why do you want to get married in church?'

The real answer was that there is nothing more unromantic than a wedding at a registry office. And because I had dreamt of a big white wedding as a child and still did, even though I knew in my head that it was seriously naff. But you don't pay any attention to your head when you're getting married, do you?

Yet to admit this would not have been particularly helpful to my cause. So I smiled as sweetly as I could and stammered: 'I… I have a great need to… in the church… in front of God…'

He interrupted me abruptly. 'Marie: I have basically never ever seen you at any of our services.'

'I… I… I have a very busy job.'

'You're supposed to rest on the seventh day.'

I did rest on the seventh day. And on the sixth day. Sometimes I even pulled a sickie, to rest on one of the first five days too. But I doubt that was what Gabriel meant.

'You were already doubting God during confirmation class twenty years ago,' he quipped.

That man certainly had quite a memory. How could he remember that? I was thirteen then and I was going out with a very cool guy called Kevin. It felt like I was in heaven in his arms, and he was the first person I ever snogged. Unfortunately that's not all he wanted to do: he was also very eager to put his hands under my jumper. I didn't let him as I felt there was plenty of time for that sort of thing. He didn't share my view, and that's why he made sure to get his hands under someone else's jumper at confirmation camp, right in front of my eyes. The world, as I knew it, ended at that very moment.

And it came as no consolation that he had felt those breasts with the same sensitivity that bakers demonstrate when kneading dough. Nor was my sister Kata, who's two years older than me, able to cheer me up, even though she said nice things like 'He didn't deserve you', 'He's a stupid fool' or 'He should be shot'.

So I ran to Gabriel and, with tears in my eyes, I asked him: 'How can there be a God if there are awful things like heartache?

'And do you remember what I answered?' asked Gabriel.

'God allows heartache, because he gave people free will,' I droned.

I also remember thinking at the time that it would have been good if God had denied Kevin this power of free will.

'I also have a free will,' Gabriel explained. 'I am retiring soon and no longer need to believe everyone whose godliness I do not feel is genuine. Wait for my successor. He'll be here in six months.'

'But we want to get married now!'

'And that's my problem, because…?' he asked provocatively.

I didn't say anything, just wondered whether it was ever OK to hit a vicar.

'I don't like my church being used as an events venue,' Gabriel explained, looking at me with his piercing eyes. I was almost beginning to feel bad. My anger gave way to a diffuse sense of guilt.

'There is another protestant church in this town, you know,' he said.

'But… I don't want to get married in that one.'

'And why not?'

'Because… because…' I didn't know whether I should say why. But it actually didn't make any difference, because Gabriel clearly didn't have a very good impression of me anyway. So I sheepishly told him. 'Because my parents got married in that church.'

Amazingly, Gabriel now became more gentle. 'You're in your mid-thirties. Shouldn't you be over your parents' divorce by now?'

'Of course I am… it would be ridiculous if I wasn't,' I replied. I had actually had a couple of hours of therapy, until it got too expensive. Parents really should be forced to open a savings account as soon as their children are born so that they can pay for psychologists later on.

'But you're still afraid that it might be unlucky to get married in the same church as your parents?' Gabriel asked.

After a moment's hesitation I nodded. 'Well, I'm superstitious.'

He gave me a surprisingly sympathetic look. It seemed that his Christian love was kicking in.

'All right then,' he said. 'You can get married here.'

I could hardly believe my ears. 'You… you're an angel, Rev!'

'I know,' he replied, smiling in a strangely melancholy way.

When Gabriel realised that I'd seen the expression on his face, he ordered me to leave right away. 'Quick, before I change my mind.'

Full of relief, I jumped up and hurried towards the door. Another painting caught my eye. This one was a depiction of the Resurrection of Christ. And I thought to myself that it really did look like Jesus might start singing *Stayin' Alive*.

CHAPTER TWO

'I told you the Reverend was a nice man,' said Sven, as he sat next to me on the sofa, massaging my feet in our cute little rooftop apartment. Unlike all other men, he actually liked doing it, which I felt could only be explained by a rare genetic defect. My ex-boyfriends had basically only ever massaged me for about ten minutes and then demanded sex afterwards as a thank you for their great efforts. This was particularly true of Marc, the air hostess-lover.

Before I met Sven in my mid-thirties, I was single and my sex life was non-existent. Every time I saw women with babies, I realised that my biological clock was ticking. And every time those completely exhausted mothers smiled at me pityingly, telling me that having children was the only way to find peace, my exceedingly fragile self-confidence took a hit. In such moments I could only calm myself down with a song that I had specifically composed for these occasions: 'I don't have no stretch marks, Doo-da, Doo-da! I don't have no stretch marks, Oh, de doo-da day, hey!'

I was already trying to come to terms with the fact that I would probably end up like one of those women whose decayed corpse is found by chance in her one-bedroom apartment by a house clearance company seven months after her death. And then I met Sven.

I had sung my stretch mark song a little too loudly at a café in Malente whilst walking past an exceedingly annoying new yummy mummy. This happy, fulfilled mother then showed me just how at peace with herself she was by throwing a cup of coffee in my face. I tripped, fell and hit my head on the edge of a table. With a gash across my forehead, I took a taxi straight to the hospital and was greeted by Sven. He was working there as a nurse. I can't say that he was particularly attractive – that's why we were very well-suited. When I cried as the wound was stitched, he gave me his handkerchief. When I moaned about the stains on my shirt, he comforted me. And when I thanked him for everything, he invited me out for a pizza. Fifteen pizzas later, I moved in and was overjoyed never to have to see my one-bedroom apartment ever again.

Another eighty-four dinners later, Sven proposed in the most perfect way imaginable – down on one knee, with a wonderful ring that must have cost him at least a month's wages. And he even got the kids' football team he trained in his spare time to make a giant heart out of roses and sing 'You Are My Heart's Delight'.

'Will you marry me?' he asked.

For a moment I thought, 'If I say no now, those kids will be traumatised for life.'

Then I answered, deeply moved. 'Of course!'

Sven was rubbing my feet when my eyes were drawn to the *Malente Post*. He had circled one of the property ads.

'You've… circled something there?'

'There's a new development area that's in our price range.'

'And why would we want to look at that?' I asked in an alarmed tone.

'Well, it wouldn't be bad with something bigger if we want to have children.'

Children? Had he just said 'children'? During my single days, I had admittedly gazed with envy at mothers, but since getting together with Sven I felt there was still some time before I became a zombie with dark circles under my eyes telling everyone how fulfilled I now was.

'I… think we should enjoy our life as a couple a bit longer,' I said.

'I am thirty-nine and you are thirty-four. With every year that we wait, the chance of us having difficulty conceiving increases,' Sven declared.

'You have a lovely way of trying to convince a woman to have a child,' I said, trying to smile.

'Sorry.' Sven was always quick to say sorry.

'It's all right.'

'But… you do want kids, don't you?' he asked.

I didn't know what to say. Did I really want to have children? My pause was turning into silence.

'Don't you Marie?'

As I couldn't bear to watch this man suffer, I joked: 'Of course, fifteen of them.'

'A football team with subs,' he smiled happily. Then he kissed my neck. That was his preferred way of initiating sex. But it took rather longer than usual to get me in the mood this time.

CHAPTER THREE

'*Sewage plant turns thirty.*'

I typed the headline of my new cover story without an ounce of enthusiasm. When I left journalism school, I had still had high hopes of getting a job at a magazine like *Der Spiegel*, but I would probably have needed better grades for that. So for my first job, I ended up in Munich at *Anna*, the magazine for the modern woman with an attention span of no more than half a page. It was not my dream job, but on good days I almost felt like Carrie in *Sex and the City*. All I needed was a five-figure budget for designer clothes and some liposuction.

I might have stayed at *Anna* forever. But sadly Marc was made editor-in-chief. Sadly he was über-charming. Sadly we became a couple. Sadly he cheated on me with that skinny air hostess, and sadly I didn't take it quite as brilliantly as I should have. I tried to run him over.

Well, not properly.

But he did have to jump out of the way a little bit.

After this performance I resigned. Between my sub-optimal CV and the dried-up journalism market the only job I could find was at the *Malente Post*. And that's only because my father knew the publisher. Returning to my hometown at the age of thirty-one was like running around with a sign that said: 'Hello. My life is a complete and utter failure.'

The only advantage of working at such a dull place was that I had plenty of time to think about the table plan for the wedding, which people say is a science unto itself. I was particularly concerned about where to position my divorced parents. Just as I was racking my brains about what to do, my father came waltzing into the office and made the whole thing even more complicated. Migraine-inducingly complicated.

'I really need to tell you something,' was how he greeted me. I was surprised. He normally looked so pale, but now he almost seemed to be glowing with happiness. He had put on plenty of aftershave and for once the little hair he did have was neatly combed.

'Dad, can't this wait?' I asked. 'I really don't have time. I need to write an article about all the things I never wanted to know about disposal of human excrement.'

'I have a girlfriend,' he blurted out.

'Well… that's… that's wonderful news!' I stammered, forgetting all about the excrement.

Dad had a girlfriend. That certainly was a surprise. I tried to imagine who this woman might be. Perhaps an elderly lady from the church choir? Or a patient from his urology clinic (although I didn't actually want to envisage their first encounter in too much detail).

'Her name is Svetlana,' Dad beamed.

'Svetlana?' I repeated, and tried to clear my mind of all the prejudices I had against Slavic-sounding female names. 'Sounds… nice…'

'She's not only nice. She's great,' he beamed even more.

Oh my God, he was in love! For the first time in more than twenty years. Although I'd always hoped that he would find love, I wasn't quite sure what I was supposed to think about it.

'I'm sure you'll get on really well with Svetlana,' Dad said.

'Oh yeah?'

'You're the same age.'

'*What?*'

'Well, almost.'

'What's that supposed to mean? Is she forty?' I asked.

'No, she's twenty-five.'

'She's what?'

'Twenty-five.'

'*She's what?*'

'Twenty-five.'

'*She's whaaat?*'

'Why do you keep asking that?'

Because my brain was about to go into meltdown at the thought of my father having a twenty-five-year-old girlfriend.

'So, so where exactly is she from then?' I asked, trying to keep my cool.

'Minsk.'

'Russia?'

'Belarus,' he corrected me.

Impatiently, I looked around to see if there were any hidden cameras.

'I know what you're thinking,' Dad said.

'That there must be a hidden camera around here somewhere?'

'OK, I don't know what you're thinking.'

'So what did you think I was thinking,' I asked.

'That Svetlana is only interested in my money, because I met her via an online dating agency…'

'You met here *where*?' I interrupted.

'On www.amore-easterneurope.com.'

'Oh, www.amore-easterneurope.com. Well, that sounds very reputable.'

'You're being sarcastic, aren't you?'

'And you are being naive,' I replied.

'It has the best ratings on www.onlinedatingagency-test. com,' he insisted.

'Well, if www.onlinedatingagency-test.com says so, then

Svetlana must be a highly respectable woman, who is neither interested in your money nor German citizenship,' I quipped.

'You don't even know Svetlana!' Dad was very offended now.

'And you do?'

'I was in Minsk last month…'

'Stop, stop, stop — stop right there!' I jumped up from my chair and sized up to him. 'You told me that you went to Jerusalem with the church choir. You were so looking forward to the Church of the Holy Sepulchre.'

'I lied.'

'You lied to your own daughter?' I couldn't believe it.

'Well, you would have stopped me otherwise.'

'Yes! At gunpoint.'

Dad sighed. 'Svetlana really is a delightful creature.'

'I'm sure she is. '

'But…'

'No buts! You're mad to get involved with a woman like that!'

Dad answered sounding sad yet defiant: 'You just can't be happy for me.'

That hit me. Of course I wanted him to be happy. Since I was twelve, since the day that Mum had left him, I had wanted to see my Dad happy again.

When he stood in front of me back then, white as a sheet, and explained that Mum had moved out, I couldn't believe it. I asked him whether there was any chance at all of her coming back.

For a long time he didn't say anything. In the end, he just shook his head silently. Then he started to cry. It took me a while to realise that my Dad was actually crying. But when he seemed unable to stop, I hugged him. And he cried on my shoulder.

No twelve-year-old should see her father cry like that.

My only thought was: 'Please God, please make everything be all right and make Mum come back to him.' But my prayer was not answered. Perhaps God was busy saving some Bangladeshis from a terrible flood.

Now Dad was finally happy again, after all those years. But instead of being happy for him, all I could feel was fear. A fear of seeing him cry again. This Svetlana would surely break his heart.

'And just so you know, I'm bringing Svetlana to the wedding,' he said emphatically.

Then he left, slamming the door shut behind him, a little bit too theatrically in my opinion. I stared at the door for a while, until I caught sight of the seating plan again. And then my migraine kicked in.

CHAPTER FOUR

Despite what the Reverend Gabriel thought of me, I often prayed to God. And although I did not entirely believe in an Almighty Lord in heaven, I really did hope that he existed. So I prayed during take-offs and landings whenever I was flying with a budget airline. Or just before the lottery numbers were drawn. Or when I wanted the excessively noisy opera tenor in the apartment below us to lose his voice.

Yet most of all I prayed that this Svetlana would not break my father's heart.

My older sister Kata, who looked rather like an unkempt version of Meg Ryan with her wild blonde hair, thought that my prayers were silly. And she told me so. She had arrived in Malente a week before the wedding, and we were on a run around the lake when she said:

'Marie. If there is a God, then please explain the existence of Nazis, wars and Bros?'

'Because he gave people a free will,' I answered, quoting Gabriel.

'And why does he give people a free will if they are going to torture each other with it?'

I pondered for a while. Then I admitted defeat. 'Touché.'

Kata had always been the more clued up one of us. At seventeen, she left school, went to Berlin, came out as a lesbian and started a career as a cartoonist of a daily comic strip in a national newspaper. It was called 'Sisters'. It was about two sisters. It was about us.

Kata was also much fitter than me. She didn't get out of breath at all, whereas I on the other hand, had stopped thinking that the lake was beautiful after only eight hundred metres.

'Shall we stop running?' she suggested.

'I still... need to lose... half a stone before the wedding,' I gasped.

'You'll still weigh 11 stone,' she grinned.

'No one likes skinny smartarses,' I panted.

'Well, I think it's nice for Dad to have sex after twenty years of celibacy.' Kata brought the conversation back to www. amore-easterneurope.com.

Dad had sex?

This was a thought that I would rather have been spared, but much to my horror I now had a very vivid image in my mind.

'I'm sure it makes him happy and…'

Kata didn't get any further. I covered my ears with my hands and began to sing. 'La la la, I don't want to hear that. La la la, I really don't care.'

Kata stopped talking. I uncovered my ears.

'Although men like Dad,' Kata cheerily started telling me, 'who haven't been in a relationship for a long time, probably do visit prostitutes once in a while…'

I covered my ears again and sang as loudly as I could. 'La la la, if you carry on talking, I'll hit you…'

Kata smiled. 'I'm always amazed at how mature you are.'

I was far too out of breath to be able to respond, and collapsed onto a nearby bench under a chestnut tree.

'And I'm always amazed at how fit you are,' Kata added.

I threw a conker at her head.

Kata just grinned. Her pain threshold was far superior to mine. While I moan when I tear a toenail, she didn't even complain when she found out she had a brain tumour about five years ago. Or, as she put it, when she was given the opportunity to find out who her real friends were.

When she was ill, I jumped on a plane to Berlin every weekend to go and visit her in hospital. It was hard to watch my sister suffer like that; she couldn't even sleep properly because of the pain. The tablets did little to ease her suffering. Neither did the infusions. And the chemotherapy turned my strong sister into a skinny, bald creature, who covered her head with a tongue-in-cheek skull-print scarf. It made her look as though she belonged aboard the *Black Pearl* with Jack Sparrow. After six weeks I started wondering why her girlfriend Lisa no longer came to visit.

Kata just said, 'We broke up.'

I was shocked. 'Why?'

'We had different interests,' Kata replied.

'What?' I asked, sounding confused.

A wry smile crossed her face. 'She enjoys nightlife. I am busy puking because of chemo.'

My sister was determined to beat the tumour. When I asked her where she got her tremendous strength from, she answered: 'I don't have a choice. You know I don't believe in life after death.'

But I prayed for Kata – without telling her, of course. That would just have annoyed her.

Now she'd almost done it. If she didn't have any relapses in the next few months, she would still have a long life ahead of her. And I would finally know whether God had answered my prayers. Because that had to be within his remit. A tumour surely had little to do with human free will.

'What are you thinking about so seriously?' Kata asked. I was not in the mood to start talking about the tumour. Kata – understandably – couldn't stand the fact that her illness always made me sadder than it made her. I got up from the bench and started to make my way back home.

'Aren't we going to run any further?' Kata asked.

'I'd rather go on a diet.'

'Why do you want to lose weight at all?' she asked. 'You've always told me that Sven loves you just the way you are.'

'Sven does. I don't,' I answered.

'And are you planning to have children soon?' Kata asked casually.

'There's still plenty of time for that,' I replied.

Kata looked at me like she always did when she was trying to make a point.

'Look! There's a black swan over there,' I tried, not particularly well, to change the subject.

'When you were together with Marc you always wanted to have children,' Kata pointed out, who incidentally never let me change the subject when I wanted to.

'Sven is not like Marc.'

'That's why I'm asking,' Kata said earnestly. 'You loved Marc so much that you announced the names of your two future children after just two weeks! Mareike and…'

'…Maja,' I added quietly. I'd always wanted to have two daughters, who would have a great relationship just like Kata and me.

'So what about Mareike and Maja now?' Kata asked.

'I want to enjoy our time as a couple,' I said. 'Those little ankle-biters will have to wait before they can start annoying me.'

'Does it have anything to do with Sven?' Kata was not letting it go.

'No!'

'The lady doth protest too much, methinks.' Kata grinned, but then stopped quizzing me any further. I wondered whether I had in fact been protesting a bit too much. Maybe I didn't want to have children.

CHAPTER FIVE

Meanwhile…

As Marie and Kata were distancing themselves from the lake, the black swan swam to the shore. From there he waddled over the pebbles to the path, shook his damp feathers and… turned into George Clooney.

Clooney ran his hands through his shiny hair, straightened his elegant designer suit and sat down on the shaded bench, on which the two sisters had recently been taking a breather. He sat there for a while, waiting for something. Or someone. As he sat there, he threw conkers at some of the ducks in the lake. They were knocked out and drowned. But even this little bit of fun did not bring the man any pleasure. He was tired. Very tired. He was suffering from burnout. This damn century!

Before things had been all right. But since, no matter how hard he tried, people were simply much, much better at creating their own hell on earth – and he was Satan!

He had of course come up with quite a few good ideas about how to torture people: neoliberalism, reality TV, Bros (he was particularly proud of the song When Will I Be Famous?*). But in general, he was no match for human beings. They were far too creative with their stupid free will.*

'Long time no see,' he suddenly heard a voice behind him.

Satan turned around and saw the Reverend Gabriel.

'It's been almost exactly six thousand years,' Satan replied. 'Since the Man upstairs threw me out of heaven. Or rather, down from heaven.'

Gabriel nodded. 'Those were the days.'

'Yes, they were,' Satan nodded.

They smiled at each other like two men who used to be friends, and who deeply regretted that they now weren't.

'You look tired,' Satan said to Gabriel.

'Thanks. Ditto,' Gabriel replied.

Then they smiled at each other even more.

'So, what's this meeting all about?' Satan wanted to know.

'God wants me to tell you something,' Gabriel replied.

'And what's that?'

'The Day of Judgement is upon us.'

Satan thought for a while, and then breathed a sigh of relief. 'Well, it was about time.'

CHAPTER SIX

Our wedding began as most weddings do – with the bride having a minor nervous breakdown. I stood outside the church door. The guests were waiting for my performance. Everything was actually almost as perfect as I had always hoped it would be. The pews were filled. Soon everyone would be admiring my wonderful white dress that I knew fitted me like a glove, as I had indeed managed to starve off half a stone. I would be giving my vows in this romantic ecclesiastical setting. Everything was indeed almost perfect. There was only one problem: my Dad no longer wanted to walk me down the aisle.

'You really shouldn't have shouted at Svetlana like that,' Kata said.

'I didn't shout at her,' I replied with tears in my eyes.

'You called her a "vodka-whore".'

'OK, maybe I was a bit harsh,' I admitted.

Before I got into the carriage to go to the church, I had been determined to act completely cool during my first meeting with Svetlana. But when I actually met this heavily made-up yet pretty, petite woman, it was clear to me that she would break my Dad's heart. A young thing like that couldn't possibly have fallen in love with him! In my mind's eye I saw my Dad crying in my arms again. And as I couldn't stand the thought of this, I asked Svetlana to bugger off back to Belarus, or just to keep going all the way to Siberia. That made Dad angry. He shouted at. I tried to explain to him that he was just being used. He shouted at me even more. Then I lost it. When I lost it, he lost it too. And that's when phrases like 'vodka-whore', 'ungrateful daughter' and 'Viagra-Dad' were thrown into the ring.

Why do you always hurt the people you are trying to protect from themselves?

'Come on,' Kata said, drying my tears and grabbing my hand. 'I'll walk you in.'

She opened the door for me. The organ started to play. Holding on to my beloved sister, I stepped into the church with as much dignity as I could muster and made my way towards the altar. Most of the people there had been invited by Sven. Many of them were related to him and the others were friends from the football club, his colleagues from the hospital, people from the neighbourhood... Well, half of Malente was either related to or friends with Sven. I didn't have nearly as many friends. Actually, I only had one real friend, and he was sitting in row number five. Michi was a skinny, scrawny fellow, with dishevelled hair, and he was wearing a T-shirt that said, 'Beauty is totally overrated'.

We'd known each other since school. At that time he was part of a truly freaky minority – he was a Catholic altar boy.

Even today, Michi was the only really religious person I knew. He read the Bible every day. He'd once said: 'Marie. What's written in the Bible must be true. Those stories are far too crazy for anyone to have made them up.'

Michi nodded at me encouragingly and I was able to smile again. In row three I spotted my father, and immediately stopped smiling. He was still angry with me, while Svetlana was nervously staring at the floor, probably wondering how we Germans defined hospitality. And kinship.

My mother was sitting in row one, deliberately far from my father. With her short, dyed red hair she looked a bit like a trade union boss. She seemed much more lively than back then, when she'd sat at the breakfast table in her blue dressing gown with a tired expression and told me and Kata: 'I'm leaving your father.'

Mum had tried to explain to us children as gently as possible that she hadn't loved Dad for a long time, and that she'd only stayed with him because of us and that she simply couldn't carry on living a lie.

Today I know that it was the right decision. She had been able to realise her dream of studying psychology, something that Dad had always opposed. She now lived in Hamburg and had her own practice specialising in relationship counselling (of all things), and she was much, much more confident than ever before. Nevertheless, a part of me still wished that Mum had carried on living that lie.

'Marriage is difficult,' the Reverend Gabriel declared during the sermon in a resounding tone. 'But everything else is even more difficult.'

It was not exactly a 'what-a-wonderful-day-let's-rejoice' kind of sermon. But I suppose that not much more was to be expected of him. I was of course relieved that he hadn't spoken about 'people who use my church to stage events'.

Sven stared at me throughout the sermon, completely overjoyed. So overjoyed that I couldn't stand not being as overjoyed as he was, even though I really did want to be overjoyed. It was probably just because I was still so shaken after my argument with Dad.

I did my best to beam now as well. But the more I tried, the tenser I became. Racked with guilt, I couldn't even look at Sven. I scanned the church and caught sight of a crucifix. At first, stupid sayings came to my head from our confirmation time. 'Hey Jesus! What are you doing here?' – 'Oh, Paul. I'm just hanging around.'

But then I looked at the red marks on his hands, where the nails had been hammered through. I shuddered. Crucifixion. What kind of brutal thing was that? Who had even thought of doing it, something so incred-ibly horrific? Whoever it was must have had a really awful childhood.

And Jesus? Well, he knew what was coming to him. Why did he allow himself to be subjected to that? Of course, to absolve us of our sins. That was an impressive sacrifice for humanity. But did Jesus even have a choice? Was he able to choose whether or not to sacrifice himself? It was his destiny – right from the moment he was born, wasn't it? That's what his father had sent him down to earth for. But what kind of a father demands that kind of a sacrifice from his son? And what would Super Nanny have said about that father? Most likely: 'Go and sit on the naughty step.'

Suddenly I got scared. It was probably not a very good idea to criticise God in church. Especially not at your own wedding.

I'm sorry, God, I said in my head. It's just that – did Jesus have to endure such a painful death? Was that really necessary? I mean, couldn't he have died from something other than crucifixion? Something more humane? What about a sleeping potion?

But then, I started thinking to myself, there would have been drinking cups hanging about in churches instead of crucifixes…

'Marie!' the Reverend Gabriel said in a penetrating voice.

I jumped. 'Yes! Here I am.'

'I asked you a question,' he said.

'Yes, yes… I heard,' I fibbed in a fluster.

'And so maybe you would like to answer?'

'Well, yes. Why not?'

I glanced over at a nervous-looking Sven. Then I looked into the nave and saw lots of confused eyes and wondered how I could get myself out of this situation. But I couldn't think of anything.

'Erm, what was the question again?' I anxiously looked at Gabriel again.

'If you want to marry Sven.'

I was having hot and cold flushes. It was one of those moments where you want to fall into a spontaneous coma.

Half of the church was laughing. The other half was appalled. And Sven's nervous smile turned into a scowl.

'Sorry. It was just a little joke,' Gabriel explained.

I breathed a sigh of relief.

'I just asked whether you were ready for your vows.'

'I'm sorry. I was miles away,' I said sheepishly.

'And what were you thinking about?'

'About Jesus,' I answered honestly, keeping the details to myself.

Gabriel was satisfied with my answer, as were the guests, and Sven was smiling and looked relieved. So it seemed that not listening to the vicar during your own wedding because of Jesus was actually OK.

'So shall we start with the vows?' Gabriel asked, and I nodded.

Suddenly, the whole church fell silent.

Gabriel turned to Sven: 'Sven Harder, do you take Marie Woodward to be your wife? Will you love her, cherish and honour her, share with her in joy and sorrow and be faithful to her as long as you both shall live?'

Sven had tears in his eyes. 'I will.'

It was unbelievable. There really was a man who wanted to marry me. Who'd have thought it?

Then Gabriel turned to me. I became extremely nervous. My legs were shaking and I started feeling queasy.

'Marie Woodward, do you take Sven Harder to be your husband, will you love him, cherish and honour him, share with him in joy and sorrow and be faithful to him as long as you both shall live?'

I was quite aware that I should have said 'I will' at this point. But it suddenly dawned on me that 'as long as you both shall live' was actually a long time. An extremely long time. That's probably something that dated back to a time when Christians had an average life expectancy of thirty, before they died in their mud huts or they were gobbled up by lions in the Colosseum. But nowadays people have an average life expectancy of eighty or ninety years. If medical science carried on like this, people might even live to be 120. But, having said that, I didn't have private health insurance, so I would probably only reach eighty or ninety. But that was still old enough…

'Hmm!' Gabriel cleared his throat, urging me to answer.

I tried, with a little sob, to win some time by getting people to think that I couldn't speak, because I was getting emotional. My gaze was now firmly focused on the door. I remembered *The Graduate*, when Dustin Hoffman steals the bride away from the church, and wondered if Marc had got wind of my wedding, driven to Malente and would speed through the door at any moment… That I had started thinking about Marc at this point was not a great sign.

'Marie. This is the moment when you should say "I will",' the Reverend Gabriel explained, sounding slightly pushy.

As if I didn't know that!

Sven was biting his lips nervously.

I spotted my mother in the crowd and asked myself whether I'd end up like she did with Sven? Would I also sit my daughters down at the breakfast table at some point and announce: 'Sorry Mareike and Maja, but I haven't loved your father for years'?

'Marie! Please answer,' Gabriel urged me. The only thing that could now be heard in the church was my noisy stomach.

'Marie…' Sven begged. He was beginning to panic.

I thought about the tears of my unborn daughter. And then I suddenly knew why I didn't want to have children with Sven.

I loved him. But not enough for a whole lifetime.

But what would hurt him more? Saying 'no' now or divorcing him later?

CHAPTER SEVEN

'What have I done? What *have* I done?' I wailed as I sat on the cold floor of the ladies' loo at the church.

'You said "no",' replied Kata, who was sitting next to me, making sure that the tear-saturated loo paper ended up in the sanitary bin.

'I know what I said!' I wept.

'It was the right thing to do. It was brave and very honest!' Kata comforted me and tore off some more loo paper. 'Not many people have that kind of courage. Most people in your shoes would probably have said "Yes" and made a massive mistake. OK, perhaps you could have chosen a slightly better moment to dump him…'

'Have the guests already left?' I asked.

'Yes. And the children will probably be traumatised for the rest of their lives when it comes to marriage,' Kata smiled kindly.

'What… what about Sven?'

'He's outside and he wants to speak to you.'

I stopped sobbing. Sven was waiting outside the door? Perhaps if I explained it all to him? Perhaps then he'd understand that I wanted to spare him even more pain? That both of us would just have ended up being unhappy. Yes, I'm sure he'd understand, despite all the grief I'd caused him. He was a very understanding man.

'Bring him in,' I asked Kata.

'I'm not sure that's a good idea…'

'Bring him in.'

'When I said "I'm not sure that's a good idea" I actually meant to say that it's an utterly ridiculous idea.'

'Bring him in!' I insisted.

'OK.'

Kata stood up and went off to get him. I dragged myself up in my crumpled dress, went to the mirror and stared at my face, all red and puffy from the crying. My make-up was all over the place. I threw some cold water on myself and the make-up started running even more.

Then Sven came in. His eyes were bloodshot. He'd obviously been crying too. I hoped that he would forgive me. He was such a sensible person, I was sure he would.

'Sven…' I began and tried to find the right words to make amends for the damage I'd done.

'Do you know what Marie?' he interrupted me.

'What…?' I answered hesitantly.

'From now on, you can massage your own bloody feet… if you can even reach them over your big fat stomach, that is!'

I was shocked.

Sven stormed out.

Kata gently put her arm around me. 'It seems that he didn't love you just as you were after all.'

I would have loved to ensconce myself in that ladies' loo at the church for the next few years, but the Reverend Gabriel had something to say about that. He asked me to leave, amazingly, without so much as a critical word. 'In the end,' he said 'there is nothing in the Bible that says that you need to answer the "Do you" question with an "I will".

As I was leaving the church, my gaze happened to fall on another painting of Jesus. I remembered how Gabriel had told us at confirmation class that Jesus could turn water into wine to keep a wedding celebration going. Well, today it seemed that there was no need for a party guest like that.

As I stepped outside, I saw that Sven's family and friends had already left, much to my relief. For a split second, I had

33

actually feared that there might be a good old village stoning. Only my little family was still there: Mum, Dad, Michi and Svetlana, who was probably beginning to wonder what kind of a family she busy wheedling her way into.

Dad was busy giving Mum a hard time. 'It's basically all your fault. She's a commitment-phobe because of you.' I overheard and immediately wanted to run back into the loo.

But Mum saw me and rushed towards me. 'Darling, if you need someone to talk to…'

Yep. That's all I needed. Psychotherapy with Mum.

'You can come back with me to Hamburg,' she suggested, but it was a mixture of guilt and therapist's reflex rather than real motherly love.

Dad joined us and said: 'You can always come and sleep in your old room.'

Even though I'd offended Svetlana and even though he was still angry, I was his daughter, and he always had a place for me in his house. That felt good.

Michi wanted to help too. 'You can sleep over at my place. I have some great horror films to take your mind off things. *Saw, Saw 2, Runaway Bride...*'

I still had to smile. Michi was always much better at making me laugh than Sven or Marc. It was just annoying that my hormones didn't share his love for humour.'

'Sleep at Michi's,' Kata whispered. 'And sleep with him.'

I could hardly believe what she was saying. I turned red – half through rage and half through shame.

'It's distracting. And he's been after you for centuries,' she added.

'Firstly, he hasn't "been after" me for centuries,' I hissed. 'And secondly, Michi and I have a platonic friendship.'

'Marie,' Kata replied. 'Plato was a complete idiot.'

I decided against horror films at Michi's and therapy at Mum's, and opted for Dad's instead. A short while later I was back in my old room. It still looked just the same, i.e. horrendously embarrassing. On the wall there were pictures of boy bands. Most of them were probably on the dole by now. I peeled myself out of my wedding dress and collapsed onto my old comfy bed in just my underwear (I didn't have any other clothes). Deeply depressed, I stared at a big wet patch on the ceiling – there was something wrong with the roof. Dad wanted to have it fixed, which was a good idea by the looks of things. It certainly seemed as though I would be spending the rest of my days in this room. I never wanted to go out into that stupid world again.

Kata sat down on the floor and leant against the bed. She didn't say anything, instead calmly working on a comic strip. After a while I inspected the result.

'So will your strip next week be all about my disastrous wedding?' I asked.

'The next two weeks' worth,' Kata grinned.

'And how long are you going to carry on with that anyway?'

'Until you grow up,' she answered lovingly.

'I am grown up,' I protested meekly.

Kata just looked at me compassionately. 'You're not.'

'Says the woman who never ever wants to have another relationship,' I answered aggrieved. Since Lisa had left her at the hospital, Kata only ever had one-night stands.

'It is clearly wiser not to tie your heart to things or people and instead to enjoy the moment,' Kata explained nonchalantly.

It was a sentence that again showed me that, deep down in her heart, she was completely disillusioned when it came to love. And hopeless. But I was far too exhausted to start talking to her about that.

'I'd like to be alone, please.' I said after a brief silence.

'Well, can you be left alone?' she asked carefully.

'I can,' I said bravely.

My sister kissed my forehead, grabbed her pad of paper and left the room. I got a pen and some paper out of my old desk and sat on the bed to write a 'Good things/Bad things' list about my life. My therapist had once suggested I do this in crisis situations, to help me see that things are not as bad as they seem.

Bad Things

- I screwed up a wedding because I didn't have strong enough feelings for the man I thought I wanted to marry.
- And far too strong feelings for a man who cheated on me with a size 6 bimbo.
- The last time I was a size 6 was when I was thirteen.

- I have a job that I hate more than your average turkey hates Christmas.
- I also have no prospects of getting another job.
- Moreover, I hardly have any friends.
- Half of Malente probably hates me for what I did to Sven.
- I'm back sleeping in my old room.
- At the age of thirty-five.
- Kata was clearly right – I really am not grown up.

I couldn't think of any more. Only ten negatives. Far off a whole dozen then. Not bad. Having said that, they all concerned the major areas of my life: love, work, friends, character.

But not everything was lost. Now for my list of positives.

Good Things

- I have a sister like Kata.

I had terrible trouble trying to think of anything else.

- Things can't get any worse.

That's when I heard my Dad moaning in the bedroom below me.
And Svetlana was screaming: 'Give it to me!'
So I crossed the second item off the list again.

CHAPTER EIGHT

Meanwhile...

Some people give up on their marriage for love; some people give up on their job. And others sacrifice their nerves. Yet compared with the Reverend Gabriel, these people were miserable victims amateurs. Thirty years ago he not only sacrificed his existence, but gave up on his wings and his immortality. All this because he had fallen in love with a mortal woman when he was an angel. Lots of angels do that, but Gabriel had never thought that it would happen to him. He was an archangel. He was the Archangel Gabriel! The head of all the angels! The one who had announced to Mary that she would have a child.

But one day he saw a young woman down on earth, who touched his heart (figuratively speaking; angels have no organs). Moreover, when he saw her he was glad that he didn't have any organs as they would probably have rearranged themselves with all that excitement.

Gabriel was lost as soon as he caught sight of this creature. And this despite the fact that he had actually seen far more beautiful women through the course of his existence: Cleopatra, Mary Magdalene, that mysterious girl that Leonardo da Vinci had painted... He had also met far more courageous women. Joan of Arc, for example, had been very impressive, even if her furore was a little annoying at times.

By comparison, the woman with whom he fell in love was actually quite ordinary. Like a thousand, a million others! He couldn't explain why he happened to be so fascinated by this woman in particular, and why he suddenly longed to do silly things like spending hours stroking her hair. Yes, love did have this annoying trait of being inexplicable. Even to angels.

For a long time Gabriel fought against his feelings, but then, finally, he asked God to turn him into a human being so that he might try and charm this woman. God answered his prayers – Gabriel lost his wings, returned to earth as a mortal, and set about winning the heart of this woman he adored. All of this in vain; she didn't love him back.

These bloody humans with their free will!

Instead, his beloved married someone else. She had two children with this man. They were called Kata and Marie.

The morning after Marie's cancelled wedding, Gabriel was standing in front of the Marie's mother's flat in Hamburg. He had stayed in touch with her over the decades. She didn't know that he still loved her. She also didn't know that Gabriel had once been an angel. God had forbidden him, and all the other three hundred angels who had become human beings over the millennia for love (including Audrey Hepburn), from ever revealing their origins.

'Have you read the Book of Revelation, Silvia?' Gabriel enquired urgently.

'Yes, and it was shocking, in a destructive kind of way,' Marie's mother replied.

'Most people do not know about it,' Gabriel said. 'Even though it makes up the last twenty-two chapters of the Bible.'

'Well, most people tend not to read books all the way through,' Silvia smiled.

'But it's important to read all of it!' Gabriel insisted. It bothered him that most people regarded the Holy Scriptures as some kind of buffet, from which they could pick and choose the things that suited their view of the world. Whenever he ate food from a buffet, he always sampled of all the dishes! At least that's what he used to do. Nowadays he suffered from heartburn. Being mortal certainly had its disadvantages!

'Come on,' Marie's mother grinned. 'In that part of the Bible it says that there will be a battle between good and evil. It reads like a binned draft of The Lord of the Rings.*'*

'It's not The Lord of the Rings,*' Gabriel protested.*

'But almost. Satan sends the Three Horsemen of the Apocalypse down to earth…'

39

'There are four horsemen!' Gabriel corrected her. 'War, Famine, Pestilence and Death.'

'And Jesus walks on earth again and triumphs over Satan and his horsies,' Silvia said mockingly.

'Yes, that's precisely what he'll do,' Gabriel insisted.

'And then Jesus will create a Kingdom of Heaven on earth,' Silvia grinned even more.

'That's how it will be!'

'Whoever wrote this must have been completely nuts'

It filled Gabriel with hellish fear that his beloved did not take the Bible seriously: 'Jesus will not allow everyone to enter into the Kingdom of Heaven.'

'Oh. So I'm supposed to start believing in my old age?' She thought it was quite sweet that Gabriel was so concerned about her.

'Yes, Damn it!' Gabriel shouted.

His outburst confused her. 'That's the first time I've ever heard you swear.'

'The non-believers will all be punished,' Gabriel explained quietly and anxiously.

'That's why we non-believers have a better life in the here and now, because we don't allow ourselves to be frightened by such terrible Bible texts,' she countered.

Silvia looked at her watch. She had an appointment with a patient. But Gabriel really was very sweet when he got angry like this. Why hadn't she seen that until now? Of course: because her ex-husband had a young Belarusian floozy, and she was suddenly afraid of growing old alone. Her psychologist's mind told her that much. But she also knew that it was entirely normal to react like that to your ex-husband falling in love again. And that you should pursue what makes you feel good.

So, as she was leaving, she turned to Gabriel and said: 'I'll come and visit you this evening'

She gave him a friendly peck on the cheek. Then she strutted off down the staircase.

Gabriel held his cheek, feeling very confused. So that's how it felt to be kissed. Now he wanted her even more than before. But he didn't have much more time to save his great love. Jesus was already walking the earth.

CHAPTER NINE

When I woke up in my old room there was no longer any doubt. I was now officially a M.O.N.S.T.E.R. (i.e. **M**ajorly **O**ld with **N**o **S**pouse, **T**ots, **E**nergy or **R**esources). I lay on my bed feeling feeble and dejected. I wasn't sure I could be more miserable. The night had been awful, and now it gave way to a horribly rainy day. Instead of sitting on a plane on the way to my honeymoon in Formentera and being served dry sandwiches by an air hostess, I stared at the growing wet patch on the ceiling, wondering whether this might be a good moment to become an alcoholic.

I took my eyes off the wet patch and caught sight of my old stereo system. When I was a teenager, I'd always listened to *I Will Survive* when I was suffering from heartache, dancing around the room like a kangaroo on ecstasy.

After that I was always on a real high for four minutes, only to collapse again, to ask myself whether I really would survive. Sweating, I then put on *I Am What I Am*, which had an even lesser effect. And when I played it, I always asked myself: 'What exactly *am I?*'

I was not going to ask myself that question today. I knew full well what I was. I am a M.O.N.S.T.E.R. And I was also sure that I would not survive all this unless there was miracle.

I put my hands together and prayed to God like never before. 'Dear God. Please, please, please make everything be all right again. Somehow. No idea how. The only thing that matters is that everything will be all right again. If you do that, then I'll go to church every Sunday. Really. Truly. I promise. No matter how boring the sermons are. And I won't yawn and I'll never ever think about Jesus again… I mean, I will of course think about Jesus, but not like the thoughts I was having yesterday. And I will also spend a tenth, or whatever you call it, a tithe of my monthly income on good causes… or perhaps half a tithe? Otherwise I might not be able to get through the month. Look, if you really want I'll give three-quarters of a tithe. That should be all right. And I could still afford to have a car. OK, OK… A full tithe if I really must! The only thing that matters is that I stop feeling as awful as I do now. That's worth all the money in the world. Who needs a car? It's bad for the environment anyway. So, what do you say? I'll become religious and selfless and will save on CO_2, and you'll make sure that everything will be all right again. Do we have a deal? If so, please give me a sign… Or no! Stop, stop, stop! We'll do it differently. If you agree, then just *don't* give me a sign.

I paused for a moment. If there was no sign now, something that was really rather likely, then everything would be all right. I would be happy, even if I'd have less money, no car and Sundays would now be spent at church. A pretty clever offer on my part.

I hoped so much that God would not give me a sign.

At that moment, the rain-soaked plaster fell down from the ceiling, right in my face. Frustrated, I stood up, rubbed my face and spat out the dusty mortar. If there really was a God, this was a sign.

It also meant the he did not want to be a part of my fantastic deal. I thought about how I could improve my offer. God could surely not expect me to become a nun, could he? On the other hand, if things carried on like this, I would never have sex again anyway, and some nuns are apparently quite fun, at least in films and books. They always seem strict at first, and then turn out to be wise and blessed with wit… And maybe a vicar would come by, on a visit or something, during the apple harvest, a guy like Matthew McConaughey… someone with an equally broken heart, perhaps his wife would have accidentally fallen off a cliff… and he would never be able to feel love again, something that would change in an instant as soon as he saw me…

And at that very moment, there was a knock on the door.

'Who's there?' I asked hesitantly.

'It's me,' Dad answered quite sternly. Although he'd taken me in, we were far from reconciled.

'What… what do you want?' I asked. A fight with my Dad was about the last thing I could cope with right now. I just didn't have the energy.

'I have a carpenter here who wants to come and have a look at the roof.'

I looked at the plaster on the floor, with the mortar-taste still in my mouth and thought: 'Why couldn't this silly carpenter have come a day earlier?'

'He needs to access the roof through the hatch in your room,' Dad shouted.

My face was covered in dust and tears and I felt absolutely awful. No one should see me like this. But on the other hand, basically the entire town now had a bad impression of me, so it probably didn't matter that much what a carpenter thought. And if I was going to spend the rest of my life lurking in this room, it was probably a good idea to prevent the ceiling coming down on my head.

'Just a second,' I shouted to my Dad. 'I just need to put some clothes on.'

It was enough to be seen with mortar dust on my face – there was no need to stand about in my underwear as well.

But I didn't have any clothes with me. Surely there had to be something in my teenage wardrobe? I opened it and found jumpers and jeans. I pulled on an old sweater that made me look like some sort of bare-midriffed Scandinavian sausage. I didn't fit into the trousers – I couldn't even get them over my hips. I had obviously added a Michelin ring around my stomach with every year that had passed.

'Marie! How long is this going to take?' Dad shouted impatiently.

I racked my brains – I wouldn't fit in Kata's clothes either, and there was no point in even asking Svetlana.

'Marie!' my father urged me.

I had no choice. I jumped back into my wedding dress. With my dusty face I looked rather a lot like a ghost. All I needed to do now was to wear my head under my arm – something that actually felt quite appealing.

I opened the door. For a brief moment, my Dad looked rather perplexed at the sight of me. 'Well, it's about time.'

Then he waved somebody in. 'Marie, let me introduce you to Joshua. He's very kindly going to fix our roof.'

A man of average build in jeans, a shirt and suede boots entered the room. He had slightly olivey skin, long, wavy hair and a stylish beard. Through my dusty eyes he looked a little like one of the Bee Gees.

CHAPTER TEN

'Joshua, this is my daughter Marie,' my Dad said. 'She doesn't always look like this,' he added.

The carpenter's gentle, dark brown eyes seemed very serious, as if they'd already seen a thing or two. Looking into them made me all confused.

'Hello Marie,' he said in a wonderfully deep voice, which distracted me even more. He reached for my hand to greet me. His handshake was strong, and somehow conveyed a deep feeling of security.

'Frblmf,' I stammered. I was completely incapable of saying anything sensible.

'It's a pleasure to meet you Marie,' he said earnestly. That voice!

'Frddlff,' I replied.

'I'm here to take a look at that roof of yours,' he explained. And I answered with a consentient 'Brmmlf'.

He let go of my hand, and I suddenly began to feel insecure. I wanted him to take hold of me again, immediately!

But Joshua opened the hatch with the pole, pulled down the ladder and nimbly climbed up the steps. He was both agile and elegant, and I caught myself staring at his bum. Only once the carpenter had disappeared up into the attic could I start thinking a bit more clearly again. I let the great bum carry on being a great bum, quickly left the room and knocked on the door of Kata's old room. My sister opened, dressed only in her underwear, and she yawned like an alligator that was busy digesting a tourist.

'Can you get me some clothes?' I asked.

'You want me to go to Sven's for you?'

'Well, if I go myself someone might end up six feet under.'

'Given how angry he was yesterday, that doesn't seem entirely impossible…' Kata conceded.

She yawned again, stretched and suddenly winced. It scared the hell out of me whenever she had a pain in her head.

Kata saw the alarm in my eyes and reassured me: 'I'm not having a relapse. I just drank some bad red wine last night.'

I was so relieved that I wanted to kiss her, but she put her arms up defensively. 'Go and have a wash before you kiss anyone.'

After I'd had a shower, I sat in the kitchen cradling a cup of coffee. Alone. Dad had taken Svetlana on a day trip to the coast. I frantically tried to put the thought out of my head that this woman might become my new mum. Once I'd succeeded, I contemplated my disastrous life. What is it people say? Crises make you stronger? I was determined to use this crisis to steer my life onto a happier course. Too right I would!

But what if I couldn't? What if my life would always be this miserable and disastrous?

Then it was preferable to think about Svetlana.

Or even better, that delightful Joshua.

He was so charming. Those eyes, that voice. I bet if he put his mind to it, that carpenter could make lots of people excited about a good cause. Like… thermal insulation.

What was it he said again? That it was a pleasure to meet me. That sounded genuine. And he wasn't even staring at my breasts, unlike most men when they said things like that.

He'd called me by my first name without even asking me. But maybe that was because he was from southern Europe. Italy or somewhere like that. Maybe he had a house in Tuscany that he'd built himself… without his top on…

But what was he doing here then? Maybe he'd had difficulties at home? Maybe work issues?

Wow. I really was thinking quite a lot about a man at whom I'd only grunted.

Kata interrupted my train of thought when she returned with two suitcases of for me.

'How is he?' I asked.

'He looks like you.'

'Like a dog's dinner?' I asked.

'Exactly.'

I felt incredibly guilty. I'd never made a man so unhappy. Normally men made me unhappy. I sighed. 'Do you really have to go today?'

I so wanted her to stay with me a bit longer.

'Perhaps it would be better if I stayed with you until you're feeling better.'

'The entire hundred years?' I asked gloomily.

'I'm sure it won't take that long,' she grinned.

I hugged her.

'You're crushing me,' she groaned.

'That's my intention!' I replied

Five minutes later, when I'd finished hugging my sister, I got changed and was happy to be back in jeans and a jumper again. We both went upstairs and wanted to do the things that most interested us at this very moment – she wanted to draw and I wanted to wallow in my own self-pity.

But as we went past my room, I heard Joshua singing up in the attic in a foreign language. Not Italian. His voice was deep and moving. I'm sure it would even have moved me if he'd been singing the theme tune from *The Smurfs*.

I told Kata that I just wanted to run and get something, and that I'd be with her shortly. Then I went into my room and climbed up the ladder into the attic.

Joshua had just taken a leaky window out of the frame and

put it down on the floor. He seemed very focused, in a relaxed sort of way. He was clearly someone who forgot everything else when he was working.

When Joshua spotted me, he stopped singing. I was curious to know what kind of a song it was and asked, 'Wddl dllll?'

This couldn't go on. I quickly looked down at the floor, pulled myself together and started again: 'So… what were you singing?'

'A psalm about the joy of work.'

'Oh… OK,' I said. I seldom used the words 'joy' and 'work' in the same sentence. And I basically never said 'psalm'.

'And what language was that?' I was now able to look at him and utter a more or less error-free sentence. The trick was not to stare into those deep, dark eyes.

'Hebrew,' Joshua replied.

'Is that your native language?'

'Yes, I'm from Palestine.'

Palestine. Not quite as appealing as Tuscany. Maybe Joshua was a refugee?

'Why don't you live there any more?' I asked him.

'My time there had come to an end,' he answered, like someone who had was completely at ease with the way things had turned out. He seemed at peace. And yet incredibly serious. Far too serious! I wondered what it would be like to see him really laughing.

'Would you like to go out for dinner with me tonight?' I asked.

Joshua was surprised at my question. Though not half as surprised as I was. Not even twenty hours had elapsed since I'd left Sven standing at the altar. And now I wanted to go out with a guy, just to see him laugh?

'What?' asked Joshua.

'Grdlllff,' I replied.

I frantically tried to think whether I should backtrack, but decide to flee forwards with a rather pathetic attempt to be witty. 'I'm sure there must be a psalm about food.'

He just looked at me, even more surprised. God, this was so embarrassing!

We both stared at each other in silence. I tried to decipher the carpenter's facial expression to see whether he actually wanted to go out with me or whether he thought I was being a pushy cow, who had about as much knowledge of psalms as she did about experimental particle physics.

But I couldn't read him at all. His face was so different to other people's, and not only because of his beard.

Ashamed, I looked back down at the floor and was just about to mumble 'forget it' when he answered: 'There are lots of psalms about bread and eating.'

I looked up at him again and he said, 'I would like to eat with you, Marie.'

That was the first time he smiled at me. It was just a small smile, certainly not a laugh. But it was divine.

With that smile he could have sold me lots of things other than thermal insulation.

CHAPTER ELEVEN

'My God. Why on earth did I just ask him out on a date?' I wailed as I was regaining my composure. I was standing in front of the bathroom mirror and trying desperately, before I went out to dinner, to fix my face with make-up after all that blubbing. My face looked like New Orleans after Hurricane Katrina.

'This carpenter is really not my type,' I explained to Kata. 'He has a beard. I really don't like beards.'

'You used to love them,' Kata grinned.

'I was six!'

Kata grinned even more and put some eye shadow on me.

'And furthermore,' I said. 'Joshua is from Palestine. And he sings psalms.'

'You're clearly trying to make a point. Are you going to spell it out for me?' Kata asked.

'Maybe he's a religious nutter. He might be one of those people who takes flying lessons but doesn't pay much attention to the part about landing…'

'Nice to see how open-minded and unprejudiced you are,' Kata said.

I wondered whether or not I should be ashamed of my prejudices. But I concluded that I was not in the mood for that right now. I had so much to be ashamed of; my shame capacity had been reached and breached.

'All this talk of beards and flying lessons,' Kata said, 'It's just because you feel bad about Sven.'

'Well it just feels wrong to be going out on a date with someone,' I conceded.

'So it's wrong to have a little bit of fun?' Kata demanded.

'How can I have fun, just one day after the wedding from hell?'

'Very simple. You'll have fun when the carpenter shows you his toolbox…'

I just stared at her blankly. She certainly didn't seem to be talking about lathes.

I turned my head back to face the mirror and realised that make-up can only be as good as the face on which it is being applied.

'I'm going to cancel,' I announced.

'And what will you do instead?' asked Kata.

'Think about my life.'

'Well, that *does* sound fun.'

She was right. I would go and lie in my bed again and think about the fact that I needed a new apartment, but had no money for either the deposit or an estate agent, because I'd taken on a huge debt for a wedding party that I'd called off. This basically meant that I would have to carry on living with Dad and listening to Svetlana demanding he give it to her at frequencies fit to drive dogs mad.

Kata read my mind and said something very persuasive: 'Go on the date. You certainly won't be more depressed if you do.'

I'd arranged to meet Joshua at Da Giovanni, an Italian restaurant with lots of advantages. It was idyllically located by the lake, had great food, and an owner, the eponymous, Giovanni, who had nicked Sven's girlfriend and sired four *bambini* with her. That meant that Sven would be boycotting the place for all eternity, and would definitely not see me with Joshua. We would thus be avoiding the *Malente Post* headline about a 'Massacre by the lake' tomorrow.

Giovanni gave me a table on the lake terrace, and no sooner had I sat down than Joshua arrived. He was wearing exactly the same clothes he'd had on while working, but amazingly they didn't look the slightest bit dirty.

'Good evening, Marie,' he greeted me with a smile. He really did have an unbelievable smile. I wondered whether he bleached his teeth.

'Good evening, Joshua,' I replied, and he sat down next to me. I was waiting for him to make some conversation. But he didn't say anything. He seemed happy just looking out across the lake and enjoying the sunlight on his face. So I tried to get the conversation going: 'How long have you been in Malente?'

'I arrived yesterday.'

That was a surprise.

'And you managed to get the job to fix our roof right away?' I asked, sounding confused.

'Gabriel knew that your father was looking for a carpenter.'

'Gabriel? The Reverend Gabriel?'

'I'm currently staying in his spare room.'

Oh my God. Hopefully Gabriel hadn't told him what a nutter I was.

'Have you known Gabriel for a while?' I asked, trying to find out whether the old vicar had told him about yesterday's disastrous spectacle at the church. 'I mean, do you know each other well enough to talk about stuff?'

Joshua answered: 'Gabriel knew my mother. He gave her the news that I was to be born.'

This was a confusing answer. Had Gabriel held Joshua's mum's pregnancy test in his hand. And if so, why? He'd never been a gynaecologist, certainly not in Palestine. I wondered whether there'd been something going on between her and Gabriel.

But these were all questions that were too direct for a first date. Probably for the seventeenth one at that. I asked him something else. 'When did you leave Palestine?'

'Almost two thousand years ago.'

Joshua was not smiling when he said that. He either had the driest sense of humour in the world, or he really was taking flying lessons.

'And where have you been living these past two thousand years?' I tried to join in without being entirely sure whether or not he was joking.

'In heaven,' he replied, without the slightest hint of irony.

'You're joking, right?'

'Of course not,' he replied.

All I could think was: Damn. Definitely flying lessons.

I tried to calm down. Joshua was probably just a normal guy who'd been here for a while. Otherwise he wouldn't have been able to speak German so well. He must just have a very strange sense of humour. The joke was probably 'lost in translation'.

We sat in silence, looking out over the lake and waiting for the menus. Joshua didn't mind the silence. I did. This wasn't exactly fun.

But what had I been expecting? There was no way we could be on the same wavelength. We were too different. He was religious. I was depressed.

The whole thing was a crazy idea. I wondered whether I shouldn't just get up and leave, and explain to him that this whole thing had been a misunderstanding. It was probably not too late for me to go home, wrap myself up in my duvet and torture myself wondering whether I would ever be happy without medication.

Joshua clearly saw that I was feeling down. He said something wonderful. 'There's a bird.'

That wasn't the wonderful bit.

'It doesn't harvest anything, it doesn't sow anything, and yet it doesn't need to worry.'

I looked at the bird. It was a nightingale. He also didn't need to worry about finding a partner for life, I thought. His only concern was avoiding ending up on someone's plate when he headed south.

'And people really shouldn't worry,' Joshua continued. 'Who can extend their life by worrying?'

He was certainly right about that. Although he did sound like someone who'd read a few too many self-help books by Dale Carnegie.

'Therefore do not worry about tomorrow, for tomorrow will worry about itself,' Joshua said.

It was a simple sentence. But a nice one. And this man's charm, voice and eyes certainly made it easier to believe what he was saying.

For the first time since my 'will not' at the altar, I felt a slight sense of optimism.

I decided to stay for now and to give the date the time it took to eat one pizza. Giovanni brought the menu, and Joshua didn't really know what to do with it. I even had to explain to him what a pizza was. Finally he opted for a Pizza Vegetale.

He explained his choice: 'Meat and cheese together are not kosher.'

'Kosher? Is that what Muslims say too?' I asked.

'I'm not Muslim. I'm Jewish.'

A Jew from Palestine. Well I never, I thought to myself. I was pleased. It would probably be easier to introduce mum to a Jew. But what if he was one of those mad Jewish settlers? Then again, if he was a mad Jewish settler he would have had curly hair, wouldn't he? How on earth did they get their hair to curl like that, anyway? With tongs?

'And you?' Joshua interrupted my train of thought about Jewish hairdressing techniques.

'Erm… what?' I asked.

'What God do you believe in?'

'Well, er… I'm Christian,' I answered.

Joshua smiled. I had no idea what was so funny about that. Had Gabriel told him about me after all?

'I'm sorry,' he said. 'But to me, "Christian" is a description of someone who is a believer. It's going to take me a while to get used to it.'

Joshua started to laugh. Just a little bit, not loudly. But this gentle laugh was enough to trigger a warm, pleasant feeling in me.

For the next few minutes we eventually got chatting properly. I asked where he'd learned his craft, and he explained that his stepfather had taught him everything he knew.

Stepfather? Was he a neurotic child of divorced parents like me? Hopefully not!

Giovanni served us and Joshua enjoyed his pizza and salad as though he really was eating for the first time in 2,000 years. He gushed about the red wine. 'I've really missed this!'

Something like *joie de vivre* seemed to awaken in this carpenter. We spoke more and more and I told him, 'As a child I used to love beards like yours. I even wanted one myself!'

This made Joshua smile again.

'And do you know what my mother responded?' I asked.

'Tell me,' he said cheerily.

'She said that a beard like that was like a cemetery for crumbs.'

Joshua laughed out loud. It seemed as though he was familiar with this problem.

It was a great laugh.

So genuine.

So free.

'I haven't laughed for ages,' Joshua declared.

He pondered for a while and then, from the bottom of his heart, he said, 'It's laughter that I've missed the most.'

And I'd never been so happy about making someone laugh. This man was strange, foreign, and unusual – but I'm telling you, he was also truly fascinating.

I wanted to find out more about Joshua. Did he have a girlfriend? And if not, was he still pining for an ex?

'So who used to make you laugh, then?' I asked.

'A wonderful woman,' he replied.

That there had been a wonderful woman in his life bugged me more than it should have.

'What… what happened to her?'

'She died.'

Oh my goodness! If I'd been interested in him – which was obviously not the case, but if I *had* been – then I was up against a dead woman. That was a bit creepy.

I therefore decided that I was never going to be interested in Joshua.

But then I looked into his sad eyes, forgot all about the 'never being interested' thing and wished that I could give him a comforting hug.

He seemed like someone who didn't often get hugged.

'Her name was similar to yours,' Joshua explained with a dejected look on his face.

'Woodward?' I asked, sounding surprised.

'Maria.'

God I was stupid!

'Maria used to make some really witty jokes about rabbis,' he swooned.

I was confused. 'Rabbis?'

'And about Romans.'

'*Romans*?'

'And Pharisees.'

I tried not to think of loose screws.

'Although you really shouldn't joke about Pharisees,' Joshua added.

'Yes... no... of course not,' I stammered. 'Pharisees are... totally unfunny.'

Joshua stared out over the lake, obviously thinking about his ex, and said, 'I will be seeing her again soon.'

That was a rather morbid announcement.

'When the Kingdom of Heaven will be on earth,' he added.

The Kingdom of Heaven? Alarm bells were now ringing in my head. Captain Kirk shouted from the bridge: 'Scotty! Get us out of here immediately!'

Scotty replied from the engine room: 'I can't, Captain.'

'Why not?'

'We haven't paid for the pizza yet.'

'How long will it take for Giovanni to bring the bill?' Kirk screamed, louder than the deafening alert siren.

'At least ten minutes. Possibly eight if we signal for attention,' came the answer from the engine room.

'We don't have eight minutes. He's on about the Kingdom of Heaven!'

'Then we're doomed, Captain.'

Since I couldn't escape, there was only one alternative. I had to change the subject. I was desperately looking for a way out of this conversation and found one. 'Oh, look Joshua! Someone's peeing in a bush.'

Not the most elegant way to change a conversation, I know.

But there really was a homeless person taking a leak in a thorn bush. After all, even in an idyllic place like Malente, there were people who were unemployed, on benefits and nutters who liked to have conversations with lampposts in the high street.

'That man is a beggar,' Joshua declared.

'Yes, it seems so,' I replied.

'We must share our bread with him.'

'What?' I said, astonished.

'We'll share our bread with him,' Joshua repeated.

'Sharing bread?' I thought. 'You only do that with ducks.'

Joshua got up and made as if to approach this slightly chubby, unshaven man and invite him to join us at the table. This date was well on its way to turning into the dinner from hell.

'We shouldn't share our bread with him,' I said, in a very loud, slightly squeaky voice.

'Give me one reason why not,' Joshua replied calmly.

'Erm…' I was trying to think of a good reason, but all I could come up with was: 'We don't have any bread, only pizza.'

Joshua smiled. 'Well, then we'll share the pizza.' And with that he went over to the homeless man and led him to our table.

The tramp, who went by the name of Frank and was probably in his late thirties, had a rather different idea about sharing than I did. He took our pizzas and all that was left for us were the side salads drenched in vinaigrette. He told us that he had been in prison last year, having robbed a mobile phone shop because of money troubles.

'So why a mobile phone shop and not a bank?' I asked.

'I felt that these service providers have earned a lot of money with their impossibly complicated tariffs.'

Frank could be accused of a lot of things, including a lack of interest in personal hygiene. But I couldn't fault his logic.

'How did you get into financial trouble?' Joshua asked after Frank had explained to him what a mobile phone shop actually was. Joshua poured Frank some more wine. He showed compassion – too much compassion, in my mind. I leaned over to him and said, 'Let's pay and go.'

But Joshua declared, 'We'll carry on breaking the bread with him.'

With that terrible stench in the air I would soon be breaking other things.

Meanwhile, Frank was answering Joshua's question. 'I lost my job at an insurance company.'

'And why?'

'I'd stopped turning up for work.'

'And was there a reason?' Joshua asked.

Frank hesitated. It seemed that this brought back painful memories.

'You can confide in me,' Joshua said in a pleasantly calming voice.

'My wife died in a car accident,' Frank explained.

Oh my goodness, I thought.

'And it was my fault.'

Now I had real sympathy with Frank and poured him some more wine.

And myself.

Frank spoke of his deep love for his wife and of the terrible night of the accident. It was the very first time that he had spoken about it in so much detail. Frank had been taking his wife Caro to a party. They were driving along a country road when a sales rep coming the other way pulled a risky overtaking manoeuvre. The cars collided head on and Caro died instantly. She was still planning to do so many things with her life. She'd just started a belly-dancing class for example.

'Were you driving too fast?' I wanted to know.

Frank shook his head.

'Could you have reacted differently?' I dug deeper.

He shook his head again.

'So why is it your fault then?' I asked, gulping.

'Because... because she died and I didn't,' he replied and

started to cry. This was the first time he'd told anyone about his guilt and it was the first time he was able to grieve freely. Joshua took his hand, allowed Frank to cry for a while and then asked, 'Was your wife a good person?'

'She was the best,' Frank answered.

'Then you should be as well,' Joshua said in his gentle, convincing tone.

Frank stopped crying. 'So I guess that means I can't rob any more mobile phone shops then, does it?' he asked ironically.

Joshua nodded.

Frank pushed the wine to one side, thanked us from the bottom of his heart, stood up and left. It was certainly possible to imagine that this guy would be off the booze for a while now. Man, Joshua could probably make loads of money with a rehab clinic in Beverly Hills.

He smiled at me. 'Sometimes you just have to listen to people to banish their demons.'

I suddenly thought how lovely it was that we'd shared the bread.

Joshua and I left the restaurant and walked silently along the lake towards the town centre. This time I didn't mind the silence. I watched the sunset with Joshua. Although it wasn't as impressive here in Malente as in Formentera, it was still nice enough to enjoy a few wonderful moments.

Joshua confused me. Sometimes I wanted to escape from him, sometimes I just wanted to listen to his voice, and other times I felt this tremendous urge to touch him. And I wasn't sure if he had this urge as well. Objectively speaking, he hadn't actually given me a single reason to think so. He had never once scanned my body from top to toe, and hadn't made any attempts to flirt with me. Why not? Was I really so unattractive? Was I not good enough for him? Who did this guy think he was? As a carpenter this guy certainly wasn't the pick of the singles market!

'Why are you looking at me so angrily?' Joshua asked.

'Nothing, nothing. My face just sometimes looks a bit strained,' I said awkwardly.

'No, it doesn't,' he responded. 'It seems friendly.'

He said that without a hint of irony in his voice. In fact, he was rather behind the times when it came to irony. I never had that feeling that any of his actions or gestures were fake, rehearsed or insincere. He really did seem to find my face friendly. Was that a compliment? At least it was better than Sven's constant refrain of 'I love every pound on you'.

I smiled. Joshua smiled back. And I chose to interpret this as flirting.

We strolled through the town centre. From a bar we could hear a crowd bellowing Meatloaf's *Bat Out Of Hell*.

Joshua was alarmed when he heard this.

'What's the matter,' I asked him.

'This music is satanic.'

Before I could reply, he stormed into the bar. I rushed in after him. There were about twenty young men and women who looked like they worked at the local building society, standing in the bar in front of a karaoke machine. The men had loosened their ties and the women had taken off their suit jackets. The atmosphere was boisterous; everyone was singing and swaying from side to side. It was the kind of karaoke party that can only be organised by people who spend the whole day battling bank transfer forms.

But Joshua was annoyed. Singing 'songs of Satan' like that did not meet with his approval. 'It's as though they are dancing around the golden calf.'

'And there is such a thing as taking things too far,' I grumbled.

'It's only a karaoke machine. Not a golden calf. And listening to Meat Loaf is indeed hellish, but nothing more than that.'

Then I went over to the building society employee who was holding the microphone and asked him, 'Can I borrow that for a while?'

The man, a typical typical product salesman with slicked back hair thought about what he was going to answer. But before he could respond, I'd grabbed the microphone off him and shoved it into Joshua's hand.

'What do you want to sing?'

He hesitated, not quite sure what I wanted him to do.

'It's fun,' I said cheerily. 'What are your favourite songs?'

Joshua got himself together and said, 'I particularly like the psalms of King David.'

I looked at the song lists on the karaoke machine. 'All right. You're getting *La Bamba*.'

I pressed the button and the machine started, but Joshua didn't get into the groove, even though he tried, as he was clearly trying to do me a favour. He half-heartedly sang along to *La Bamba*, but at the *Soy capitán, soy capitán* bit he put the microphone down. It wasn't for him. I'd made a mistake. And I was sorry that I'd coerced him into doing it.

The slick-back man came up to me. 'So, are you done killing the mood?'

I looked around and saw lots of annoyed faces. 'Yes. It looks like it.'

I was about to pass the microphone back to him. But then Joshua joined us. 'I would like to sing. Is there perhaps something more meaningful in this machine?'

'We don't want anything meaningful,' the building society guy shouted. 'We want *99 Red Balloons*!'

I saw that Joshua really did intend to sing. He clearly didn't want to let me down. That was kind of sweet.

So I pulled the building society man aside and quietly whispered, 'Let him sing or I'll kick your red balloons. Then there'll only be 97.'

'Well, it sounds like a good idea with a calmer song for a change,' he answered fearfully.

I went over to the machine, perused the song catalogue for a while and found *Landslide* by Fleetwood Mac. Joshua took the microphone and started singing in his wonderful voice. By the time he'd finished, half of the building society lot were in tears. The rest of them were shouting: 'We want more! We want more...!' A young, quite petite woman approached Joshua and said, 'How about *We Will Rock You?*'

Quite annoyed at this suggestion he asked: 'Is it about a stoning?'

But he wasn't half as confused as the young woman and I were.

I looked through the song catalogue again and was only able to find tracks that I did not think were particularly suitable for Joshua, like *Do Ya Think I'm Sexy?*, *Bad* or *Who Let the Dogs Out?*

'I think, we can go,' I suggested to him. But the building society gang simply didn't want to let him leave, and so Joshua asked the crowd: 'Am I allowed to sing a psalm as well?'

The slick-back answered. 'Yeah sure. Whatever that is.'

Joshua showed him what it was. He sang a wonderful psalm, which he had – seemingly instinctively – chosen for the bankers, as it included the line: 'If riches increase, set not your heart upon them.'

When he'd finished, the building society people clapped their hands excitedly. 'Bravo', they shouted. 'We want more!' and 'Encore'.

So Joshua sang another psalm. And, fired up by the bankers, he sang yet another. And another. In total he sang eight of them, until the bar closed. The bartender was deeply moved and decided not to charge for the wine. Even the building society lot had switched from Jägerbombs to red wine. Everyone said farewell to Joshua and thanked him, and as I looked back at the cheerful crowd, I got the impression that they would be just a little bit happier processing overdraft applications the next day.

Joshua accompanied me to my father's house. I was euphoric and slightly tipsy. It had been a long time since I'd drunk as much wine as I had done with this man (who seemed to be completely sober – was he used to drinking or did he just have a better metabolism?) It was also almost certainly the strangest evening that I'd ever spent with a man, not counting the day when Sven seriously suggested that we could share a room with his mother for a night at a fully booked hotel in Formentera.

Joshua had a way of touching people. And he touched me as well. But I was But I was totally unsure whether the feeling was mutual. Did he find me attractive? He'd still not taken a peak at my breasts. Maybe he was gay? It would certainly explain why he was such a nice guy.

'It's been a wonderful evening,' Joshua said and smiled.

Maybe he did find me attractive?

'I have dined, sung and, more than anything, I have laughed,' Joshua explained. 'I haven't had such a wonderful evening here on earth for a long time. And I have only you to thank for that, Marie. Thank you!'

He looked at me gratefully with his wonderful eyes. It almost seemed as though he really hadn't had this much fun for a long time.

Maybe he fancied me! That's how I was taking it, in any case. If my knees had been shaking just a little bit more they would have been dancing the Charleston.

'So would you like to come upstairs for a bit?' I asked, without thinking. I was immediately shocked by what I'd said.

'What do you want to do upstairs?' Joshua asked innocently.

No, I couldn't sleep with him. That would be wrong on three counts – because of Sven, Sven and Sven. And because of Kata, who would then spend the coming years making comments about screwing.

'Marie?'

'Yes?'

'I asked you a question.'

'Yes, you did,' I confirmed.

'And are you going to answer my question?'

'Sure.'

Neither of us said a word.

'Marie?'

'Yes?'

'You wanted to give me an answer.'

'Erm, what was the question again?'

'Why should I go upstairs with you?' Joshua repeated gently. It seemed as he really didn't have a clue.

It was mad. He was so innocent. Somehow that made him even more attractive.

But if he didn't have a clue what I wanted to do with him upstairs, I could probably still get myself out of this situation pretty easily and protect myself from making another error. Or worse – from being rejected.

I could probably just defuse this whole thing. I just needed to make sure that my drunk self didn't answer something incriminating like 'have a coffee'.

'So what do you want to do with me?' Joshua asked again.

'Screwing.'

'Screwing?'

Damn the red wine.

'Erm… I mean scrawing.'

'Scrawing?'

'Yes,' I smiled awkwardly.

'What's that?'

Oh my God. How was I supposed to know?

'I… erm… did mean screwing… in the attic,' I added hastily.

'You want us to go and work on your attic together?'

'Yes!' I answered, delighted to have turned the conversation around.

'But at this time of night, we'll wake up your father and your sister,' Joshua said.

'Yes. And that's exactly why we won't be doing that!' I announced slightly insanely.

Joshua looked a little bewildered. I grinned awkwardly.

Then he said, 'Good! Let's do some screwing together tomorrow then.'

'I heard that!' bellowed a slurring, aggressive voice behind us. I turned around, and Sven appeared from behind the plum tree at the edge of our large front garden. Had he been waiting outside my house this whole time?

He looked terrible. He was drunk and incredibly angry. 'You've been cheating on me!' he yelled at me.

'I haven't,' I replied.

'No, of course not,' he sneered. 'I bet that you've been carrying on with this long-haired ape the whole time.'

'My friend,' said Joshua calmly, standing in between us. 'Don't raise your voice to Marie.'

'Piss off, hippie. Or I'll kick your arse!' Sven threatened.

'Don't do that,' Joshua warned softly. But then Sven hit him in the face with the flat of his hand.

'Oh my God!' I exclaimed, looking at Joshua. He was holding his cheek. It looked like Sven had hit him hard.

'Come on. Fight, if you're a man!' Sven shouted at Joshua.

But Joshua just stood still. He did nothing. Absolutely nothing. I'm sure that he could have trounced him quite easily. He seemed much fitter than Sven. And besides, he was nowhere near as drunk. But Joshua didn't make any attempts to respond to this provocation: 'I will not fight you, my frie…'

'I'm not your friend!' Sven hit him again, this time with his fist.

'Ahh…' Joshua grunted. That must have hurt a lot.

'Defend yourself,' Sven urged him.

But Joshua only stood in front of Sven, peacefully, without any kind of aggression. He'd gone all Gandhi. Sven, on the other hand, swung another punch. Joshua fell to the ground. Sven jumped on top of him and carried on hitting, screaming: 'Defend yourself, you poof!'

Panicking, I thought, 'Yes, Joshua. Defend yourself!'

But Joshua did not fight back. Sven carried on punching him. I couldn't bear to watch it any longer. I grabbed Sven by the collar and pulled him off Joshua. 'Stop it immediately!'

Sven stared at me, eyes full of rage, and coughed in my face. He reeked of alcohol. For a short moment I feared that he would hit me as well. But he didn't. He got off Joshua and turned to me and said 'I never want to see you again'. And then he left.

As loudly as I could, I yelled after him, 'Great!'

Then I looked at Joshua and his split lip. He stood up. I felt awful, as it was my fault that Sven had lost it like that. But I was also annoyed with Joshua. If he'd only defended himself a little bit, he wouldn't have ended up in such a state. And I wouldn't have felt so bloody guilty!

'Why didn't you defend yourself?' I asked angrily.

'But whosoever shall smite thee on thy right cheek, turn to him the other also,' Joshua answered calmly.

That made me really angry. 'Who do you think you are?' I snapped. 'Jesus?'

Joshua stood up. He was shaking. He looked deep into my eyes.

'Yes, actually.'

CHAPTER TWELVE

'Get us out of here!' Kirk screamed.

'But Captain…'

'No buts! He really does think he's Jesus!' Kirk insisted.

'But we can't just escape!'

'Why not?' Kirk was about to lose it.

'Because he's hurt.'

Kirk thought for a moment. Scotty was right. Joshua couldn't be left alone in this state.

But Kirk wasn't happy about it.

'Scotty?'

'Yes, Captain.'

'There's something that I've always wanted to tell you.'

'And what would that be?'

'That you're really annoying.'

I looked at Joshua, who was just about standing up, his lip still bleeding. 'I expect you want to know why I'm here,' he said calmly.

No, I didn't! I also didn't care which loony bin he'd broken out of. So I went on: 'Don't speak. You need to rest. I'll take you to Gabriel's.'

'That's not necessary. I can make my own way there,' Joshua said, and I hoped that this was the case. I just wanted to get away from him as quickly as possible.

After two steps, he collapsed. Damn it!

Sven had hit him harder than I'd thought. I helped him all the way back to the vicarage. Joshua tried again: 'I came to earth because…'

But I just said, 'Shhh!' I didn't want to hear that. I had enough madness going on in my life right now. I didn't need his on top of that.

I rang the vicarage bell and Gabriel opened the door in a vest. The vision of him standing there in his underwear was something that I really could have done without.

Gabriel ignored me. He was deeply shocked to see Joshua in such a state.

'What did you do to him?' he demanded.

'I knocked him out in the twelfth round with a wonderful left hook,' I snapped.

'This is not the time for clever remarks,' Gabriel replied, sounding much stricter than he ever had during confirmation class.

I explained to him what had happened. Gabriel looked at me angrily, took me aside and hissed: 'Leave Joshua alone!'

I hissed back. 'My pleasure to the power of a million.'

Gabriel led a stunned looking Joshua into the house. I noticed three odd things. Firstly, Gabriel treated Joshua as a servant would his master. Secondly, Gabriel had two massive scars on his back. And thirdly, I heard a voice calling 'What's going on?' – and that voice sounded remarkably like my mother's.

I hurried over to a window, looked into the vicarage and sure enough – my mother was walking around inside. Dressed in her underwear.

I was now well and truly sober.

Meanwhile…

Gabriel took Joshua into the spare room, treated his wounds and caringly sat by his bed until he'd fallen asleep. Why on earth had the Messiah got involved with Marie? Gabriel couldn't think of any plausible answer to that question and finally returned to Marie's mother, who was lying curled up in his bed. For this former angel, this was quite a remarkable sight. For decades he'd longed to be reunited with her, and now his dream had finally become reality. He smiled. Angels always knew that God had an unusual sense of humour, but it was not until now that the full extent of God's humour had become clear to Gabriel. That people had sex like a saw – backwards and forward – was simply one of the Almighty's delightful jokes.

And it was a wonderful activity.

The only downer was that the world was going to end soon, and the chances of Gabriel's beloved getting into heaven were close to zero. He had tried to convert Silvia, but she'd tossed the Bible on to the bedside table and started nibbling on his earlobes. Then he'd forgotten all about wanting to convert Silvia.

Yet even if his great love did manage to enter into the Kingdom of Heaven, he doubted that this wonderful sawing action was permitted in the domain of the Almighty.

'Why are you looking so worried?' Marie's mother asked.

Gabriel appeased her, telling her that everything was all right, and gave her a kiss.

'Does it have something to do with that carpenter?' Silvia was not letting it go. She was a psychologist, after all.

Gabriel thought for a while. He couldn't let her in on it all. He couldn't tell her that Jesus just wanted to spend some time among the people working as a carpenter, something he loved doing, before heading off to Jerusalem for the great battle against evil. He couldn't say that the Messiah had come to him because he was the angel whom he loved the most, nor that he, Gabriel, had warned Jesus how much times had changed and that walking among the people would not bring him any joy. How could he explain that the Messiah was actually very stubborn, and wouldn't be put off doing anything once he'd got an idea into his head – something the rabbis in the temples could vouch for? Gabriel certainly couldn't tell Silvia that the son of God had gone on a date with none other than her own daughter.

But what did he want from Marie?

'Are you going to answer my question today?' Silvia demanded to know. He just turned to her and said, 'The carpenter is a great man.'

'I'm sure he's not as great as you are,' my mother smirked, making Gabriel blush. One thing was certain – he would not be getting used to her remarks about his tool, even if the end of the world was very nigh.

Then Silvia started kissing him again. Sure, she was interested in his problems, but on the other hand, she'd been without a man at her side for far too long. There would be plenty of time for psychological discussions later.

But Gabriel was only half-heartedly responding to her advances. He was thinking about Joshua. He had a great task ahead of him. He had to create the Kingdom of God on earth. And no one was allowed to interrupt him – least of all an exceedingly ordinary person like Marie.

CHAPTER THIRTEEN

I was still in a state of shock when I got back to my father's house and bumped into Svetlana. She was barefoot, dressed in a bathrobe, leaning against the kitchen sink and drinking a coffee in the middle of the night. In my mind's eye, all I could see was her indulging in some sort of tantric sex marathon with my father. I wished I could rip my mind's eye out of its socket.

'What was all that noise out there earlier? Sounded like a fight?' Svetlana asked. Her German was really good. It seemed like she'd been to university, though it was probably the Belarusian University for Applied Sham Marriage.

I was furious. It was none of her business what that noise was all about. Why did I even need to be conversing with her? Why hadn't she stayed in Minsk? Why did that stupid Iron Curtain have to fall? Where were those totalitarian regimes when you really needed them?

'Leave me alone,' I replied snarkily. 'And put some clothes on.'

Svetlana looked at me angrily. I met her gaze – perhaps I would be able to outstare her?

'You're very rude to me,' she countered. 'I want this to change.'

'OK, I can be even ruder if you like,' I replied.

'You want me to leave,' she declared.

'Not necessarily. You could also spontaneously combust.'

'Well, believe it or not, I love your father.'

'Sure. I mean, you've already known him for, what, three weeks?' I quipped.

'Sometimes all you need is a moment to fall in love,' she replied.

Why on earth was Joshua racing around in my mind now? I shook off my thoughts about the carpenter and turned to Svetlana: 'You only signed up to a dating agency to get into the west.'

'Yes, and thank the Lord that I met someone like your father. He's a wonderful man.'

I snorted disapprovingly.

'And he's going to be a wonderful father to my daughter.'

'Your what?' I shouted.

'Daughter.'

'Your *what*?'

'Daughter. She's still with her Grandma in Minsk.'

'YOUR WHAT?'

'You know, you tend to repeat yourself.'

'YOUR. *WHAT*?'

'That's what I'm saying.'

I couldn't even begin to compute this information. Was my Dad also going to have to finance her bloody child?

'My mother is flying to Hamburg with her today.'

'So Grandma is coming here as well, is she?'

'Don't worry. Grandma is taking a flight straight back to Minsk.'

'That doesn't sound cheap.'

'My little girl is not allowed to fly on her own, and my mother can only take one day off from her job.'

'So who's paying for all this flying about?

'Who do you think?' Svetlana replied with a hint of sadness in her voice.

'You really are despicable,' I hissed.

'You have no idea what my life is like,' Svetlana countered. 'And you have no right to judge me.'

'Yes, I do. This is my father we're talking about!' I tried to look as menacing as possible.

Svetlana took a deep breath and then, incredibly calmly, she promised: 'I understand that you are worried about your father. But I will never hurt him like you hurt your groom.'

I gulped. I had nothing to say to that. Svetlana walked out of the kitchen. At the door, she turned back to me again and said, 'Judge not, that ye be not judged.'

Then she left the room. I wanted to judge her to death.

I really wanted a coffee now too – the caffeine would probably have calmed me down I was in such a terrible mood. But then I looked at Kata's sketchpad, which was lying on the kitchen table. She'd drawn another comic strip, which seriously distracted me.

I put Kata's comic strip down. Was it true? Did I only ever fall for the wrong men?

As I lay on my bed and looked at the wet patch on the ceiling for a change, I thought about the men in my life – about Kevin the breast-kneader, about Marc the cheater and especially about Sven. I never dreamed that he could be so violent. Even though I was feeling guilty that he had lost it like that because of me, I was suddenly overjoyed that I'd hotfooted it at the altar.

Joshua on the other hand was completely different to the other men – so gentle, so unselfish and compassionate. And he was a great singer. It was a real shame he was completely bonkers.

I was keen to know just how bonkers he was. So I did some googling on my father's laptop and found two articles about people who claimed to be Jesus. One of them was just a nutter.

His delusions were not curbed until he jumped off a garage trying to prove his divine capabilities. The other one was a vicar in Los Angeles, who claimed to be Jesus so as to be able to con his followers out of hundreds of millions of dollars. Looking at this unscrupulous sect leader made you think, 'Hey! Let's nail him to a cross and see whether he really is Jesus.' Joshua was not likely to be one of those who used their delusions to trick people out of money. He was more likely to be one of the garage types. What had happened to make him go off the rails? Perhaps the death of his ex?

I was thinking far too much about a carpenter who was a few teeth short of a fretsaw.

I lay down in my bed again, turned off the light and decided to think about something other than Joshua... and his wonderful voice... and his great laugh... and his charming ways... and those eyes... those eyes... those... Damn!

I tried to think about someone else. Any great man. George Clooney, for example. Good idea. The best actor in the universe as we know it... but his laugh was not as great as Joshua's... and his eyes weren't as wonderful either... those eyes...

Oh my God! Not even George Clooney could stop me from thinking about Joshua.

Now there was only one thing left to do – I had to think about Marc. After all, the remaining feelings I had had for him had caused me to ditch Sven at the altar. I thought about Marc... about his looks... his charm... that could not be compared to Joshua's... because Joshua had a better aura... and he was a kinder person... and he had a better voice... and those eyes... those eyes... eyes... eyes... eyes...

Oh no! Although Joshua was mad, not even Marc could get him out of my thoughts. My sister was right – if anyone could fall for the wrong men then it was me.

CHAPTER FOURTEEN

'*Jesus?*' Kata had a minor laughing fit at the breakfast table, and I regretted telling her about my date at all. After a long moment she finally stopped laughing and suddenly looked at me, deadly serious: 'Have you done a pregnancy test yet?'

'I didn't sleep with him!' I answered indignantly.

'But what about the Immaculate Conception?' Kata said, and starting laughing hysterically again.

I threw a bread roll at her. And a spoon. And an egg cup. She didn't stop laughing until I picked up the marmalade.

'It's not funny,' I grumbled.

'No, of course not,' Kata snorted, and burst out laughing once more.

When she'd finally calmed down, she reached for a bread roll and winced. She had a stabbing headache again.

'Well, it's not because of the red wine this time,' I said anxiously.

'Yes it is,' she insisted, a little bit too adamantly.

'When do you have your next check-up?' I asked.

'In three weeks.'

'Can't you get them to see you earlier?'

'It's nothing.'

'And what if it is?'

'Then,' Kata grinned, 'your Jesus can do some miracle healing.'

I threw another bread roll at her head.

Then the doorbell rang. We looked out through the kitchen window. Joshua was standing there with his toolbox.

'Speaking of the Messiah…' Kata joked, slurping her coffee.

'Am I going to have to listen to Jesus jokes for the rest of the day now?' I demanded.

'You'll be able to read some of them in my next comic strips,' Kata replied.

The doorbell rang again.

'Aren't you going to open the door for the Son of God?' she asked me.

'No. I want to hit the urologist's daughter,' I smiled, rather more sweetly than sourly.

'Jesus wouldn't like all this anger one bit,' Kata said disapprovingly. She grabbed the *Malente Post*. I only had another five day's holiday. Dad wasn't there to open the door; he'd gone to Hamburg Airport with Svetlana to collect that bloody child of hers. I stood up, sighed, went to the door, opened it – and was amazed at what I saw. Joshua was completely unscathed. No black eye. No scratches. No swollen lip.

'Good morning Marie,' he greeted me. He was visibly pleased to see me again. And his cheery smile made me go weak at the knees again.

'I'm ready to screw with you now,' he announced soberly.

I heard Kata having a laughing fit in the kitchen.

I closed the kitchen door. 'I'm not sure that's such a good idea,' I told Joshua.

'You don't believe that I'm Jesus,' he declared.

Why couldn't he just say, 'This whole Jesus thing has been a pretty stupid joke and I only did it because I smoke too much dope.' I could have lived with that. We could have built a future together based on that.

'You don't have faith,' Joshua stated baldly.

And you don't have a straightjacket, I thought.

'Listen, if you really are Jesus,' I said irritably, 'then go and jump off a garage.'

'Excuse me?' Joshua was mildly surprised.

'Or turn water into wine or walk over a lake, or turn the lake into wine to make people happy. Or make there be a sweetener that actually tastes good,' I urged.

'I think you have misunderstood why miracles occur,' he answered sternly. Then he walked past me and up the stairs to the first floor.

Who did he think he was, scolding me like that? I would love to have thrown the marmalade at his head. And then licked it off his body.

Oh dear. My hormones really did run riot whenever I saw him.

Should I go after him now? Or was it better to keep away from him, and do silly things like trying to get my life in gear again? Perhaps I should think about a career change. But I knew I couldn't get a better job with my qualifications.

I opted for the next-best thing – hanging out with a friend.

Michi owned a video store, his love life was about as disastrous as mine, and before I met Sven, I'd spent more or less every evening with him. When he closed his video store at nine o'clock (really late for Malente), we liked to consume a balanced diet of takeaway pizzas, crisps and Diet Coke, while watching DVDs and providing our own running commentary, such as:

'Leonardo looks a bit cold.'

'I bet he wishes he hadn't won that ticket now.'

'There… now Kate has let go of him…'

'… and he's sinking down into the icy water.'

'I think that the message of this film is that you sometimes just have to let go.'

As I stood slurping a coffee at the counter in the video store, I told Michi, who was very knowledgeable about the Bible, all about Joshua. I kept a few minor details – such as the fact that I had feelings for this carpenter – to myself.

Michi told me that those beautiful words that Joshua had said by the lake on the subject of 'How to Stop Worrying and Start Living' had already been spoken by Jesus in the Bible. I also found out that Jehoshua was the Hebrew version of the Latin word Jesus, and that Joshua was the modern Anglo-Saxon version of the name.

'Your carpenter is a pretty well-informed nutter,' Michi said admiringly.

'So he's a professional nutter,' I noted.

'Yes, and professionals are always impressive.'

I sighed, and Michi looked at me disapproving. 'Marie! You don't have feelings for this guy, do you?'

'No, no,' I replied, staring at the cover of a DVD.

'Since when do you like porn films?' asked Michi.

I immediately threw the cover on the floor, trying not to think about what kind of men had held it after whatever they did with it.

'You really are keen on the carpenter,' Michi declared.

'Am I that easy to read?'

'Do you want me to tell you the truth?'

'No, lie.'

'You're not easy to read at all,' Michi began. 'Far from it, you are a mysterious woman, whose thoughts are as difficult to read as those of Mata Hari. No, Mata Hari is like Jane Bennett in comparison to you!'

'Liar,' I said. 'I don't want to be easy to read.'

'There are worse things,' Michi tried to comfort me. 'Like being alone in the world.'

'Well, I am!' I wailed.

'No, you're not,' Michi retorted, giving me a hug.

He really was like a brother to me (even though Kata always claimed that if this were true, it would have been an incestuous relationship).

'If you feel anything for this Joshua, you need to find out whether he is psychologically disturbed or whether he's just pretending to be for some reason.'

'How am I supposed to do that?' I asked. 'Steal his medical records?'

Michi grinned. 'Well, either that or ask the Reverend Gabriel. He knows him, doesn't he?'

'You're right. Although I'd rather go after the medical records,' I sighed.

I bumped into my mother in front of the vicarage. She was whistling away cheerily as she came out. She looked very pleased and I realised that both my mother and father currently had better sex lives than I did. This was a fact that could easily have pushed a woman into her mid-thirties with weaker nerves than mine in a depression. Mum smiled at me. 'How are you, Marie?'

'I've been better,' I replied, wondering whether or not I should question her about her relationship with Gabriel. But then we'd just end up arguing again, as we did every time I asked her about her love life. My God, why couldn't my parents just do what all other married couples did at their age – sit down on the sofa together and be bored?

'You're probably wondering what I was doing at Gabriel's. And you have a right to know.'

I didn't know whether I wanted to claim this right. But the prospect of having Svetlana as a stepmother and maybe even Gabriel as a stepfather led me to ask: 'OK. Why were you at Gabriel's?'

My mother broke into song: *'Girls just wanna have fun.'*

'The last time you were a girl it was in the last millennium,' I snapped.

'Right back at you,' she quipped.

'This is just too much right now,' I muttered, trying to get past her. But Mum stood in front of me.

'If you need help…' she began.

'I'll be very unlikely to come and lie on your couch,' I interrupted.

'Well, I am responsible for all your problems, because I got divorced,' she answered tersely. I nodded..

'You know, Marie, at some point you reach the age when you have to stop blaming your parents for everything. You have to take responsibility for your own life.'

'And when exactly do you reach that age?' I asked sharply.

'In your early twenties,' she grinned. And as she left, she added, 'But if you decide that you do need some psychological help, then I can put you in touch with a great therapist.'

I watched her go. Her haughtiness made me so angry I felt like getting in touch with a great hitman.

As I stepped into Gabriel's office I looked at the painting of the Last Supper again, and saw that Jesus did indeed look like Joshua, even more so than a Bee Gee. That was actually quite creepy. Gabriel was busy clearing his calendar for the coming week for some reason. Without looking up he asked, 'So, planning another wedding?' Thirty years of laughter-free sermons, and Gabriel had still not understood that he had no sense of humour worth speaking of.

'I… I want to ask you something. About Joshua.'

Gabriel looked up at me sternly, but I wanted to know, so I bravely stammered on: 'He… says that he's Jesus. Is… is he mad?'

Gabriel answered me with a stern question: 'What do you want from him?'

Thank God I was sober and didn't answer 'screwing'.

'Is he mad?' I repeated instead.

'No, he's not.'

'So why did he lie?' I demanded.

Gabriel did not delve into this any further. He just said, 'Marie, Joshua will never reciprocate your feelings.'

'Why?' I asked, without noticing that I was admitting to having feelings for Joshua.

'Trust me, this man is not going to fall in love with a woman,' Gabriel explained emphatically.

And I thought, 'My God. Joshua is gay after all.'

By the time I got home my head was buzzing. But Joshua had told me about another woman. Could he really be gay? But on the other hand, Palestinian carpenters probably had a hard time coming out, much like football players. Perhaps people there preferred to tell the women they weren't interested in that they were Jesus, rather than having to explain themselves.

Kata wasn't at home, so I couldn't talk to her about my suspicions. Instead I climbed up to the attic where Joshua was. He was busy sawing a new wooden beam and was singing another one of his psalms. When he saw me, he stopped singing and a gentler expression came over his face. His anger must have been short-lived. Right away, I began with my 'Inconspicuous Questioning' mission.

'Joshua... did you have to sing your psalms alone at home as well?'

Joshua was surprised at my question. 'No, I didn't.'

'So whom did you sing them with then?'

'I had friends.'

'Men?'

'Yes, men.'

So he was gay, I thought.

'So were there people among them whom you loved?' I was really going for it now.

'I loved them all.'

All of them? I was aghast. 'How many men were there?'

'Twelve,' Joshua answered.

Good grief! 'Not all of them at the same time?' I giggled nervously.

'Oh yes, of course!'

Oh my God!

'They were all very normal people. Fishermen, a tax collector...'

One of his lovers was a tax collector? Well, the world is a colourful place. I gulped and played my final trump card: 'But... what about Maria?'

Joshua noticed my confusion and asked: 'You think that these men and I shared a physical love for one another?'

'No, no, no, no...' I sputtered. But I just couldn't lie to this man. 'No, no, no... yes,' I admittedly sheepishly.

Joshua laughed out loud. The whole attic vibrated. But this time I didn't think his laugh was quite so wonderful.

Then we suddenly heard a child screaming loudly. Joshua stopped laughing and we listened.

'We need to put her on the floor,' Svetlana was saying on the stairs. She sounded very worried. Joshua and I rushed downstairs and saw her pinning down her eight-year-old daughter on the floor with my father's help. This fragile blonde little girl was having an epileptic fit. She was twitching uncontrollably and frothing at the mouth.

'Is Lilliana in pain?' my father asked anxiously.

'She wasn't screaming because of the pain. It was because she was frantically sucking in air,' Svetlana explained, trying to remain as calm as she possibly could. 'A fit like this generally lasts two minutes,' she added.

My father nodded and held the child so that she would not hit anything and injure herself. Joshua approached them and bent down over the twitching child.

'What do you want?' Svetlana asked him aggressively. You could tell that this mother would enter a Kung Fu tournament for her child. And she'd probably win, too.

Joshua did not answer. Instead he placed his hand on the girl. She immediately stopped twitching. Then she opened her eyes and smiled as though nothing had happened.

'From this very hour the girl is cured,' Joshua declared.

Svetlana and my father stared at the child in amazement.

CHAPTER FIFTEEN

This was definitely a 'holy moly' moment. Dad, Svetlana and I were completely perplexed, but the girl was not unnerved at all. She wiped the foam from her mouth with her sleeve, walked towards Joshua and smiled. She said something to him in Belarusian. (If such a language even existed. There is no such thing as Belgian after all, so on second thoughts it was probably Russian.) Joshua answered her in that same guttural language. Then they chatted until Joshua started laughing and went back up stairs.

I turned to Svetlana and asked her (very nicely with no nasty undertone) what they had been talking about.

'First Lilliana asked what had happened to her,' Svetlana explained. She was also far too confused to think about making snide remarks. 'Then that man said that God had healed her, and then Lilliana asked whether God could do everything, and the man confirmed that God really could do everything. Then Lilliana asked God for a PlayStation Portable. And for me to find a man who was much younger.'

Dad looked a little offended. At this moment in time it was hard to imagine that he could ever be fond of this little girl.

'And what did Joshua say to her?' I asked excitedly.

'He laughed and explained that Lilliana still had a lot to learn about God.'

I asked her whether she'd ever witnessed such a speedy recovery after one of her daughter's fits and she answered that she'd never seen anything like it. And by 'never' she meant 'never in the known history of medical research on epilepsy'. It was basically totally uncharacteristic for this disease.

I didn't want to know any more. I rushed after Joshua and caught up with him in my room, as he was about to climb up into the attic. I asked him, 'You... you can speak Russian?'

It might have been more pertinent to ask him if whether he could perform miracles. But as I wasn't sure about what I'd just witnessed, I decided not to. I was also far too scared of what he might answer.

'That was Belarusian,' Joshua corrected me.

'Who cares?' I barked at him. 'Just answer my goddamn question!'

'I can speak all the languages of the world.'

Of course he was unable to answer a question without seeming even madder.

'Prove it,' I blurted out.

'If you wish,' he smiled and then began a little address that started with '*Have faith in God*' and then continued in various different languages. I didn't know all of them. Some sounded like English, Spanish or whatever it was those Lebanese waiters babbled at the pizza place just around the corner. One made him sound like he had laryngitis – that was probably Dutch.

If this was some kind of a trick, it was a pretty good one. After this short speech I certainly no longer dared to ask Joshua about the miracle healing. I was even more afraid of what he might answer.

'So would you like to work with me now?' he offered. He really did want to spend the day screwing in the attic.

'I... I am not a great help.' I made my excuses and left. This whole thing was just too creepy.

A short while later I stormed into the vicarage. I wanted some answers from Gabriel and no cryptic waffle that would get me into any more embarrassing 'Oops, I thought you were a homosexual' situations.

But Gabriel wasn't there. I stormed out of the vicarage and into the empty church. For a moment I just stood there enjoying the cool air. It was quite humid outside as it can be on a late summer's evening. I looked at Jesus on the cross again, reflecting that if Joshua really had been through all that, then he had a remarkably friendly disposition…

What I kept to myself was that I was actually starting to believe this whole 'Saviour of the World' business!

Then I suddenly heard Gabriel's voice coming from the crypt. At first, I couldn't understand what he was saying, but then, as I came closer to the entrance of the crypt, I heard: 'You're wonderful…'

Oh no! He wasn't doing it with my mother in the crypt, was he?

'…Our Father which art in heaven…'

Phew, it was a prayer.

I plucked up my courage, went down the steps into the dank, musty old cave. It had a low ceiling; basketball players would certainly not have been able to stand upright in here. Then I saw Gabriel on his knees, praying. He noticed me, but carried on with his prayer. Was he expecting me to kneel down next to him? But then what? I didn't know any of the official church prayers; only my own improvised 'Please, dear Lord, make…' version.

I decided to keep schtum until Gabriel had finished.

I'd always found it quite weird that people knelt to pray. Why did God require that? Why did you have to kneel in front of him? Why did you have to submit to him like that? Was the Almighty in need of something to boost his self-esteem? That would make for an interesting therapy session. 'Dear God, please lie down on the couch… and now tell me, why do you want everyone to kneel before you?'

I was still imaging the therapist asking God about his childhood (an interesting proposition: who had created God? Did he create himself? How did that work?) when Gabriel looked up. 'Why didn't you kneel down next to me?' he demanded

I explained to him that I had minor textual insecurity when it came to prayers.

'Everyone can speak to God, however they like,' Gabriel replied.

I also shared my thoughts on the matter of kneeling down.

'God is concerned with more important things than how people pay homage to him, or even, whether people do so at all.'

'And what things would those be?' I asked, not entirely uninterested.

'Maybe you'll find out one day,' Gabriel answered. But judging by his tone, he seemed to think that this was unlikely. I changed the subject and excitedly began telling him about Joshua – his linguistic capabilities and the miracle healing.

'What was going on there?' I demanded an explanation.

Gabriel didn't say anything for a while. Then he asked me a question. 'What would you say if I told you that the carpenter really is Jesus?'

'I would say that you were bullshitting me,' I said sounding annoyed.

'Good,' Gabriel smiled. 'Then I'll tell you that the carpenter really is Jesus.'

I grimaced.

'How many more signs do you need?' Gabriel said. 'Joshua speaks all the languages of the world and has performed a miracle healing. The only thing that speaks against it, is…'

'Common sense?' I suggested.

'No, your lack of faith.'

'I can bullshit myself,' I snapped.

'Yep. I saw that at your wedding,' Gabriel responded drily.

His attempts at humour were beginning to get on my nerves.

'Let me give you some advice,' said Gabriel.

'What would that be?' My interest in his advice was minimal.

'Find faith,' he said very, very insistently, almost like a warning. 'Quickly.'

'Faith, schmaith,' I cursed, sitting on a pedalo in the middle of the lake. I didn't want to go home because Joshua was there, as was Svetlana and her child, who thought my father was far too old. I couldn't go to Michi's either, because after hours the video store was always filled with shifty-looking customers who came to rent porn films. As I was also unable to reach Kata on her mobile – what was going on there? – I decided to hop on a pedalo, something that I'd last done as a teenager. Back then, I used to pedal out into the lake whenever I was feeling a bit down. So pretty much every other day.

I had the lake to myself. The holidays were almost over and nowadays depressed teenagers obviously had better things to do than take pedalos for a spin, like searching the web for instructions on how to build bombs. It had also become unbearably humid, and it felt like there was thunder in the air, which I hadn't really paid any attention to with all my 'Who the hell have I fallen for?' thoughts. Not even when the first raindrops started falling. That's how confused I'd been because of Joshua and my conversation with Gabriel. But then the thunder made me jump. I looked to the skies and saw black clouds approaching at lightning speed. An icy wind was blowing my face. I quickly looked towards the shore and thought that it would have been nice if it were a bit closer.

I put my foot down, so to speak. I couldn't be on the lake when the lightning started. The thunder came ever closer, unlike the shore, which was still quite far away. I should have noticed this storm earlier. To hell with love! It just confuses you.

Suddenly the rain set in. It lashed against my face. Within just a few seconds, I was completely soaked. I was becoming increasingly out of breath from all the pedalling. My lungs were aching, not to mention my legs, and no matter how hard I tried, I just wasn't getting anywhere. The waves kept pulling my pedalo back. The next thunderclap was deafening and I was scared shitless. It was quite obvious that I wasn't going to make it to the shore. Hopefully the lightning wouldn't strike on the lake!

I was terrified and wanted to pray to God. For a second I even considered kneeling, since it made him so happy. But it isn't that easy to kneel down in a pedalo, so I decided just to clasp my hands together. But before I could begin with my prayer, a lightning bolt struck the other side of the lake. There was an almighty bang and I was momentarily dazzled. The pedalo tipped over and I fell into the water.

I was overcome by panic and a fear of death. But I tried to calm down. I could swim after all. Even if not particularly well. My sports teacher at school had always made derogatory comments like 'Oh well, I'm sure you have other talents' (although none of us had a clue what those talents might be). But paddling up to the surface seemed feasible. If I could make it up before I ran out of air, and then hurl myself into the pedalo, I might actually survive. With all my might I kicked my legs and tried to swim upwards. Just when I had almost reached the surface, I got cramp in my leg. I screamed, which isn't a clever thing to do underwater. My lungs filled up and burned so much that I thought they were going to explode. The air escaped through my mouth and I saw bubbles rise to the surface as I sank deep down into the lake. I frantically kicked my legs, but I didn't have enough strength to swim to the top with my burning lungs and a cramp-incapacitated leg. Suddenly the realisation hit me – I was going to die.

I was no longer able to struggle against my fate. I stopped fighting and sank further down. Pain and panic flashed through my body and soul, but it only felt like a faint echo.

I wondered whether I would go to heaven. Or to hell. I'd actually never done anything really bad in my life, except leaving Sven at the altar. Which was pretty bad, of course – I felt incredibly guilty about it. But what about all the good things I'd done in my life?

I couldn't think of anything particularly impressive. I'd never done any aid work or volunteering in a third-world country. I wasn't even a particularly charitable person. Saint Peter probably wouldn't be rejoicing at the gates of heaven: 'Welcome Marie, you who always gave your small change to the beggars on the high street.'

The bubbles had actually stopped coming out of my mouth. I lost consciousness, and everything around me went black. My feet were touching the bottom of the lake. I closed my eyes. I was about to find out whether heaven and hell existed.

And then someone grabbed my hand.

I was pulled up to the surface and gasped for air. My lungs were burning even more now. The water from the churned up lake was beating against my face. It was still raining, and I heard loud claps of thunder. Bolts of lightning dazzled me. And in the middle of this inferno, I saw who was holding my hand.

It was Joshua.

And he was standing on the water.

CHAPTER SIXTEEN

Joshua carried me over the lake.

Yes, he really carried me *over* the lake. I remember thinking 'He's carrying me *over* the lake'.

Of course, I could have thought a lot more about what just happened like, 'Joshua pulled me up from the bottom of the lake', or 'He saved my life', and more than anything 'Holy shit, he really is Jesus!'

But my brain didn't get any further than, 'He's carrying me over the lake'. It got stuck on this thought like a computer program that is 'not responding'. It was not able to compute thoughts like 'Holy shit, he really is Jesus'.

When my brain finally made some baby steps in the right direction, it decided to stick to harmless stuff like, 'No man has ever managed to carry me before'. When Sven had once tried to carry me over the threshold in a burst of romance, he almost slipped a slipped disc.

The wind and rain continued to lash against my face until Joshua threatened the skies and shouted 'Silence, be still!' at the lake.

The wind settled and a serene calm befell the scene. This man did not need oilskin or an umbrella.

When Joshua stepped onto the shore with me five minutes later, all the dark clouds had yielded to dusk. He put me down on a bench. I was completely drenched, unlike Joshua, and I'm not sure I'd ever been that cold. My lungs were still burning. 'I can take away your pain,' Joshua said calmly.

He wanted to touch me, like he had touched Svetlana's daughter. But I just screamed: '*Noooooo!*' I didn't want him to touch me. This was all too much for me already. Far too much!

Joshua paused. He didn't let on whether he was confused by my hysterical shouting. 'But,' he said, 'you're completely frozen.' He tried to touch me again.

'Don't!' I yelled at him. I was so afraid of him, probably quite a natural reaction to a supernatural being.

'You're afraid of me?'

He was pretty quick on the uptake…

'Fear thou not,' he said gently. But it had no effect on my panicked state.

'*Don't touch me!*'

He nodded. 'As you wish.'

'Go away!' I shouted at him with my last remaining energy, before succumbing to a coughing fit.

Joshua was still looking at me with great concern. Did I mean something to him or was he just caring to anyone whom he'd saved from drowning.

'By "go away" I meant "piss off".' I was desperately gasping for air and carried on coughing.

'As you wish,' he repeated calmly and respectfully. Then he left. He'd left me alone on a bench, completely soaked, because that's what I'd wanted.

Joshua disappeared from view around the corner. The rain had disappeared thanks to his invocation, but I was trembling much more than before, and this cough was unbearable. Somehow I had to get home. Otherwise I'd die of hypothermia here on the park bench. Bravely, I sat up. I would almost certainly make it home. This was a piece of cake. I stood up, took one step, and collapsed in a heap.

CHAPTER SEVENTEEN

'Beep, beep, beep,' I heard as I woke up. I was lying in a hospital bed. I was attached to a 'beep, beep, beep' machine. Why on earth was it so loud? Should sick people be plagued by such beeping? Shouldn't they be left in peace? I looked down at myself. I was wearing a hospital gown, so somebody had clearly undressed and dressed me. It was already dark outside, and I wondered whether I should call the nurse.

The first thing I did was to hit the machine until it finally stopped beeping. Only then did the thoughts that should have occurred to me on the lake start flashing through my head. He had saved my life. And most important of all – holy shit, he really was Jesus.

And another even more important thought struck me. 'Oh my goodness! I wanted to nibble Jesus' bum!'

I took a deep breath and tried to calm down. Maybe I'd just imagined the whole thing. Maybe I was injured and I'd been hallucinating. Then it would not have been Joshua who'd saved me; I'd have saved myself. No idea how. Just somehow. But how would I have saved myself? There's no way in hell I was fit enough to swim to the shore. But what was the alternative? If I hadn't been hallucinating, then Joshua really was Jesus. And if that was the case, then I could be very happy that I hadn't drowned, since I would definitely have ended up in hell, as I'd almost asked Jesus to come up to my room to sleep with me.

Well, most likely he would have rejected me.

But I was sure that it would not be considered meritorious at the gates of heaven to have been hitting on the Saviour of the World.

And to make matters worse I'd now gone and told him to 'piss off'.

Good Lord, if this was a matter of life and death, things were not looking good!

Then the door opened. For a moment I feared that it might be Joshua entering the room. Or floating in. But it was Sven. This was the hospital where he worked, and he was doing the night shift. Had he changed my clothes? I really didn't like the idea of that.

Sven looked at me compassionately. 'Are you all right?'

'No! Nothing is all right. Either I'm completely mad or I've seen Jesus and I am going mad because of that!' is what I would have liked to have replied. But instead I just nodded slightly.

Sven approached my bed. 'A passer-by found you by the lake, completely soaked. What happened?'

I told him about the pedalo, nothing more. He smiled sweetly and sang an old Neue Deutsche Welle song by Fräulein Menke about sinking pedalos and sunsets.

'I'd forgotten that song for a reason,' I replied cattily.

Sven took my hand. 'I'm here for you. I even made sure that you got the only single room available.'

It felt so wrong for him to be holding my hand. The only hand I should have been holding was Joshua's – that's what I felt, anyway.

I pulled my hand away from Sven and asked him not to touch me again. That shocked him. It seemed that he'd hoped I would find my way back to him in my moment of weakness. He no longer hoped that now. In fact he looked offended. 'Fine. Now it's time for your injection,' he declared in a professional voice.

'Injection?' I asked in a panic.

'You need an injection in your bum. Doctor's orders.' He pulled back the plunger of a syringe that had been lying on my nightstand.

I gulped. Injections aren't exactly a cause for jubilation, particularly not if your ex is the one administering them…

Reluctantly I turned over onto my front. If holding hands with Sven had felt wrong, then this was far worse. I squeezed my eyes shut, and things got even more uncomfortable, because Sven hit a cramped up muscle. I yelped.

'Oooops, sorry, I missed,' he said innocently. 'I'll have to go again.'

He stuck the needle into my bum again.

'*Ahhhhh*!' I yelped again.

'And I've missed again. Silly, silly me,' said Sven.

I looked at him. 'The doctor… the doctor hasn't asked you to give me an injection, has he?'

He didn't even try to act innocent. 'If I do it twice more you'll almost have a smiley on your arse,' he smirked and stuck the needle in again.

'*Ouch!*'

I jumped out of bed and screamed 'You're sick' at him.

Then I ran to the door, but Sven stood in my way. 'We're not done yet. The doctor wanted me to give you some laxatives, too.'

It was a precarious situation. My leaving him at the altar had clearly unleashed some dark side from deep within him. But I remembered the advice that my sister had given me about such situations. 'There's no problem that can't be resolved with a swift kick in the balls.'

Sven squealed and I ran out of the hospital onto the street, which was still wet after all the rain. I didn't stop until I couldn't run any further. Sven hadn't followed me. He was probably still wailing like a moonstruck coyote.

I hastened through Malente in a hospital gown in the middle of the night. My bare feet were almost completely numb from the cold and my whole body was shaking. When I'd finally reached my father's house I had no other option but to ring the doorbell. Fortunately it was not my father who opened the door, but Kata. She looked at me with great astonishment.

'Don't ask,' I said quietly.

'OK,' she answered, but immediately asked, 'What happened?'

I told her about the pedalo and Sven, but obviously didn't say a word about Joshua walking on water. I wanted to avoid my sister having me committed to a mental asylum.

Kata took me into the bathroom for me to wash away the smell of the lake. She told me that Dad, Svetlana and her little girl were already asleep. But I didn't want to go to sleep. I was still in an emotional state between heaven (Joshua) and hell (Sven). I showered, got changed and went into Kata's room. She had just finished drawing a new comic strip:

It was a surprising comic. Little Kata was never quite so self-pitying. God only appeared in her comics when she was particularly frustrated with life. It was clear that something was bothering her.

'You went to see the doctor,' I realised anxiously.

'Yes.'

'And?'

'I need to wait for the test results,' she said, trying to play it cool.

'Is there any cause for concern?'

'Just a routine check-up; no need to worry,' she explained straight-faced.

I didn't know whether to believe her or not. My sister was very good at lying, especially when it came to her own fears. But I also knew that I couldn't push her too much. So I looked for clues, to see whether there really was any reason to worry. There was a second comic strip on the table that she'd drawn today.

This comic was much more cheerful than the first, so she wasn't feeling like the world was going to end. So there probably wasn't any need to worry.

If I hadn't been so confused and shaken by the whole 'Joshua walking on the lake' business, I might have noticed that it was quite strange for Kata to be drawing comics for Christmas at the end of the summer. And I would have noticed that Kata had drawn a comic in which she questioned the existence of friendly old men with white beards. At least that was one of the possible ways of reading the Santa comic. The other was that Kata had a deep-seated desire to be absolved of all her sins by a friendly old man with a beard.

CHAPTER EIGHTEEN

Meanwhile...

Gabriel woke up in the kitchen of the vicarage and waited for Jesus to return. His beloved had a meeting in Hamburg, which is why she couldn't spend the night with him. God! He missed Silvia so much, even though he'd only been apart from her for a few hours. In difficult situations like these, Gabriel was firmly convinced that this love business had more cons than pros, and that God was going through a bad patch when he created love, as imperfect as it was.

Of course, the Almighty never had bad patches. As a former angel, Gabriel knew this, but his love-induced yearning could simply not be explained in any other way. What was the point of it?

It was rather like heartburn. He could not quite understand the divine purpose of this either.

Jesus was now finally back at the vicarage. He seemed very deep in thought.

'What is on your mind, my Lord?' Gabriel asked.

'What do you know about Marie?' Jesus asked.

Oh no, Gabriel thought. Is the Messiah really still thinking about this woman?

'Forgive me, Lord,' he answered. 'But Marie really is what we would somewhat profanely consider to be rather "ordinary" here on earth.'

'She does not seem ordinary to me at all. Quite the contrary, I see something special in her.'

'Special?' Gabriel's voice squeaked a little. 'Are we talking about the same Marie?'

'She made me laugh,' Jesus interrupted.

'Did she fall over?' Gabriel asked. As soon as he had spoken he was

shocked at himself. He felt anger bubbling up inside him. Why couldn't she just leave the Messiah alone?

'No, she didn't walk into a wall. What makes you say that?' Jesus asked, and Gabriel was suddenly relieved to learn that irony was a foreign concept to Jesus.

'Is she somewhat lacking in faith?' Jesus wanted to know.

'Somewhat?' Gabriel sighed, thinking that she was lacking faith 'somewhat', in the sense that Goliath's manhood was 'somewhat' large.

Jesus looked thoughtful.

'You don't want to convert her do you?' Gabriel asked hesitantly. 'You don't have time for that. Think about your task.'

'I just want to find out more about her,' Jesus replied and then disappeared into his room.

Gabriel stared at the closed door and wondered whether Jesus actually had feelings for Marie. He laughed at himself for thinking such an absurd thing. While Jesus was clearly capable of such feelings, Marie was certainly not in the same league as Mary Magdalene. Nor Salome. She was possibly on a par with Lot's wife. Maybe Jesus just wanted to convert a sheep that had lost its way.

CHAPTER NINETEEN

After everything that I'd been through, I didn't think I'd be able to get any sleep at all. On the other hand, I'd almost drowned and had run through half of Malente trying to get away from Sven. My spirit was shaken up, but my body just wanted to fall into a coma. I fell asleep at record speed and had a wild dream. I was standing in front of the altar and Gabriel asked me the 'Will you?' question, except it wasn't Psycho-Sven standing next to me, but Joshua. The cross on the wall behind him was bare. It seemed as though he'd jumped down and slipped into a very stylish wedding suit.

I answered Gabriel, from the bottom of my heart. 'Yes, I will.'

Joshua moved closer to kiss me. His hands gently touched my face. It was amazing to be touched my him. My heart was pounding. His lips came closer and closer. I was shaking with excitement. His beard was already touching my face, electrifying me. He wanted to kiss me… I was longing for him to do so… Our lips touched… And then I woke myself up screaming.

When I'd finally stopped, I realised that my subconscious self wanted to marry Joshua.

Why couldn't my stupid subconscious just stay out of my life?

I looked at the clock. It was 8.56 a.m. That late already? In four minutes, Joshua would be standing in front of my door. He always arrived at nine to work on the attic. I didn't want to see him. I was afraid of him! It was partly rational fear – that same fear that women in horror films probably experience when the guy with the manic chainsaw fetish is approaching. And partly it was the fear of my own feelings.

I grabbed my clothes, skipped unnecessary things like showering, hair brushing, tooth brushing and shoe tying, rushed out of the house and fell flat on my face. Damn shoelaces!

Svetlana's daughter was drawing on the road with some chalk. She saw me fall and burst out laughing. I pulled myself together, tied my shoelaces and listened as this little girl told me, 'Your hair looks stupid.'

Her mother had taught her German. I was not a fan of this kind of cultural diplomacy.

'My mother has much nicer hair than you,' the girl said in her Belarusian accent with a 'Na-nana-naa-nah' voice.

'How old are you?' I asked the girl.

'Eight.'

'If you carry on like this, you won't make it to nine.'

She was shocked and almost dropped her piece of chalk. Then I saw Joshua turning down into our road. I ran away like Forrest Gump on steroids. I prayed the whole time that Joshua had not seen me escape. That was until it dawned on me that I should probably not pray to God when it came to matters concerning Joshua.

Eventually I reached the lake, completely out of breath, and sat down on a pier. When I felt that I could start breathing again, I watched the sun sparkling on the water. Some tourists were already out on pedalos. There was a light breeze. Everything that had happened yesterday seemed so unreal. Like a dream. I'd probably just imagined that Jesus saved me – that was the logical explanation. And a calming one, even if the consequence was that I would now have to hear sentences like: 'Marie, those two hefty men are here to take you to your electroshock therapy.'

In that case Joshua and I would both have been nutters. He because he claimed to be Jesus, and me because I believed him. So we were ideally suited. We could make some super-cute crazy babies…

Hang on. I didn't just want to marry him – I wanted to have his babies too?

Like with Marc. All that was missing was giving them names. I was much more in love than I thought.

Than I'd ever been before.

Shit!

No sooner had I realised this than I heard his wonderful voice behind me. 'Marie?'

Joshua was standing on the pier. He had followed me after all.

'I'm happy to see you.' He smiled sweetly.

'Grdll,' I replied.

'You're afraid of me,' he stated calmly.

'Brdll.'

'And that's why you ran away from me.'

'Frzzl.'

'Fear thou not.'

He said these words so incredibly gently that all the fear in my body vanished in an instant.

'I have a question for you,' said Joshua.

'Just ask me,' I said. Without this stupid fear, I was once again able to speak properly.

'Would you like to eat with me again this evening?'

I could hardly believe it. He wanted to go out with me again!

'It would mean a great deal to me,' he added.

He really meant it. I could feel it. It really meant something to him.

That meant that I really meant something to him!

Yippee!

I was grinning like a Cheshire cat on dope as Joshua sat down next to me. Very close to me. My knees became weak at the sight of him, and my stomach turned wonderfully queasy. Our feet were now dangling next to each other over the water. It could have been an amazing moment between two nutters. But unfortunately, Joshua said something that dashed any hopes I had of us not needing to be put in a loony bin: 'The sea is much calmer than yesterday.'

'So you were by the lake yesterday as well?' I asked aghast.

'I carried you over the lake. Don't you remember?'

So it had not been a hallucination. I hadn't told anyone about what had happened. How could Joshua have known about it if it hadn't happened just like that?

'So... you really are Jesus?' I asked in a muffled voice.

'Yes, of course.'

'Oh!' I groaned. I couldn't think of anything else. No 'I'm standing in front of the Son of God!' No 'He walks the earth again.' No 'It's a miracle.' Just a pathetic 'Oh'. My whole self was a single exhausted, paralysed and overwhelmed 'Oh'.

'Are you feeling OK?' Jesus asked compassionately.

'Oh.'

'Marie, is everything all right?' He was sounding quite worried now.

I wasn't feeling well at all. Someone like me really should not have been in the presence of Jesus.

'Why on earth do you want to go out and eat dinner with *me*?' I asked flatly.

'Because you're just an ordinary person.'

'An ordinary person?'

'Exactly.'

There are better compliments. Thousands. But who was I to want compliments from Jesus? That was absurd in itself. Ridiculous. Pathetic.

I looked out over the lake, and it was getting calmer by the second. No waves, no storm, no lightning. Although that would have been pretty apt. I was sitting next to Jesus after all.

'You're very quiet.'

How observant, I thought to myself.

'What's up?'

'I... I don't think it's right for you to be associating with me.'

'Why not?'

'I'm not worthy of that. You should be sitting with the Pope, or someone like that.'

Or give the Dalai Lama a fright, I added in my head.

'You're worth just as much as the Pope,' Jesus replied.

'You have to say that. You're Jesus. You have to regard all human beings as equal. But trust me, I'm not worthy of being with you.'

'You are.'

That just proved that he didn't know what a loser I was. To know that you hadn't accomplished anything particularly worthwhile in your life was one thing; to do so in the presence of the Son of God was quite another.

'I want to ask you something,' Jesus said, looking deep into my eyes.

'And what would that be?'

'Spend the evening with me, like you'd spend it with any other person.'

'But you're not just any other person.'

'Yes I am. Everyone can be like me if they want to.'

Sure, I thought to myself. I'll just go and have a stroll across the lake then, shall I? 'Why do you want to do that?' I asked.

'Because... because... ' This was the first time that I'd seen him hesitate. Did he have feelings for me? Is that why he wanted to meet up?

No, to even think such a thing was blasphemous! The Son of God was obviously not able to fall in love with an earthly being. Especially not me.

Jesus cleared his throat. 'Because I'm eager to know how people live these days,' he answered in a determined voice.

So that was it. He needed a tour guide. I nodded affirmatively. And he seemed to be genuinely pleased about it.

Joshua went back to our house to finish the attic while I stared blankly out over the lake. I had agreed to go on a date with Jesus. Yes. My life was pretty crazy.

But if the Son of God wants you to show him the world, what are you supposed to say? Not tonight, I'm washing my hair?

I carried on sitting for a while and tried to process all of this. The thought that a ridiculous person like me could fall in love with Jesus was high up on the 'things to process list'. Yet it was quite easy. The realisation of having had anything to do with Jesus sent me into a state of shock. I no longer felt anything for him. Thank God.

Instead I just started thinking about how we were going to spend the evening. What would someone like Jesus want to experience? I realised that I didn't have a clue. And then I also realised that I hardly knew anything about him, either.

I proceeded to Malente's beautiful bookshop and asked the assistant for a copy of the Bible.

'Which version?' she asked.

I didn't have a clue what she meant. Were there different Bibles? If so, why? Was there a director's cut?

'Standard,' I replied, acting like I was in the know.

She sold me a Bible.

I went to a café, drank a latte, leafed through the Bible and realised that it bored me just as much as it did during confirmation class. Even now when I had a qualified interest in the subject. So I decided to switch formats. I went to Michi's video store and rang the bell. He opened the door looking dopey and unshaven. He was wearing a T-shirt adorned with a quote from Yoda, which was not entirely unfitting for my current situation: 'You must unlearn what you have learned.'

'What do you want?' he yawned, rubbing the sleep out of his eyes.

'I… I… just wanted to see you,' I replied.

'In the middle of the night?'

'It's eleven o'clock.'

'Exactly. The middle of the night.'

'I'd like to watch a couple of films.'

'What kind of films?' Michi asked.

'Ones about Jesus…' I said meekly.

'This Joshua is really confusing you,' Michi said. He sounded concerned and – if I'd heard correctly – there was a surprising note of jealousy.

'No, no,' I tried to deny it. But of course my voice sounded completely unconvincing after all I'd experienced in the last few days.

'I can assure you of one thing,' I explained to Michi. 'I no longer have any feelings for him.' At least that was true.

Michi clearly liked the sound of that. We crept into the video store and he put the coffee machine on.

Michi showed me a little Jesus compilation on the flat screen TV in the video store. First we watched *The Passion of the Christ*, Mel Gibson's film about the crucifixion.

'What are they babbling about?' I asked. I couldn't understand a word of what the actors were saying.

'Gibson filmed this movie in Aramaic and Latin,' Michi explained, and I thought that Gibson may as well have let the characters communicate in signal flags.

The Passion of the Christ was a pretty gruesome account. A horror film for Bible fans. The Jews certainly didn't come out of it terribly well. When Jesus was finally brutally crucified, it was so graphic that I was very happy that I had an empty stomach. I couldn't imagine that this man, who'd been sitting with me on the pier this morning, had gone through all of this.

In contrast, Michi then showed me the seventies musical film *Jesus Christ Superstar*. After just a few minutes, I was already longing for a second helping of *The Passion*. Jesus singing musical hits was far more horrific!

The actor was grimacing as though he was in a Louis de Funès film and he seemed similarly balanced. He was only outperformed by the black actor who played Judas dancing around in a white disco outfit.

After fifteen minutes we turned it off and watched Scorsese's *The Last Temptation of Christ*. I much preferred this film to the other two. Jesus was a real person. A neurotic person, but a person nevertheless. And who would not have been neurotic with such a dominant father figure?

That he'd had the opportunity to marry Mary Magdalene, whilst hanging on the cross, to become a mortal was pretty stirring. You just wanted to shout, 'Do it!' at him.

It was obvious that this Maria, whom Jesus had talked about during our date, must have been Mary Magdalene. So I got Michi, who was au fait with the Bible, to explain who she was. Whore? Wife? Lover? Groovy boogie dancer?

Michi explained that there was no evidence at all that she was a converted whore or Jesus Christ's ex-wife. And there were certainly no indications as to her funky dancing abilities. Having said that, there was some evidence that they'd kissed. It was not actually written in the Bible, but there was another old text from the second century BC, the so-called Gospel of Mary. If what was written in this text was true, it occurred to me that Jesus was indeed a person who could love an earthly woman.

Perhaps he was still capable of that today…

I didn't want to allow my thoughts to develop any further. Such a train of thought that was far too dangerous for someone in my position.

CHAPTER TWENTY

Meanwhile...

'So you've arranged to meet up with Marie again?' Gabriel couldn't believe what Jesus was telling him. *The Messiah was sitting at the kitchen table in the vicarage drinking coffee, one of the things he liked most about the modern age. Like pizza.*

'You heard correctly. I'm going to be spending this evening with Marie,' Jesus replied calmly, *as he poured himself another cup.*

'But why?' Gabriel asked aghast.

'Because I believe that I can learn a lot about humanity through Marie. How people live, what they feel and believe these days.'

'There are plenty of other people who could help you with that,' Gabriel interjected. *A couple of churchgoers immediately sprang to mind, people who would have been far more suitable for the Messiah to spend the evening with than Marie. He could even think of atheists who were more suitable than this woman, whom he was beginning to dislike more and more, even if she was the daughter of his beloved Silvia.*

'I am not going to cancel a planned appointment ,' Jesus said emphatically. *'And I happen to enjoy spending time with Marie.'*

As soon as he heard these words, Gabriel's heartburn made a reappearance. *'But don't you need to prepare for your task?'* he asked, in the hope that he might still be able to get Jesus to cancel.

'You do not need to lecture me,' Jesus replied cuttingly.

Gabriel stopped talking. No one could lecture Jesus. He knew that much.

'You should prepare for the final battle yourself,' Jesus warned.

'That's... that's what I'm doing,' Gabriel stammered, *suddenly very defensive.*

'No, you're just having fun with that woman.' The Messiah's tone was a little critical.

Gabriel turned red. He had indeed spent most of the last couple o f days in bed with his great beloved. Had Jesus heard them? Silvia was not exactly quiet, which was irritating, but also quite nice, and sometimes, even Gabriel lost control of his own voice whilst they were 'sawing'.

'I, er… just want to convert her,' Gabriel stammered. It wasn't even a proper lie. He could never have lied to the Messiah! But Silvia could not be converted. She was determined not to let her life be dictated by the Bible.

'What is lingerie?' Jesus asked.

Gabriel had a coughing fit.

'I happened to overhear when you told this woman that you love lingerie.'

'Erm… it's a French dish…' Gabriel replied. He was shocked to discover that he was more than capable of lying to the Messiah.

'And what is a thong?' Jesus asked.

'Thong… that's… that's the name of her cat,' Gabriel replied. It seemed it wasn't all that hard to lie to Jesus. The Messiah then got up from the kitchen table: 'I am off to see Marie,' he declared.

Gabriel didn't want him to go. He was afraid that Marie was a bad influence. If she was only half as determined and well versed in the arts of seduction as her mother… then… they'd also do some s… Oh God! Had he lost his mind? Even to think such a thing! This was abominable! 'Would you not rather have dinner with me tonight?' he asked despairingly.

'Haven't you arranged to meet Silvia?' Jesus countered.

'We could all eat together,' Gabriel suggested.

'Lingerie?' Jesus asked.

'No!' Gabriel answered, his voice cracking slightly.

'Why not?'

'Erm… it gives you heartburn.' This lying business was quickly becoming routine.

Jesus laughed. 'Why would I be afraid of heartburn?'

Before Gabriel could provide him with a halfway reasonable expla-
nation, the doorbell rang. Jesus opened the door. It was Silvia. Gabriel
seriously hoped that Jesus would not mention the lingerie or the thong.
Silvia came in and gave Gabriel a kiss on the cheek. In the presence of the
Son of God, the former angel found this incredibly embarrassing.

'Is something wrong?' Silvia asked, noticing that he was a bit nervous.

'No… no,' Gabriel said, trying to appease her. He realised that he
actually wasn't doing much other than lying.

'Do you mind if Joshua spends the evening with us?'

Silvia's expression suggested that she minded a great deal.

Jesus explained: 'I have arranged to meet someone else tonight.'

Silvia was relieved.

'I'd like to try your lingerie another time,' Jesus added politely.

That really did surprise Silvia. 'My lingerie? You want to try on…?'

Gabriel quickly interrupted her. 'Please let's talk about something else,
I have a spot of indigestion.'

Silvia was very perplexed.

Jesus turned to her and asked: 'So, where is your lovely little thong?'

Silvia couldn't believe it.

'Gabriel told me all about it.'

At this moment, Gabriel suddenly regretted ever becoming a mortal.

'Does it have a glossy coat?' Jesus asked politely.

'Erm… I'm sure there are thongs with fur, but…'

She didn't get any further. Gabriel was completely overwhelmed. 'Aren't
you going to be late?' he asked Jesus.

He just wanted to put an end to all this and saw no option but to
throw the Messiah out. He didn't even care that the Messiah was going
to see Marie.

Jesus nodded. 'You are right, my loyal friend.'

He bid farewell and closed the door behind him. Gabriel breathed a
sigh of relief.

Silvia watched Jesus leave through the window. She was rather bewil-
dered. 'Is he gay?' she asked Gabriel.

Gabriel closed his eyes. It was all too much for him. He had made the Son of God utter the words 'lingerie' and 'thong'. And he had lied to him. And above all, he'd allowed him to go and meet up with Marie again!

CHAPTER TWENTY-ONE

'So what do you wear for a date with Jesus?' I asked myself after I'd had a shower and brushed my teeth. I stood in front of my wardrobe and looked for the most demure and high-necked garments I could find. A shirt, a jumper over the top and a pair of black wide leg trousers. I hadn't looked this prim since I was confirmed. So I'd solved one problem, but not the other. Where to go with someone like Jesus?

I would have loved to discuss this issue with my sister, but she'd left me a note saying that she'd gone to the lake to draw. And that I shouldn't worry, the test results had been fine.

Who knows what Kata would have suggested anyway? Probably something like, 'Hey, why not show Jesus a couple of people who have a tumour and ask him about God's love of humanity?'

Part of me wanted to ask him about that. And, if Jesus existed, whether hell did too. And whether you should even think about things like that if you wanted to be able to sleep at night.

Then Dad came into the room. 'Can we talk?' he said.

'Dad, I have to go soon,' I replied, hoping to avoid a 'Svetlana is not like you think she is' conversation.

'Svetlana is not like you think she is,' Dad said.

I sighed, 'Oh, is she even worse?'

His eyes filled with sadness. My God, old men have such an amazing ability to look sad.

'She loves her daughter very much.'

'How lovely,' I snapped. As if that would change anything.

'Is it so hard to imagine that someone loves me?' he demanded.

'No, just that someone *like that* loves you,' I replied, a little too honestly.

He didn't say a word. He seemed to know that I was right. But then he said: 'Well, what if she makes me happy? Does it really matter whether she loves me?'

I wasn't sure if I'd ever heard a more desperate statement.

I would have loved to shake Dad until the part of his brain where he'd stored Svetlana plopped out of his ear. Instead I just stroked his old, wrinkled cheek. But he pushed my hand away. 'If you can't be friends with Svetlana, then you need to leave this house,' he said emphatically.

He left. I was stunned. My own father was threatening to throw me out.

As I went outside I walked past the kitchen, where Svetlana and her monster child were playing Ludo. Svetlana looked happy and much less uptight than she'd seemed before. It was as though a she was relieved about something. Either because she and her daughter were now able to deplete my father's bank account, or because her child's epilepsy had been cured. It was probably a combination of the two. I paused. I now realised that we'd all been witnesses to a miracle yesterday. I was overcome by a profound feeling of awe. Perhaps I should tell Svetlana that her daughter was cured forever. That would surely create a human connection between us. We could put all this strife behind us. This miracle would have forged a union between us forever…

Then the little girl saw me and stuck her tongue out. I gave her the finger and left.

Jesus and I had agreed to meet by the pier where we'd sat this morning. For many people, such an encounter would have been a fantastic experience. But I was just Marie from Malente. What on earth was I going to talk to him about? I felt completely overwhelmed.

I stepped onto the pier. Jesus was already there, standing in the evening sun. It was such a wonderful sight. I'm sure that it would have made Michelangelo rethink his concept for the Sistine Chapel. Jesus was still wearing the same clothes that never got dirty. This was probably one of the more practical aspects of being the Messiah. This morning, my feelings would still have been all over the place at the sight of him, but now I was just extremely intimidated.

'Hello, Marie,' Jesus greeted me.

'Hello…'

I had trouble saying 'Jesus', so I left it at 'Hello' and did up the top button of my shirt. My feelings for him were still out for the count.

'What shall we do?' he asked.

'I… I'll just start by showing you around Malente,' I suggested in a fluster.

'Lovely,' Jesus smiled.

So-so, I thought.

I took Jesus to the other church in our little town, the one in which my parents had got married. A house of God, I thought to myself, seemed to be fitting for our rendezvous. And surely better than a visit to the local salsa club.

'Do you come here often?' Jesus asked, as we stepped into the small, modest church.

What was I supposed to say to that? The painful truth? Or should I lie? But it was probably not appropriate to lie to Jesus, particularly if hell really did exist.

'Sometimes,' I replied. A wishy-washy answer seemed the right approach to tackle this situation.

'So what's your favourite prayer?' Jesus asked inquisitively.

Oh God, I didn't know the texts of any prayers. I racked my brains and answered: 'Come, Lord Jesus, be our guest and bless what you have given us.'

Jesus was surprised. 'Do you eat in the church?'

God, this was so embarrassing. I decided to shut up before I put my foot in it any more. We slowly sauntered towards the altar. Jesus was not really pleased at the sight of all these crosses – they must have brought back painful memories – but he seemed to be quite happy that people paid homage to God in this place.

The only thing was that I wasn't exactly great at doing so myself. So I felt pretty awful. How was I going to get through this evening?

Jesus looked at the pictures on the walls, while I frantically stared at the floor, and noticed that it was high time that someone ran a mop over it.

Suddenly Jesus started laughing.

'What is it?' I asked inquisitively, shifting my gaze from the ground to look at him.

'My mother looked very different.' He looked at the pictures of the Madonna, in which she had a halo and seemed as though she was carved out of ebony. Mary was in the manger with the Baby Jesus in her arms.

'She had more frown lines,' Jesus smiled.

No wonder with those family relations, I thought to myself.

'And her skin was darker.'

'It was difficult for her back then,' Jesus continued. 'Very difficult. At first everyone thought she was mad.'

I looked at Joseph, who was standing next to Mary, and thought to myself that he must have been high on the list of people who thought Mary was mad. Just imagine this woman saying to this man, whom she has never had sex with: 'Hey, Joseph… erm… you'll never guess what happened to me…'

Jesus had noticed me staring at Joseph. 'Initially Joseph wanted to dissolve the engagement quietly and secretly, to avoid shame being brought on Mary. But then an angel appeared to him in a dream and explained who was growing in Mary's womb. And then he took her to be his wife.'

A man who marries a pregnant woman. Noble. Not everyone would do that these days.

'From that moment he embraced me lovingly and raised me as though I were his own child,' Jesus continued.

'How do you bring up Jesus?' I asked.

'With a firm hand. For a while, Joseph would not allow me to leave the house.'

'What did you do to deserve that?'

'At the age of five, I fashioned twelve sparrows out of clay on the Sabbath.'

'And why was that so bad?'

'Because you are not allowed to do that on the Sabbath. And because I brought them to life.'

Imagine Mary and Joseph explaining something like that to the neighbours.

'I also withered the son of Anna like a willow branch.'

'What?' I shouted aghast.

'We were playing by a stream. I diverted the water into small ponds with my willpower, and he then destroyed these pools of water with a willow branch. So I cursed him and he withered away.'

Gosh… If Joseph only grounded him for that he got off pretty lightly. I'm sure that mothers in Nazareth weren't busy arranging playdates with Jesus.

'But when I was six I also saved a child's life. My friend Zeno fell off the roof and died, so I brought him back to life.' He smiled and added, 'I was scared that people would blame me for his death.'

Jesus clearly did not develop selflessness until later in life.

'I also argued with a teacher.' He really was in a storytelling mood now. 'This man was not good at teaching. I told him so, and he scolded me…'

122

'Did you wither him as well?' I asked nervously.

'No, of course not.'

I breathed a sigh of relief.

'I made him faint.'

Why didn't we get taught about these stories in confirmation class? This would give teenagers something to relate to.

Jesus looked at the picture of his parents again and mused, 'Joseph's face was much more furrowed by the sun… and the hardship…'

I looked at Mary and Joseph a little more closely. It was actually the first time that I'd looked at a picture in a church this carefully. These parents must have had a hard time bringing up Jesus. But how hard must it have been for this little boy? He'd already noticed that he was different from all the other children at the age of five. And at some point he must have realised that this furrow-faced man was not his real father.

I felt really sorry for junior Jesus.

Something that senior Jesus immediately noticed. 'Is there something wrong, Marie?'

'No… no… It's just that it must have been hard for you as a child. So alone. No friends.'

Jesus was clearly surprised that someone felt sorry for him. Normally it was he who expressed sympathy, even to people who raided mobile phone stores. But my comment really confused him for a moment. Then he gathered himself and said: 'Well, I did have siblings.'

'Siblings? I thought Mary was a virgin!' I blurted out.

'Is it not impolite in your society to talk about older people's love lives?' Jesus said reproachfully.

In my opinion, the older people in our soci ty – in particular my mother – spoke a little bit too much about their love lives, but I decided that I'd better keep that to myself.

Instead I meekly said, 'I'm sorry.'

'My siblings were born after me.'

'So it was afterwards that Mary…' I was just able to stop myself before the words 'had sex' crossed my lips.

'You think very logically,' Jesus said, and I thought that it almost sounded a little sneering. Then he told me that he had both sisters and brothers. He'd also save one of their lives. His brother James was bitten by a viper and Jesus rushed to the scene and blew on the wound. James stood up and was healed. The viper exploded.

The viper exploded? Jesus was probably the world's coolest big brother back then.

'So why doesn't the Bible say anything about your siblings?' I asked.

'They are mentioned briefly, but…' Jesus hesitated.

'But…?'

'They did not follow me on my path,' he said sounding disappointed.

So Jesus had abandoned his siblings to fulfil his mission. It still seemed to sadden him even today. I would have loved to hold his hand to console him. But that was obviously ridiculous. He was the Son of God. He didn't need to be consoled. Particularly not by me.

'Do you always spend evenings at church?' Jesus asked, when he had suppressed his sorrow again.

'Well… not every evening,' I replied, which was technically not a lie, since 'not every evening' could also mean 'no evening'.

'I want to spend the evening with you doing what you would normally do,' Jesus explained.

Fine. But what did I normally do in the evening? I'm sure that Jesus didn't want to zap through the TV channels with me, getting irate about paid-entry phone quizzes. What is the capital of Germany? a) Berlin or b) Lufthansa?

I also didn't think that it would be a good idea to take him to my favourite hangout. How would I explain the 'over 18s only' section in Michi's video store?

So I had to think of something innocuous, like having an ice cream at the world's best Italian ice-cream parlour, right in the centre of Malente. The owner had even scattered some sand to create a Mediterranean feel, which led to frequent altercations with dog owners.

'This is the best invention of all time,' I said pointing at banana split.

'This does not say much for your times,' Jesus explained. He could certainly have done with a few lessons in irony.

We gobbled the ice cream without saying a word. For quite a while. I found this awkward. So I casually tried to get the conversation going again. 'So you're living with Gabriel?'

'Yes,' he answered, in a short but friendly manner.

'Do you have a nice room?'

'Yes.'

I had to stop asking yes-no questions. So I asked, 'How do you like Malente?'

'Lovely.'

Ahhhhh! The conversation was, like earthly beings, destined to die. The silence grew ever longer. Every minute became unbearably drawn out. I would have loved to have gone home, as I had no idea what else I could possibly talk about with a Messiah. But then I would probably have been the first woman who'd ditched Jesus on a date. Or maybe I wouldn't? It would be interesting to know whether someone had done that before? Mary Magdalene perhaps? But this was not really an appropriate topic of conversation.

'OK,' I said eventually. 'You wanted to know how I live. So ask me. Anything. Whatever you like.'

'Very well,' said Jesus. 'Are you still a virgin?'

I almost choked on a piece of banana. 'What… what makes you ask that?' I spluttered.

'Well, you don't have any children.'

'That's true.'

'And you're old.'

Well, thank you very much.

'Very, very old.'

He clearly also needed some lessons in charm too

'In Judea women of your age would already have been grandmothers. Unless they had succumbed to leprosy.'

I pushed my banana split aside. How was I going to explain to him that I didn't have any children? Should I tell him about Marc, whom I'd wanted to run over after finding out he was cheating on me? Or about Sven, whom I'd ditched at the altar? Or about the fertility computer that I used, which had a reliability of ninety-four per cent when used as a contraceptive, which was at least six percent too little in my eyes?

No. That would all be too embarrassing and awkward. He would probably judge me and tell me that I'd burn in hell. The only good thing is that it would almost certainly bring an end to our date.

But before I could even answer, I saw a group of Sven's footie mates approaching. After the episode in the church, I was probably not in their good books. And more importantly, Jesus would find out what I'd done to poor Sven. I wanted to avoid that at any cost.

'Let's go,' I said to Jesus.

'Why?'

'Let's just go.'

'But I haven't eaten all my banana split.'

It was bizarre to hear Jesus say 'banana split'.

'You don't need to eat it all,' I replied impatiently.

'But it's really delicious.'

'Forget the bloody ice cream,' I shouted.

Jesus looked at me in astonishment. It was too late anyway – Sven's teammates were already standing over us. They were four typical footballers in their mid-thirties. They reeked of alcohol. You could probably have sterilised surgical instruments with their breath.

The striker, a small guy with a sharp tongue, immediately had a go at me. 'You broke Sven's heart…'

'Get lost,' I interrupted.

'Are we interrupting your date?' the midfielder asked. His Don Johnson mullet was not very becoming.

'You're a slut,' said the gigantic defender, a vulgar man who was simply known in the club as 'Not man, Not beast'.

'Hmmm!' the goalie grunted affirmatively. It seemed that this guy had taken a few too many shots to the head.

I looked at Jesus and wondered whether he was now going to judge me. The guilt about Sven I'd felt when I'd almost drowned in the lake was overwhelming me again.

But Jesus just got up. 'Let he who is without sin cast the first stone,' he declared.

'He wants us to throw stones?' the gigantic defender snapped.

'Not a bad idea,' the forward said maliciously.

'Hmmm,' the goalie grunted affirmatively.

Yes, my dear Jesus, the times have changed. The foot-ballers were so drunk they would happily have stoned me to death. With all that alcohol, a couple of stones would probably have missed the target, but I still felt pretty uneasy.

'We really should go now,' I whispered to Jesus.

'We will eat our banana splits in peace,' he insisted, as the goalie picked up a small stone.

'I'm sorry, but I think that we're not going to get very far with your "turn the other cheek" attitude,' I warned.

'I'm not going to show them my cheek,' Jesus explained as he stood up again.

Oh my goodness. He wasn't going to wither them, was he?

But Jesus did no such thing. Instead he wrote something in the sand without saying a word. I couldn't figure it out. To me, it looked like illegible hieroglyphs. But the footballers stared at the sand for a long time. Then they hurried off. Jesus blew on the sand and the inscription disappeared.

'What… what did you write?' I asked.

'Everyone could read their own worst sin in the sand,' Jesus smiled.

It seemed that he'd read their minds.

Oh God. Had he also seen what I'd done to Sven?

Jesus looked at my guilt-ridden face. 'Don't worry Marie. I did not read your memory to see your sins, only the men's. That's why you couldn't read what I wrote.'

Phew.

'What exactly is S&M?' Jesus asked.

I wondered which footballer's mind he'd read to see that word. And how on earth was I going to answer the question without blushing.

'What does "tax evasion" mean? And what is it to abandon your mother in a damp nursing home?'

I didn't know which question to answer first, or whether I even could. Instead I opted to tell Jesus what had happened with Sven. How sorry I was, but that I just had to leave him at the altar, because I didn't love him enough, and that I'd broken his heart. And how guilty I felt. I probably would not be able to forgive myself as long as I lived.

'Are you judging me now?' I asked fearfully.

'No,' he replied. 'And do you know what that means?'

'That I shouldn't judge myself either?' I asked hopefully, so as to be able to rid myself of my bad conscience.

'Erm,' he cleared his throat and looked for the right words.

'You meant something else, right?' I asked nervously.

'I actually wanted to say that you shouldn't do something like that again.'

'Oh,' I said disappointedly. 'Well I wasn't planning on ditching someone at the altar again…' I added.

'Rightly so,' Jesus stated.

And after thinking for a while he explained: 'But it would be a good idea to forgive yourself.'

'Yeah?' I was surprised.

'I should have thought of that myself,' he explained. 'I've learned something.'

And for that he smiled at me gratefully. That was nice. His smiled warmed my heart. As did the fact that I could now forgive myself.

'You stopped a stoning once didn't you?' I asked Jesus, who was now focused on his ice cream again. For the first time that evening, I was able to breathe easily again.

'Yes. A whore's,' he explained.

'Mary Magdalene?' I asked.

'Mary Magdalene was not a whore!' Jesus replied angrily.

Jeeeeeez, someone still had strong feelings for the ex. If she even was an ex.

'Mary Magdalene was just an ordinary woman,' explained Jesus, more calmly.

'So how did you meet her?' I asked.

'She and her sister Martha invited me into their home. She anointed my feet.' Did Mary Magdalene do pedicures? Surely not. They probably didn't even exist back then.

'And then she dried my feet with her hair.'

Whatever floats your boat.

'From that day on, Mary Magdalene was one of my followers,' Jesus smiled. This smile made me feel jealous. A particularly silly feeling when it's because of Jesus, and with the dancing Mary Magdalene from *Jesus Christ Superstar* still in my mind.

Nevertheless, I couldn't stop feeling jealous. It seemed that my feelings were not quite as dead and buried as I would have liked. I just needed to know whether Jesus and Mary Magdalene had shared a bed. How was I going to ask this subtly?

'So, you and your followers… er… did you spend the night in small caves… where you had to… huddle together to keep warm?'

Not very subtly then.

Jesus shook his head. 'Mary Magdalene and I never lay side by side.'

What was it my sister always used to say? Plato was a complete idiot.

'Mary had said to me…' Jesus carried on talking, but then stopped.

'What had she said?'

He didn't want to answer.

His eyes were now really sad again. He had not just forsaken his family for his mission, but his love as well. Too much forsaking, if you ask me.

Jesus had now finished up his ice cream, and one of his hands was resting on the table. Again, I wanted to touch his hand to comfort him. And this time I didn't hold back. I didn't care that he was the Son of God. Right now he was just a sad man, who I happened to like very much. Maybe even too much. My hand approached his, but he saw and took his hand off the table in a controlled movement. He didn't want to be comforted. Not by me.

But he wasn't able to comfort himself right now either – he was still making a melancholy face. I tried to think how I could get him to stop thinking about his memories. He wanted to see how people lived today, so maybe I should take him to the place there was most life in Malente right now.

'I know what I'm going to show you next,' I smiled.

'What?' Jesus asked eagerly.

'Salsa!'

CHAPTER TWENTY-TWO

At about eleven o'clock we entered the only place that was still open at this time in our little town – the salsa club. Its name was typically unoriginal for Malente. Club Tropical was located in a cellar, and the smoking ban was a foreign concept here. But the atmosphere was tremendous – there were lots of young people dancing to fantastic South American rhythms. Jesus and I raised the average age considerably, and not just because he was over 2,000 years old. All this was clearly alien to him – the wild dancing, the skimpy clothing and the men's shirts that revealed unpleasant amounts of chest hair.

'Is dancing forbidden in any way?' I asked. I was suddenly afraid that I was making a mistake by bringing him here.

'No. King David danced virtually unclad to honour God.'

Virtually unclad? Good Lord.

We squeezed our way through the crowd. Some of the women were clearly a little too unclad for Jesus' taste, judging from his disapproving glances.

'Do you want to leave?' I asked him.

'No, I'm used to being among sinners,' he replied.

'But… you're not going to write their sins on the ground, are you?' I asked.

'No.'

'Good.'

'But I will convert the people.'

He made to approach a woman whose top was clearly communicating to men that she wanted to take it off.

But I followed Jesus, overtook him and stood in front of him. 'No one is going to be converted here,' I warned. I suspected that most people in the club weren't real sinners anyway, at least not according to my definition.

'But…' Jesus tried to protest.

'Otherwise this evening will be ruined!'

He raised an eyebrow.

'You want me to show you how people live today. But I just can't do that if you are the Son of God.'

'Well, I *am* the Son of God,' Jesus replied. This was the first time that I'd seen him look confused.

It suited him. He looked so gentle and vulnerable.

'But you're a person as well,' I explained. I'd felt it when he spoke about his parents and Mary Magdalene.

Now he raised his other eyebrow as well.

'Just be Joshua this evening.'

He thought for a while. 'Agreed,' he said at last.

I immediately set up some 'be a normal person' rules for the salsa evening:

No singing of psalms.
No breaking of bread.
No confrontations with sinners.
No unclad dancing.

The last rule made Jesus laugh out loud. He seemed to like laughing at my jokes. 'You needn't worry about that,' he said.

He even seemed amused by my other rules and accepted them gladly. But it wasn't only Joshua who had to blank out that he was Son of God – I had to do so as well. But when it came to men, it seemed I was more than capable of blanking things out… Marc's continuous flirting with other women, Sven's unpleasant habit of cutting his toenails in the living room… I'd blanked out all of these things, typical of a woman desperate to stay with a guy. This female aptitude for self-deception was something I was going to take advantage of tonight.

'Are you thirsty?' I asked.

'Do you want to have some wine with me again?'

'I was thinking of mojitos.'

I ordered two drinks at the bar and wondered whether this might be construed as an attempt to seduce the Messiah. Surely a mojito wasn't going to do too much harm to a man with a divine metabolism? Once he'd found out how to sip past the little umbrellas, he smiled with genuine pleasure. 'That really is a tasty alternative to wine.'

Joshua – yes, it worked, I could call him Joshua again – was smiling from ear to ear. His mood got better by the minute. I looked at the crowd that was dancing to the hot rhythms. Should I ask Joshua to dance? Why not? He was just a person now!

I gathered up all my courage and, with a pounding heart, I asked, 'Shall we dance?'

He hesitated.

'Come on.'

'I… I've never danced before in my life.'

'Well, then King David really has one up on you,' I smiled, trying to challenge him a bit.

'But these are not the Lord's songs,' he pointed out.

'They're not the devil's either.'

Joshua weighed up this argument, but as he was still weighing I just dragged him onto the dance floor.

He was completely overwhelmed. It suited him to be overwhelmed. I grasped his waist, and he let me do so, now firmly determined to engage with all of this. Then I started to push him over the dance floor. Admittedly he was a little stiff at first. We stumbled and bumped into another couple, who complained loudly. 'Can't you watch where you're going?'

shouted the man, who was dressed like Antonia Banderas, but looked like Andrew Marr.

'Watch your mouth – or he will wither you,' I grinned and pushed Joshua onwards.

'I would never do that…' he protested.

But I interrupted him. 'Some time I'll teach you what irony is.'

Then I pulled him towards me. He stepped on my foot.

'Ouch!' I cried.

'Forgive me.' He was really embarrassed.

'Don't worry,' I replied and really meant it. I actually thought it was a good thing. It finally made me forget that I was not dealing with an ordinary person.

Slowly but surely we found our rhythm. Joshua stopped stepping on my feet quite as much, and at last we were moving as one – as one who wasn't dancing very well. But as one nevertheless.

I'd never before shimmied across a dance floor quite so harmoniously with a man. To me he was Joshua again, the carpenter with the wonderful voice, the amazing eyes and the… yes, I even let myself think it again… great arse.

We danced salsa. And merengue. And even a tango. Even though we didn't quite know all the right steps, and garnered one or two disapproving looks from the people around us, seeming to wonder 'What are those klutzes doing jumping about here?' I had fun. Loads of fun. And so did Joshua. Tons!

Between two dances he beamed at me and said: 'I never knew that physical exertion not tied to work could be so fun.' Then, much more earnestly, he added: 'And that it could be this much fun just to be Joshua.'

After the salsa club had closed we headed towards the lake to watch the sunrise. It had been such a great evening, and I wanted the works! In fact, it had been the best evening I'd had in years.

We sat down on the pier. Yes, it seemed like we were almost regulars here. A romantic place, the ideal spot to watch the sun go up... and for a first kiss... a nice, gentle kiss... My God! I couldn't think about things like that now! Or ever, really. I punitively hit myself on the head.

'What's the matter?' Joshua asked, clearly confused by my mortification.

'Oh, nothing. It was just a mosquito...' I answered untruthfully.

Joshua took off his shoes to cool his feet in the lake. I saw his scars.

I gulped. That's where the nails had been hammered in.

'That must have been horrendously painful,' I blurted out.

Joshua glanced at me sternly. I quickly looked down. Had I just crossed a line?

'I was supposed just to be Joshua,' he reminded me.

'The... the evening is as good as over,' I replied. I couldn't get the images from the Mel Gibson film out of my head, which were – to make matters worse – accompanied by the soundtrack of *Jesus Christ Superstar*.

I could no longer pretend that this man sitting next to me was not Jesus. That made me very sad. I would so have liked to carry on pretending.

Joshua stared into the break of dawn and nodded. 'Yes, I suppose the evening has come to an end.'

It sounded as though there was a note of melancholy in his voice.

He let his feet dangle in the water.

'How... how did you cope with the pain?' I asked. It really was bothering me too much to be able to keep quiet.

Joshua just kept looking at the sky. He simply didn't want to talk about it. I was such a stupid cow. It seemed that I really had crossed the line with my questions. I was just about to hit myself on the head again when Joshua answered: 'My faith in God helped me to bear it.'

His answer sounded a little too dramatic and valiant to be the whole truth.

'You believed in God the whole time, despite the pain?' I added.

He didn't say anything. He was clearly thinking. Finally he replied in a melancholy voice: 'Eli, Eli, lama sabachthani?'

'Excuse me, what?'

'A psalm of David,' he replied.

'Oh…' I stammered. I didn't understand a word of course. But this psalm probably didn't have anything to do with his naked dancing.

'It means, "My God, my God, why hast thou forsaken me?"' Joshua said quietly.

'That… that… sounds sad,' I said.

'I shouted it on the cross, just before I died.' His eyes were now filled with pain.

In this moment I felt sorry for him again. Immensely sorry. So much that I once again stretched out my hand to touch his. But this time he did not immediately pull back. I carefully touched his hand. He still didn't pull back. Then I clasped it. Tightly.

So we sat there – Joshua and I – hand in hand on the pier, without saying a word, watching the sun rise over the lake.

CHAPTER
TWENTY-THREE

A couple of hours earlier…

For the first time in ages, Satan felt a fire burning within him. The final battle would now finally begin. Existence suddenly made sense again.

He decided to start by recruiting those people on whom he could confer supernatural powers, so that they would become his Horsemen of the Apocalypse. For the first horseman, 'War', the forty-third president of the United States was at the top of the list of candidates. He was currently bored to tears in his holiday home in Kennebunkport. For the second horseman, 'Pestilence', he had a cardinal who told Africans that it was a great idea not to use condoms. And for 'Famine', Satan had selected that supermodel who presents that show for aspiring models and tells skinny girls that they are flabby monsters.

The fourth horseman, 'Death', did not need to be recruited. He'd been working on earth since the beginning of time. Satan decided to wait as long as possible before looking him up. He was the only being other than God whom he did not like to meet in the dark.

But he was still not entirely satisfied with his candidate list for the first three horsemen. He needed the best companions to be able to win against God. This time it was essential, since it was going to be the final battle for the fate of humanity. And Satan was the underdog. The Almighty had always been a whisker (metaphorically speaking of course) ahead of him. Pensively he sat down on a bench by the lake, next to a woman who was drawing.

'You're blocking my light,' the woman complained.

He engaged his George Clooney smile. 'But I'm George Clooney.'

'You're quite similar, be happy about that. But don't get too excited,' she replied. 'Anyway, I'm a lesbian.'

Then she told him to get lost.

Satan had always had a thing for strong-willed women. He particularly enjoyed breaking their will. Of course he knew that it was because of his envy. Yes, he envied people's free will. What wouldn't he do, to have this himself? He would then give the key to hell to some lowly demon and make himself comfortable on a tropical desert island, without having to be annoyed by people's thoughts, desires or sins. He would never again have to listen to strange sexual fantasies that people were willing to sell their souls for… That really would be paradise.

He called himself to order. He urgently needed to stop dreaming. After all, he had no free will and had to fulfil his destiny, and for that he needed to gather the troops for the final battle. Then his gaze fell on the woman's sketchbook, and he saw that she was drawing a comic strip.

It seemed that she had similar feelings about God as Satan did himself. He looked at her more closely and saw the tumour in her head – a disease that he hadn't thought of, would never have thought of, and hadn't really ever understood. Maybe Death had been involved. That guy was seriously unpleasant.

One thing was certain though. This strong-willed woman didn't have long to live. No more than a month or two.

And she was filled with anger towards God. What a great candidate for Pestilence.

CHAPTER TWENTY-FOUR

As we sat hand in hand on the pier, and the first rays of sunshine shone down on us, I felt close to Joshua. Joshua. Not Jesus.

As Joshua was gripping my hand, both tightly and gently, it seemed as though – this much I dare to hope – he felt the same.

Here and now, during the sunrise at the lake in Malente, we were just Marie and Joshua. Not M.O.N.S.T.E.R. and Messiah.

But I had an extraordinary talent for destroying special moments, no matter how lovely. Because when something was lovely, I wanted it to last forever. As that's impossible (at some point we all have to go to the loo), I wanted lovely experiences to be repeated over and again.

'Do you think that we can have another lovely evening like this together?' I asked cheerily.

Joshua looked at me with sadness in his eyes. What was wrong? Was the Son of God not allowed to be together with a mortal woman? Had we done something that was forbidden? Why didn't I have an inbuilt gag that would stop me from talking every time I was about to ask something stupid?

'It really was a wonderful evening.'

He had a nice evening too! No, a *wonderful* evening!

'But unfortunately we will not be able to experience another one together.'

That cut me to the quick. 'B– but why not?' I asked wistfully.

'Because I have a task that I need to complete.'

He didn't sound very happy about it. And I was confused. A task? Wasn't he just on a little holiday from heaven?

'What kind of a task?' I wanted to know.

'Haven't you read the Bible?' he asked looking surprised.

'Yes, yes, sure, of course…' I stammered. I didn't dare to tell him that I had no idea that I felt that it needed a stylistic update.

'Then you'll know why I am walking the earth.'

He pulled his hand away. I felt a twinge in my heart. Then he took his shoes and got up. 'Farewell, Marie.'

'Farewell? Are we… never going to see each other again?' I asked. This was getting harsher and harsher.

Instead of giving me a straight answer to my question, Joshua said something truly wonderful. 'You have given me a lot.'

I had given him a lot? I could hardly believe it.

Then he gently stroked my cheek.

I was on the verge of a coma induced by an enormous sense of wellbeing when he removed his hand from my face.

I suddenly felt very cold.

And Joshua headed back to the shore.

I wanted to call out 'Stay!', but I was unable to make a sound. I was too choked watching him walk out of my life along the edge of the lake.

Of course, any hopes of spending another evening – thousands of evenings – like that with Joshua had been absurd. But knowledge does not protect you from pain.

My sorrow almost overwhelmed me completely. Then a thought crossed my mind. Task? What kind of a task?

Shortly afterwards I was frantically ringing the doorbell at Michi's video store. He opened up, even more bleary-eyed than the day before. He was wearing a T-shirt that said, 'There's nothing to see here!'

'What is Jesus' task?' I just blurted out.

'Eh?'

'What is Jesus' task?!?'

'Don't yell at me.'

'I'm not yelling!'

'Then I don't want to know what it's like when you are.'

'*Like this!*'

'You have a great career as a foghorn ahead of you,' Michi replied.

I was annoyed.

'Come in and I'll explain it to you,' Michi said.

He sat down at the counter, drank a black coffee and told me of the prophecies about Armageddon in the Bible. There were some in the Book of Daniel and even Jesus himself had predicted the end of the world in the Gospels. But it was described in most detail at the end of the Bible, on the last pages, in the Book of Revelation. I was spellbound as Michi told me about the final battle of good against evil. And about the Horsemen of the Apocalypse, about Satan, and about how Jesus conquers them all in a battle and creates a Kingdom of Heaven on earth, in which believers can live in peace for all eternity. Without hardship, without sorrow and, above all, without death. I now knew why Joshua was here.

'You're paler than Michael Jackson,' Michi declared. 'What's wrong?'

Should I tell him? Would he believe me? Not likely. But it didn't matter; I just had to tell someone what I'd experienced.

I told Michi everything. About how I'd been rescued in the lake, about the miracle healing of the little girl, about the scars on Joshua's feet and about his task. The only thing I didn't tell him was how I felt about Joshua.

When I was finished with my tale, Michi gasped. 'Wowzers.'

'You… you believe me then?' I asked hopefully.

'Of course I believe you,' Michi replied, in a tone that you normally use to explain to children that the horse they've drawn is really, really good, although it actually looks like a giraffe.

'You don't believe me,' I said flatly.

'Well, you've had a rough time, with the whole wedding fiasco and stuff… so you're probably trying to suppress your feelings for this carpenter, so as not to get hurt again, and that's why you're imagining that he's Jesus…'

'I am not mad!' I interrupted him.

'*Mad* is a strong word…'

'I'm about to punch you.'

I was angry and disappointed. I really could have done with someone to share the madness of the last couple of days with. Michi went quiet for a moment, then gently explained: 'I don't really want to believe all this either.'

'Why not?'

'Our world being turned into a Kingdom of Heaven would have disadvantages for some people.'

'Why so? I thought that there'd be no more death, no more shortages. And it sounds like there mightn't be any heartache either. Or acne.'

'Well yes, but not everyone will be getting an invitation.'

I stared at him in bewilderment.

'All people,' Michi explained, 'will appear before God. Even those who have already died. They will be brought back to life. God will open the so-called Book of Life, which details what every single person has done.'

'Must be a pretty thick book,' I said feeling pained.

The idea that everything I'd done in my life was written down did not please me greatly. Were God's angels monitoring my every step? Even when I showered? Or when I had sex? Or the sex I had alone? If so, I'd like to give those Peeping Toms a piece of my mind.'

'People will be judged on all their deeds. Those who've been good will be allowed to enter the Kingdom of Heaven.'

'And the rest? What will they do if the world no longer exists?'

'The rest will, according to the Book of Revelation, be cast into the lake of fire.'

'Sounds unpleasant,' I said shuddering.

'I guess that's the idea.'

'And the Bible really says all that?'

Michi nodded.

'But I thought God was benevolent,' I asked hesitantly.

'He is the same God who flooded the earth at the time of Noah, completely destroyed Sodom and Gomorrah, and hurled the Egyptians into a major recession to make them free the Israelites.'

'I'm not sure I like this God,' I said gloomily.

'If the Book of Life really exists, it will include what you just said.'

'Oh no!' I exclaimed.

'I also prefer the God who helped David against Goliath,' Michi said.

'Isn't he the same one?'

'This question has been giving theologians a migraine for centuries.'

'And what do you think? Who is the true God?'

'I'm hoping for the benevolent one, but when you look around at the world…'

He didn't say anything more. He did not want to articulate any doubts he had about his faith, so as not to acknowledge their existence.

The facts, as they were presented, were unpleasantly clear. Jesus was walking the earth and said that the task that he was now preparing for could be found in the Bible. That thing about the Day of Judgement was probably his task then. The world, as I knew it, would end. And there were probably loads more awful things about me in that stupid Book of Life. So was I going to end up in the lake of fire for all eternity?

CHAPTER TWENTY-FIVE

Meanwhile...

Gabriel had been worrying about Jesus the whole night. He wasn't worried that something might have happened to him, but rather that that wretched Marie would have turned his head and messed up God's plans. He felt so guilty that he'd let the Messiah go and that he hadn't gone after him. But the night with Silvia had just been too wonderful. His flesh was not just old – it was weak and exceedingly willing.

When Jesus finally came into the vicarage at seven o'clock in the morning, Gabriel had a hard time not treating him like one of his students at confirmation camp. As calmly as possible, but still somewhat sternly, he asked Jesus: 'So where were you?'

'Dancing salsa,' he replied.

It took a while before Gabriel was able to close his mouth again.

'It was very nice,' Jesus declared, smiling misty-eyed.

My God. Gabriel asked himself again whether his absurd suspicion was true – did the Messiah really have feelings for Marie? That girl whom Gabriel had almost advised to change denominations after listening to her moaning on about heartache during confirmation class, only so as not to have to endure her anymore?

Gabriel just needed to know what was going on. Jesus had a task to fulfil – there was no room to allow his feelings to get in the way of that.

'You... you have feelings for this woman?' Gabriel asked carefully.

Jesus clearly found this question awkward. He didn't want to speak about his emotions. But since he hadn't ever lied before and didn't want to start now, he said: 'She affects me, unlike anyone else has done for a long time.'

Gabriel wanted to scream! Go berserk! And use angelic powers to travel back in time to ensure that Marie was never born! But since he was no longer an angel, just a mere mortal, he simply asked, 'How... how can that be?'

'Since I was a young boy, everybody has only ever regarded me as the Son of God,' Jesus explained. 'But Marie... she... she sees something else in me.'

'A salsa dancer?' Gabriel snapped.

'Just an ordinary person.'

'But you're not an ordinary person,' Gabriel protested.

'Yes, and I told her that too,' Jesus grinned.

'And Marie...?' Gabriel asked.

'Didn't want to hear about it.'

'Of course,' Gabriel snorted.

'For a very short time I felt completely unburdened,' Jesus explained, smiling. Gabriel didn't want to hear it and snorted again.

'I even learned something from her,' Jesus said.

'How to swing your hips?'

'That too. But the main thing that I learned from Marie,' Jesus continued, 'is that you can teach people to forgive themselves.'

Gabriel stopped snorting. This was surprisingly wise, particularly coming from Marie. She... she had... really taught the Messiah something... unbelievable!

'And she comforted me, too,' Jesus said wistfully.

Gabriel knew that expression. Jesus used to make that face around Mary Magdalene. It was that awful 'I, too, need a person in my life' expression.

Jesus actually had romantic feelings for Marie! Perhaps he wasn't entirely clear about them himself – he lacked experience in such matters, but Marie had touched his heart. That was now very clear!

Love really was one of God's more bizarre ideas. But that his own son would be hit by it twice – well, that can't be something that the Almighty had reckoned with.

148

Or had he? After all, he was also called the Almighty because he was omniscient. This was now all very confusing to Gabriel.

'But…' he asked hesitantly, 'are you going to abandon your task for Marie?'

'What?' Jesus asked in surprise.

Gabriel was annoyed at himself. Had he put this stupid idea into Jesus's head? Would the Kingdom of Heaven on earth now not be realised because he couldn't keep his mouth shut?

'Are you asking that because of your love for Silvia?' the Messiah asked Gabriel. Then he put a stupid idea in Gabriel's head. If the Day of Judgement did not come, Gabriel could carry on living happily with Silvia. And sawing. And all the things she still wanted to show him. That Kama Sutra *thing certainly sounded interesting…*

'Do you think it might be a good idea to wait a little while?' Jesus asked nervously. It was obvious that he wanted to spend more time with Marie.

Gabriel grappled with himself. He and Jesus were just being led into temptation. He had to fight these emotions. He had to remain steadfast. For God's sake!

'Travel to Jerusalem today,' he urged the Messiah. 'You have to create the Kingdom of Heaven on earth.'

Jesus thought for a while, remembered his duties and declared: 'You are right of course.'

He got his toolbox and took his leave. 'Farewell, old friend.'

'Farewell,' Gabriel replied.

Then the Messiah left the vicarage. Gabriel watched him go, aghast that something as ridiculous as love had almost messed up God's plans.

CHAPTER TWENTY-SIX

When I'd found my voice again, I asked Michi: 'And… and Jesus predicted that as well?'

I still could not imagine that Jesus – that Joshua – would be a part of such a thing.

'With the threat of the end of the world, he got many people to think about their actions and find God,' Michi explained.

'I… I don't believe it.'

Michi leafed through the Bible. 'It says so in several places, look. In Matthew 25 Jesus proclaims: "Then shall he say also unto them on the left hand, Depart from me, ye cursed, into everlasting fire, prepared for the devil and his angels."'

'You know your stuff…' I stammered. 'Do you know what the admissions criteria are for the Kingdom of Heaven?' I asked anxiously.

'You actually believe that this man is Jesus,' Michi realised. He was pretty shocked now. My fear slowly seemed to be transferring to him. Or maybe he was just really worried about me.

'What you need to do,' he then explained, 'is not precisely detailed in Revelations. But I guess that if you've lived your life according to the many commandments in the Bible, you shouldn't have any problems getting in.'

'Many? I thought there were only ten.'

'There are many more. Lots more. Probably more than seven hundred,' Michi explained. He giggled nervously, as there were pearls of sweat forming on my brow. I didn't even know the Ten Commandments, except the obvious ones: 'Thou shalt not kill'; 'Thou shalt not steal'; 'Honour thy father and thy mother'…

Oh, dear. Honour thy father and thy mother. There was the first problem. And what about the commandments I didn't even know I'd broken?

I asked Michi to show me the others.

'But there are lots in there that don't even concern you.'

'Like what?'

'In Deuteronomy it says that men should not wear women's garments.'

'Not great for David Beckham then,' I said.

Michi showed me another commandment in the Bible: 'Leviticus 19:19: "Thou shalt not let thy cattle gender with a diverse kind."'

'I'll let the guinea pigs and the dogs know then,' I declared. It seemed that we weren't really getting anywhere with these rules.

Michi carried on leafing through the Bible. 'Deuteronomy 25: 11–12: When men strive together one with another, and the wife of the one draweth near for to deliver her husband out of the hand of him that smiteth him, and putteth forth her hand, and taketh him by the secrets: Then thou shalt cut off her hand.'

'A case taken straight from real life,' I said impatiently. I was scared shitless and was listening to these pointless rules.

Michi was about read me the commandments on bathing and ejaculation from Leviticus, but I took the Bible from him. 'I really don't want to hear that now.'

He nodded understandingly and said: 'I really think it's enough if you stick to the Ten Commandments.'

As I wasn't readily acquainted with these either, I got Michi to show me where to find them. And that's the first time in my life that I'd read the Bible with full concentration. Talk about the powers of self-preservation…

The first three commandments would probably not present too much of a problem. God is the Lord, I shalt have no other gods and no graven images or likenesses. That was all OK.

Except maybe that image I had in my head of God lying down on a psychiatrist's couch talking about being a control freak...

The fourth commandment was fine as well. I should rest on the seventh day. I'd actually heeded that advice my whole life. I'd never been workaholic slaving away all weekend. It amused me to think that the champions of the meritocracy would end up not getting into heaven. Nor had I murdered anyone or committed adultery (I was never married and married men have never been interested in me). I'd also never stolen (except things that I'd borrowed and not given back) and had coveted neither my neighbour's house nor wife (there was nothing about coveting husbands in the ninth commandment).

Michi felt that my fear for the lake of fire was causing me to take a rather one-sided perspective. He was right of course. I had often coveted the husbands of other women. Far too often. But I hadn't got them as often as I might have liked.

I'd also violated the tenth commandment by almost constantly coveting other people's things: Marc's convertible, my colleague's shoe collection, Jennifer Aniston's figure...

But what was giving me the biggest headache was commandment number five, the one about parents. I wondered whether I'd get that sorted by the time the world ended.

A short time later, I nervously entered my father's urology clinic. I asked his receptionist Magda, who'd been there for decades, whether I could see him. She immediately led me into his room and offered to make me a hot chocolate, completely ignoring the fact that I was now thirty-five years old.

My father was wearing his white coat and was busy sorting out-of-date medicine samples in his cupboard to give to charity. He was surprised to see me. 'What are you doing here?'

'I wanted to tell you that I respect your decision about Svetlana.' The Bible had said nothing about lying while honouring your father and mother.

'Oh…' my father said, looking puzzled. 'I'm… I'm pleased to hear it.'

I remained silent and played with a paperweight that was lying on his desk.

'So you don't mind if she moves in with me?' he asked.

'If that's what you want, it's OK by me,' I lied, tightly clutching the paperweight.

'I'm toying with the idea of marrying her,' Dad confessed.

He was clearly afraid that I would react badly, but now that I was coming in peace, he dared to say it out loud.

'If that's what you want…' This honouring your father and mother thing was not easy.

My father was happy about my response. And he wanted seize the opportunity. 'We're also planning to have a baby.'

'*No fucking way!*' I screamed.

My father was shocked. I slammed the paperweight on the desk and stormed out of the clinic. I didn't dignify Magda's hot chocolate with a second look.

Outside the door of the clinic, I leaned on the wall. 'Damn, why the hell can't I do this?'

An elderly man, who was just about to go into the clinic, asked me: 'Oh, do you have problems urinating too?'

I gave him a dirty look, and he nervously scurried into the clinic. Then Magda came out with the hot chocolate.

'I don't want the bloody hot chocolate,' I snapped.

'You will,' she said sympathetically.

'I won't.'

'Your father asked me to tell you that he never wants to see you again. You are to pack your belongings and get out of his house,' she whispered meekly, passing me the cup. I dejectedly slurped on my hot chocolate.

Once I'd finished it, I remembered that I had another parent whom I could honour. Even if I did find it extremely difficult.

My mother and I arranged to meet at a café in town. We ordered our cappuccinos and I began honouring her. Just as sincerely as I had honoured my Dad earlier. 'I'm... I'm sorry, that I've been so aggressive towards you these last few years.'

'I don't believe a word,' my mother replied.

'Wh... why not?'

She explained that I had been looking away when I spoke, which suggested I was lying. And that I was grasping my spoon, a sign of suppressed anger.

'What's the matter?' she asked.

'Oh, forget it,' I replied, preparing to leave. This whole thing was just ridiculous. When Moses had come down from Mount Sinai with the Ten Commandments no one could have known anything about mothers with degrees in psychology.

'There's something on your mind.' She grabbed my arm and gently pushed me back down into my seat. She seemed to be happy that I'd taken a step towards her for the first time in years, so she didn't want me to disappear again.

'Is it something to do with my relationship with Gabriel?' She'd got it all wrong.

But since I didn't reply – I could hardly tell her that the world was about to end and I wanted to save my big arse from the lake of fire – she assumed that it really was about Gabriel. The man who I had to assume knew that the man he was harbouring was Jesus. So I thought about why Jesus had mentioned that Gabriel had announced his birth to Mary, but I simply couldn't think of any reasonable explanation – he didn't seem to be the kind of person who invented time machines.

'I'm lonely. That's why I'm with him,' she explained. 'Very lonely.'

I looked at her in surprise. This was not her typical psycho-logical mumbo-jumbo. It was honest. And that scared me.

'Do you regret it?' I asked carefully.

'Leaving your father?'

'Yes.'

She didn't say anything for quite some time. That made me impatient. 'Are you going to answer this month?'

'I only regret it because it meant that I ended up losing you,' she replied sadly.

It was the first time that I understood she hadn't wanted to leave me – just my father. But back then you couldn't do one thing without doing the other. This realisation immediately helped me let go of so much of the pain that had been weigh-ing on me for the past twenty years.

'It would be silly if we hugged now, wouldn't it?' I said in a croaky voice.

'And cheesy,' she replied.

'Totally.'

'But absolutely fine as well,' she said. That's when the psychologist in her was speaking again. And for the first time in my life it didn't make me angry. Hesitantly I got up. She did too. And we hugged.

Perhaps this 'honour your father and mother' thing wasn't so stupid after all.

On my way home I was relieved, and not just because things were looking up with respect to my admission into the Kingdom of Heaven.

Then, suddenly, I thought I saw Sven on the other side of the road... talking to George Clooney?

I only saw the two of them very briefly, before they went around the corner and disappeared from view. I rubbed my eyes. I could have sworn that it was George Clooney.

Malente was getting weirder and weirder.

Back home again I ignored Svetlana and her daughter – nowhere in the Ten Commandments did it say that you had to honour sham brides or their children. I went to Kata's room to tell her that Dad had thrown me out. She wasn't there. But she'd said she was going to stay in Malente to look after me...

I looked at her latest drawing. And I noticed that Kata's current criticism of God was just a tiny bit less subtle than the last one.

Kata's holy wrath now knew no bounds – it was harsh and crude. That scared me. I leafed through her sketchbook and saw another comic strip. She was yelling at the Almighty about having a tumour.

Had the tumour returned?

Oh no!

God hadn't answered my prayers.

I was even angrier now that I knew he existed.

What was God's problem? Why didn't he help Kata? Sure, he'd heard a lot of prayers. But he wasn't a call centre, he couldn't get overloaded. Was he? 'Welcome to God's service centre. If you have a prayer for a loved one, please press one. If you wish to confess a sin, please press two. If you are a victim of an Act of God, please press three… We're sorry, all the lines are currently busy. Please call back later.' Beep-beep-beep…

'Why are you making beep-beep noises?' Kata asked as she came in carrying croissants. I was so shocked, I'd actually been making beeping noises. My mind was becoming increasingly fragile.

'The tumour has come back,' I confronted her.

'No, it hasn't,' she said emphatically.

'But the drawings…'

'I'm just processing old memories,' she countered. She sat down and groaned – she obviously had a terrible pain in her head.

I rushed over to try to help her, but then she exploded. 'Just get out of my room!'

She'd only be this aggressive towards me once before, when I'd cried at the hospital as she told me about the terrible pain she in. My tears had made her furious, and she'd screamed at me loudly then as well, telling me to get lost.

Kata's eyes were blazing just as they had in the hospital. It was this mixture of anger and physical pain. Now it was definite.

I felt sick. My whole body was shaking. Partly because I was angry at God, but mostly because I feared for my sister. I didn't want to see her suffer again. Never again!

And if God wasn't going to save her then perhaps it was a job for that son of his.

CHAPTER
TWENTY-SEVEN

I ran to the vicarage as fast as I could and rang the doorbell. Gabriel opened the door, looked at me and… slammed the door shut in my face. I rang the bell again, and when Gabriel opened up I put my foot in the door. He slammed the door shut again and I screamed with pain, jumped about on one leg swearing, then rang the bell a third time, waiting in vain for the door to be answered. I bent down and shouted through the letter box: 'He told me that he's Jesus!' One millisecond later, Gabriel opened the door again.

'Where's Jesus?' I demanded. Now that the carpenter was going to have to heal my sister, he was no longer Joshua but Jesus, the Son of God.

'That's none of your business,' Gabriel replied abruptly.

'You bet it's my business.'

'It's not.'

'It is.'

'It's *not*.'

'It *is*!'

'This conversation is going around in circles.' Gabriel said smugly.

'In a minute I'm going to hit you so hard that *you'll* be going around in circles,' I replied. I had neither the time nor the nerves for diplomacy.

'Your association with Jesus has not rubbed off on you it seems,' Gabriel noted disparagingly. He was just about to close the door again when I threatened: 'If you don't help me, then I'll tell my mother that you… that you…'

'That I what?' asked Gabriel.

I didn't have a clue what. I just knew that there had to be something fishy about Gabriel, but my time machine theory wasn't plausible. So I bluffed. 'That you are carrying a strange secret within you.'

Gabriel gulped. I had hit a nerve. Now he thought that Jesus had told me his secret, whatever that might be.

'He's on his way to Hamburg,' he explained.

I was confused. 'What's he going to do there?'

'Get onto a freighter to Israel.'

Israel! Of course! According to Michi, the final battle was going to take place in Jerusalem. Was it getting close? Or would Jesus spend a few months or even years preparing for his task? Whatever. Kata was in pain again, terrible pain, and she had to be spared this agony. Immediately!

Michi was pretty flabbergasted when I told him that I wanted to borrow his car, a rickety old VW Beetle, to try to stop Jesus from getting on a ship. Until now Michi had thought that I was just a bit confused. Now he firmly believed that I was either a) completely nuts, b) being hypnotised by the carpenter, c) on drugs or d) all of the above.

In my state of irate determination, or madness as Michi saw it, there was no way that he was going to leave me alone, particularly not at the wheel of his beloved vehicle. He closed the video store and we headed off towards Hamburg in his VW. On the motorway I kept complaining at him that he took silly things like speed limits and no overtaking on the inside lane too literally, particularly when he disregarded my suggestion of avoiding slow-moving traffic by driving on the hard shoulder.

So I made him stop at a car park, dragged him out of the driving seat and took the helm myself. We were soon hurtling towards Hamburg at breakneck speed.

It was very loud in the Beetle. Michi frequently closed his eyes, especially during my overtaking manoeuvres. When I turned off the motorway without removing my foot from the accelerator, Michi actually started reciting the Lord's Prayer. I was far too angry with Our Father, but I didn't share my thoughts with my friend. I started hurtling towards the harbour, where I hoped to find the ship that was going to take Jesus to Israel, along with a massive shipment of gummy bears, Twixes and Kinder Eggs.

I safely parked the car without ending up in the water, despite what Michi had predicted just moments before on account of the speed at which we were travelling. A sailor was standing at the railing of the ship. He had a dragon tattoo on his left arm. It seemed that the man didn't know that most people nowadays associated images of dragons with youth literature rather than exotic aggression. I asked him about the carpenter, and he replied that the ship would be setting sail half an hour later than planned and that Joshua had wanted to stretch his legs a bit. After asking him where exactly he was stretching his legs, the sailor answered: 'He's at the *Moulin Rouge*.'

'*Moulin Rouge?*' That didn't sound good. A joint like that was hardly likely to be home to avant-garde theatre, particularly not in a harbour.

The sailor gave us directions and warned that the women who worked there tended not to be overjoyed if other women entered the establishment.

'I expect Jesus wants to use the time to convert fallen women,' I explained to Michi.

'Yeah, sure. And I expect he only reads *Playboy* for the articles.' He still didn't believe that this was the Messiah we were talking about.

The *Moulin Rouge* was located in a bungalow. Only some of the neon signs were working. A plump woman opened the door. Her best years – and those of her lingerie – were long gone.

'We don't *do* women,' she snarled.

Hard to imagine that she generated much of an income with her looks and unpleasant manner.

'Well, is he allowed in?' I asked, pointing at Michi, who went bright red.

'Sure!' The woman laughed, flashing her decaying teeth, and pulled my completely dumbfounded friend inside before he could protest.

'Send Jesus to me,' I shouted at him as he grudgingly went in. Then I waited a while until the door reopened and Jesus stepped outside. A young woman in red lingerie followed him. She seemed quite distraught, but he calmed her down: 'Neither do I condemn thee: go, and sin no more.'

Relieved, the woman slid away. Jesus was visibly happy to see me, but also surprised. I was pleased to be near him again. I wished I could get myself a berth on the freighter too. Now I understood why Mary Magdalene had left her home back then to follow Jesus. But how on earth she managed to keep her hands of him the whole time was a complete mystery to me.

'Why did you come here?' Jesus asked me, and I concentrated on my request again. This was about Kata after all! Words spilling out of me, I told him about her disease and her terrible pain.

'I am very sorry for your sister,' he said empathetically.

'But you can heal her,' I smiled optimistically. 'Like Svetlana's daughter.'

Jesus remained silent.

'Erm… did you hear what I said?' I asked.

'Yes, I heard your words.'

'And… why do I get the feeling that there's a "but" coming?'

'Because I can't do anything to help your sister.'

'What?'

'I can't do it.'

'Erm… I'm sorry,' I stammered, 'But… all I hear is "I can't do that".'

'That's because it's what I said,' Jesus explained softly.

'That explains it,' I replied, feeling utterly confused.

Why couldn't he do it? He was Jesus, for Christ's sake, who commanded the wind, healed the sick and walked over water. He could do anything he wanted!

'Don't you want to?' I asked.

'I am on a mission from God.'

'God?' I asked. I couldn't believe it. 'God is keeping you from saving my sister?'

'It's not that simple…' Jesus added.

'I prayed to God, asking for my sister to get well again,' I interrupted. 'But he wasn't interested!'

'Did you pray often?'

His question threw me off course a little. Often? What was often? Whenever I feared for her life!

Jesus spoke: 'If you go to a friend at midnight and ask him for three loaves…'

'What?' I asked. 'Why are we talking about bread?'

Jesus carried on speaking, unmoved by my interruption. 'If he is your friend, he will rise because of your importunity and give you as many as you need.'

Jesus looked at me, as though I should somehow have understood some of this. But in all honesty, all I understood was bread.

'That was a parable,' he explained.

No kidding, I thought. Then I asked myself whether the people in Palestine also had trouble understanding what he was on about.

'You have to persevere with God, in order to make sure that you are heard,' Jesus explained.

Should I have prayed more?

'So God is a diva?' I snapped.

Jesus was surprised at my outburst. I clearly hadn't understood the parable as he'd wanted me to. But before he could reply anything in return, we heard the horn of the *Bethlehem Four*. The ship would set sail any moment.

'I'm sorry, I must board the ship now,' Jesus said.

I'd come here in vain. Kata would not be healed. I was in total despair and was trying to find the right words. Then Michi came charging out of the brothel. He looked at me wide-eyed. 'I saw things in there that no man should see, ' he exclaimed, aghast.

A perturbed Michi disappeared off in the direction of his Beetle. The horn sounded again. 'Farewell, Marie,' said Jesus.

And off he went.

My desperation turned to anger. If you had to go knocking at his door more often to get that bread, then that's what I was going to do now.

'Jesus, wait!'

He didn't turn around.

'Jesus!'

He still didn't turn around.

'*Eli, Eli, llama, sabathi*,' I finally shouted, filled with grief.

He stopped and turned around to face me: 'That means "My God, my God, my llama is infertile".'

'*Eli, Eli, lladara sabathi*,' I tried again.

'And that means, "My God, my God, my hat is infertile."'

'You know, what I mean!' I yelled.

I wanted to run up to him and pummel his chest in sheer desperation.

'Yes, I know,' he replied.

And then he quietly spoke, adding his own pain: '*Eli, Eli, lama sabachthani.*'

'My God, my God, why hast thou forsaken me?' I translated. Accusingly. Angrily. Unhappily.

Jesus thought long and hard. Then he declared: 'I will travel on another ship.'

I could hardly believe my luck. Overjoyed, I ran up to him and hugged him.

And he let me. He even enjoyed it. I pulled him close to me. And he enjoyed that too. Because in this instant, he was Joshua again.

Have I mentioned that I have a talent to destroy even the most special moment?

Exuberantly, I kissed Joshua on the cheek. For a brief moment, he enjoyed that too. I could feel it! And then, shocked by his own behaviour, he let go and declared: 'We need to hurry to your sister.'

I wondered whether I should be ashamed of myself. But I didn't feel any shame. After all, that kiss was born out of a deep gratitude. And love. It surely couldn't be wrong to love Jesus.

Love Jesus?

Oh dear! I knew that he was Jesus, and I loved him anyway? Then I did feel ashamed.

I didn't say a word in the car on the way back to Malente. Jesus sat on the back seat and prayed in Hebrew. I wondered whether he might be asking God for forgiveness for reacting to my kiss like that. In any case, he managed to create a distance between us. As I awkwardly stared out of the window, Michi was hardly able to focus on steering. The presence of Jesus was making him nervous. He still wasn't entirely convinced that he had the Son of God sitting in the back seat of his shabby VW Beetle, but Jesus's charming manner, to which he was being exposed for the first time, was slowly dispersing any doubts he had.

'How am I to believe you that you are the Messiah and not just some nutter?' Michi asked.

'By just believing it,' Jesus answered coolly.

'I can't!'

'That's what many people in Judea felt, particularly in the temples,' Jesus replied.

This really ate away at Michi. As a believer, he had until now never identified with the haughty rabbis in the temple.

While Michi was grappling with his faith, I noticed that the last time I'd gone to the toilet was at the salsa club. We drove into a car park, and I bravely headed into one of those typical motorway toilets, the kind that would drive any environmental health officer to an early grave. As I emerged, rather relieved, Michi approached me and said: 'You're sure that that man is Jesus?'

'Yes.'

'Do you swear?'

'On my sister's life.'

Michi pondered and pondered and finally said: 'Then I'm going to ask him to forgive me my sins.'

I was pretty taken aback and followed my friend back to the Beetle. Then Michi started recounting his sins to Jesus, in chronological order. He began with a story featuring a Bunsen burner, a can of deodorant and the frizzled beard of a chemistry teacher. Then he moved on to latter day sins and he told him about his Beetle, which he loved dearly, even though it produced more CO_2 than most African states. He confessed that he was a meat eater despite the fact that he knew how livestock were tortured, and that he even had a T-shirt that said, 'Vegetarians are eating my food's food'.

He confessed that he enjoyed drinking coffee, even though he knew that farmers in developing countries were being exploited, just like the girls that appeared in adult movies like *I Saw it Cumming*, which he had in his store.

Then Michi asked me to move out of earshot.

'Why?' I demanded.

'I'm now going to talk about sins that belong to the "Thou shalt not covet your neighbour's wife" category.' He hung his head in shame, and I began to feel queasy, fearing that the neighbour's wife might be me. So I decided to move away.

From a distance, I watched my friend, who turned bright red, confessing all manner of sins to Jesus. Then I wondered whether it might be a good idea to tell Jesus about all my sins as well. Telling him about Sven had certainly helped. The prostitute also looked very relieved after she'd poured her heart out to him, and it was clearly doing Michi good. Even if the Messiah furrowed his brow once or twice while listening to him.

He really did look great when he furrowed his brow like that.

Good God, I really was in love with Jesus.

It probably wasn't a great move to confess all your sins to a man for whom you have feelings of that kind.

When Michi had finished, Jesus put his hand on his shoulder, and shortly afterwards my buddy looked much happier than I'd ever seen him look before, except maybe when the iPhone was launched the market and he became one of the first one hundred owners in Germany. I was also pleased that Michi finally believed me. Now all we needed to do was to convince Kata to allow Jesus to heal her. Then everything would be fixed. Well yes, except for the thing about the final battle and all that hullabaloo.

Kata looked pretty taken aback when we turned up in her room. I quickly explained why the carpenter was there and that he wanted to heal her. 'Wow,' Kata replied after I'd finished my little speech. 'Tom Cruise seems completely stable in comparison to you.'

Jesus confirmed my story, and that he really was the Son of God.

To which Kata replied: 'And compared to you Lindsay Lohan seems stable.'

'Who's Lindsay Lohan?' asked Jesus.

Michi started telling him. He used words like 'rehab' and 'rap sheet'. He carried on speaking until I gave him a signal that made him realise that all this wasn't really that important right now.

'What have you got to lose?' I asked Kata.

'When I got ill the first time I didn't turn to quacks, miracle workers or witches, and I'm not going to do so now!' she protested.

'Ha! You just said something about a first illness. That means you must have a second one,' Michi concluded, looking very pleased with himself.

Kata looked at him, visibly annoyed. Then Michi realised that looking pleased was seriously inappropriate at a time like this.

'Why should I start with this hocus-pocus now?' Kata asked me.

'Because I'm asking you to,' I explained, sounding almost desperate.

'You're the second person who's tried to cure me today.'

'The second?' I asked.

'Forget about it,' Kata said.

She hesitated for a while and then turned to Jesus: 'All right then. At least Marie will realise what a nutter you are. But I hope that you're certain of one thing. If you really are Jesus, we really need to have a chat about why God has such a poor job performance.'

In that instance, I saw a little crack in Kata's tough exterior. A tiny part of her really did hope that this guy standing in front of her wasn't on day release from a mental asylum. If someone as hard-boiled as Kata could hope for a miraculous salvation, then no wonder so many sick people gave their money to faith healers.

Jesus approached Kata. He would soon be laying his hands on her, she would be cured, I would start crying tears of joy, and start hugging him and snogging him until he could no longer resist snogging me back!

Jesus put his hand on Kata and then quickly pulled it away again.

Had he cured her already? That was pretty speedy.

But why was he looking at me like that?

'This woman is not ill,' he announced.

We all looked at him in astonishment.

Then he looked at me reproachfully. 'You kept me from my task for nothing.'

His eyes were blazing angrily, and for a moment I feared that he was going to show me exactly what this 'withering away' was like in practice.

He was trembling with rage, but did not say a word and left the room silently.

So much for snogging.

CHAPTER
TWENTY-EIGHT

A couple of hours earlier...

The people of Malente had once again reminded Satan how much people cursed God. A man ditched at the altar. A fourteen year-old girl who was still a virgin. And a bank employee,…

In fact, people in Malente cursed God three times a day in their thoughts. That's more than Satan did himself. But no more than in other places around the world. Malente was actually in the lower middle ranks in this regard.

But that didn't matter. Almost every person had the potential to become a horseman of the Apocalypse – that was now very clear to Satan. So it made no difference if his warriors came from this dump. And as he was so fascinated by the artist; she would become Pestilence.

While Kata did her best to fight against her pain at the drawing board, trying to get something down on paper, the doorbell rang. Satan had been waiting to catch her while she was alone in the house. People were always at their most vulnerable when they were alone. Or in a crowd.

Kata went downstairs. She just hoped that it wasn't her sister at the door again. Of course she was going to have to talk to Marie about the disease some time, but she wasn't ready yet. Kata just knew one thing – this time she would just give up honourably. She couldn't cope with another fight against the tumour. Not the chemo and particularly not the baby-faced doctors, most of whom were still wondering why they hadn't gone into investment banking.

Kata opened the door, and there, to her amazement, stood George Clooney's doppelgänger.

'What do you want?' she asked impatiently.

'To make you an offer.'

'Didn't Avon sales reps die out long ago?' she quipped.

'I can cure you of your tumour,' Clooney-Satan smiled charmingly.

Kata was speechless for a moment. How did this guy know about her disease?

'You just need to give me a little something in return,' Satan explained.

He so loved these 'Deal or No Deal' conversations. People were so quick to sell their souls to get what they wanted – be that success or the promotion of their favourite football team, or even just a takeaway coffee after a spot of shopping in town. And not to be forgotten – the eternal bestseller – sex.

'I… don't have a tumour,' Kata replied.

'Of course not,' Satan grinned. 'But if you did, and I cured it, would you give me a little something in return?'

For a short moment, Kata was filled with hope, however absurd it was. And nothing made a moribund woman more nervous than the fear of having her hopes dashed. That's why she wanted to get rid of this unpleasant guy as soon as possible. 'Yeah, yeah… sure… anything as long as you get out of here,' she replied.

'Don't you want to know what that little something is?' Satan asked.

'No,' Kata declared, slamming the door shut.

Wow, Satan smiled. These human beings did have a free will, but they were very negligent when it came to their souls.

CHAPTER TWENTY-NINE

Nothing made sense any more. What had happened? Had I made a mistake? Was Kata not ill after all? She seemed pretty disconcerted by Jesus's performance herself. 'Those people at the psychiatric ward really should check the locks,' she said, trying slightly too hard to sound cool.

I was confused. And what made matters worse was that I had offended Jesus. He would have forgiven me the kiss on the cheek, but now he thought that I'd conned him. He most probably thought that it had all just been a trick to get him to stay with me.

I looked at Kata's sketchpad despondently. What I saw distracted me from both her tumour and from Jesus's withering glare:

Kata just snapped: 'You'll never get back those parts of your life that you have spent being afraid.'

I couldn't stand it when Kata made 'seize the day' comments. But this time it turned out to be pretty prudent since it made me remember something that I had been successfully suppressing due to her alleged illness. That question was, how many days did I actually have left to seize? Or to put it another way, when would the Day of Judgement be upon us?

Once Kata had thrown us out of her room and we were back at Michi's video store, I articulated this question for the first time: 'Well, it does make a difference whether you only have a couple of months or years to live.'

'Especially, if you're still a virgin,' Michi let slip.

I stared at him.

'Erm, what I mean is... an old friend... who... who's a virgin,' he stammered.

'What friend is that then?' I wanted to know.

Michi was so nervous that he was about to start hyperventilating. He caught a glimpse of the *Bourne Identity* shelf and quickly said, 'Julian Styles'.

'Julian Styles?' I replied suspiciously.

Michi turned red.

I was very surprised. I knew that Michi's sex life was currently pretty non-existent, but I had thought that he'd had a sex life at some point. He'd had girlfriends. Well, one, to be precise. Her name was Lena. And, come to think of it, she was Catholic too.

Gosh. Religion could be so rotten.

'Is this Julian a repressed homosexual?' I asked.

'No, no, no, what makes you think that?' Michi stammered. 'Julian is very straight.'

'But?'

'He has just been in love with the wrong woman for decades,' he admittedly wistfully.

I felt even queasier than I had before. My illusion, that mine and Michi's friendship was entirely platonic, could now officially be laid to rest. Michi was preparing to declare his love to me. I didn't want to hear it. So I looked away. My gaze fell on a shelf of DVDs and I implored Michi, 'Please tell me that she's called Brenda Pitt.'

Michi was surprised.

'Then I won't be losing a friend,' I explained.

Michi thought about what I'd said and then replied with a sad forced smile: 'Her name is Brenda Pitt.'

'Thank you.'

We didn't speak for a while. Then Michi asked me a question that had been weighing heavily on his mind for some time. 'Do you love Jesus? I mean, in the same way that normal Christians don't? And probably shouldn't?'

'Looks like it,' I admitted contritely.

This admission really hit him hard. Michi had been honouring Jesus his whole life. And now he was the only person in the world who was jealous of the Son of God.

Bravely he tried to brush this feeling aside, and he said something that really upset me: 'The world deserves to end.'

I was stunned. He explained himself: 'There are so many awful things on this globe – civil wars, environmental destruction, human trafficking…'

I also thought of things that were reason enough to put humanity in the dock: Morris dancing, tramp stamps, Russell Brand, toilet paper adverts, Filet-O-Fish burgers, 'Gangsta' rappers, parents who call their children *Chantelle*… So was Michi right? Would it actually be a good thing for there to be a heaven on earth? Should I even be asking that question? Or was it a fast track to a dip in the lake of fire? Was that my destiny? Was there still time to change it?

But what if there wasn't?

Then I could kiss goodbye to all my dreams of having children… sweet, easy to care for girls that sleep through the night and tell me: 'Mummy, you're the best and not really *that* fat…'

And on the subject of kissing goodbye to things, I could add never doing anything of any great significance in this life to that list. I would depart this earth as a M.O.N.S.T.E.R.

So I really did have to find out when this Apocalypse was planned for, even if Jesus was incredibly angry with me.

CHAPTER THIRTY

Meanwhile...

The Reverend Gabriel was sitting in the bath, surrounded by bubbles. Silvia was with him and she was enjoying having her back washed. She was much more relaxed today and more focused on caressing than sawing. She'd even said that she had feelings for him, which made his heart race as only the presence of God had done before. Silvia, the psychologist, explained to him why she was suddenly able to open up to him like this. After more than twenty years, she had finally made peace with her daughter, which cleared emotional blockages. Until now, she had not been able to get involved with another man because of her constant feelings of guilt towards Marie. While Silvia spoke of her heartache that she'd had with her daughter all these years, Gabriel thought that families were another one of God's bizarre inventions. Nothing gave people more pleasure and sorrow at the same time, more reason to rejoice and froth at the mouth, than a family. Humans really would have a much easier life, Gabriel thought, if God had designed them more like earthworms in matters concerning reproduction and breeding.

At least Gabriel no longer needed to listen to the family problems of his congregation, because he'd gone on sick leave for the rest of time on earth. His successor, Dennis, had taken up his new position a little earlier than planned – this morning to be precise. Dennis was one of those typical gym-body vicars, who loved church fêtes and gospel singing, but had also lost all faith during their theology studies, and wondered why they hadn't chosen a more lucrative profession like investment banking.

Gabriel enjoyed parties and coffee mornings with his congregation about as much as the fact that his human self had a prostate. Not a single person had ever found to God through eating cake as far as he was concerned.

When the doorbell rang, Gabriel thought that it was the gym-body vicar. And he wasn't going to get out of the bath for an atheist like him. . Then he heard the door open and a voice calling 'Gabriel!' It was Jesus.

'Your carpenter is back,' Silvia stated factually. Of course she didn't understand what this meant. Gabriel didn't understand it either for that matter. Wasn't Jesus supposed to be on the open sea bound for Israel by now?

He heard the Son of God approaching. Any moment now Jesus would catch him in the bath with Silvia.

'You look like a husband who is about to be caught having an affair,' Silvia grinned.

'The carpenter is Jesus,' he blurted out. Silvia looked at him aghast for a short moment and then burst out laughing.

Jesus came into the bathroom and saw Gabriel in the bathtub with Silvia. She had turned red with all the laughing.

Gabriel wondered whether it might be a good idea to submerge himself in the bath and remain under the surface until the Day of Judgement was over.

But Jesus apologised. 'Forgive me, my friend.'

Gabriel had not broken a marriage and had also not gone against the bathing guidelines in the Third Book of Moses (which did not interest the Son of God anyway – he was a man who elevated faith above rules), and so Jesus did not chastise him. The Messiah merely wanted to speak to him urgently, and left the bathroom to wait for him in the kitchen. Gabriel jumped out of the bathtub and dried himself hastily.

Silvia was astonished. 'You're behaving like that man really is Jesus and I am Satan.'

'Satan?' Gabriel looked at Silvia.

Was there a chance that he had a hand in it?

With Marie?

And with Silvia?

Yet even madder was the idea that Jesus could have fallen in love with someone like Marie without Satan's influence.

Gabriel got dressed and ran into the kitchen with wet hair. Jesus told him what had happened in the harbour and that there was no tumour in Marie's sister's head, even though Marie had claimed there was.

'Do you think she lied to me on purpose?' Jesus asked his old friend.

Gabriel briefly wrestled with himself, and then told Jesus of his suspicions. 'We have to consider the possibility that Satan has a hand in all of this.'

'He wants to lead me into temptation?' Jesus asked aghast.

'Do you feel tempted by Marie?' Gabriel's worst fears seemed to be becoming a reality.

Jesus paused. Was Marie really leading him into temptation? He felt drawn to her, yes. But was there more to it?

'I am probably being misled as well,' Gabriel explained. 'Satan gave us what we desire most. He gave me the woman I'd always loved. And he gave you the woman who sees the man in you.'

Gabriel did not say that he thought it was particularly perfidious of Satan to have chosen a woman like Marie, as it was hard to imagine her seducing a man, let alone the Son of God.

Jesus disputed this. The suspicion that Marie was linked to Satan was just too horrific: 'Satan has tried once before to tempt me. In the desert. He promised me water, food, kingdoms... but not love.'

'Well he's perfected his methods,' Gabriel explained. 'Kingdoms are not for everyone, but love... that gets everyone sooner or later. Even angels.'

Jesus protested: 'I... I just can't believe that Marie is in cahoots with Satan.'

'There is no other explanation.' Gabriel had now convinced himself. This meant that he would have to banish Silvia from his house (and from the bathtub).

Jesus was so confused – he wanted to retire to pray and so looked for a calm place to do so. But the search did not lead him to the church, nor to the garden behind the vicarage. It led him to the pier, where he'd so enjoyed sitting with Marie. He sat down, looked at the water sparkling in the evening sun and began to doubt. Not Marie, but himself. Because *there was yet another explanation as to why he had not climbed aboard the freighter, something that he had not wanted to admit. Perhaps… perhaps he didn't want to head into the final battle? A part of him doubted his task. Punishing people did not fill him with joy. In Judea he'd only ever made threats about the wrath of God so that people would choose a better path. That was helpful. But they'd only been threats.*

Quite probably he was so drawn to Marie because of his own doubts, and that's why he was only too willing to be distracted from his task.

CHAPTER THIRTY-ONE

I was absolutely delighted to see Joshua sitting on our pier. It showed me that this place meant something to him too. His anger had subsided, and it seemed that he was not even particularly surprised to see me, just a bit subdued and thoughtful. I sat down and let my feet dangle over the water next to his.

We sat there silently, like two people with a couple of wonderful dates and a great kiss on the cheek behind them, who knew very well that they couldn't be a couple as their family backgrounds were too different.

Joshua also looked at me searchingly, as though he was somehow suspicious of me. Did he really believe that I'd just invented Kata's disease so that he'd stay with me?

'What brings you to me?' he asked eventually.

'I… I have a question.'

'Ask away.'

'When is the Day of Judgement coming?'

Jesus waited what seemed like a very long time before answering: 'Next week, on Tuesday.'

The realisation that the world would only exist for five more days came as a deep shock to me. Everything I knew… everything that had ever touched me… everything I loved… would soon no longer exist. And I would have to lay all my dreams to rest. I reacted to this news like any other person would have reacted. I threw up in the lake.

While the ducks bid a hasty retreat, Jesus sympathetically passed me a tissue. After I'd wiped my mouth, I carefully asked whether this Book of Life and God's Judgement and the lake of fire really did exist. I'd hoped that this was just a transmission error and that the Kingdom of Heaven would be for everyone. But unfortunately, Jesus confirmed: 'It will happen just like that.'

I went very pale and declared: 'That... that bit about burning eternally is quite harsh.'

For a moment, I thought he might agree, but then something hit him, as if he wanted to rid himself of any burgeoning doubt. His expression darkened, he stood up and walked off the pier towards an apple tree on the shore that didn't bear any fruit. Angrily he said to the tree, 'Let no fruit grow on thee henceforward for ever.'

The tree withered away before my eyes.

Jesus looked at me sternly. Like an authoritarian teacher with a stomach ache looks at his pupils just before they're about to do an exam. I had no idea what he was trying to tell me.

'That's what happens to everyone who fails to live according to God's rules,' he said threateningly.

'You really could do with working on your metaphors,' I let slip. 'They really are quite complicated at times.'

Jesus did not let my objection stop him. 'God's commandments are recorded in the Bible for all to read. No one can say that they didn't know them. Those who have done good things in their lives will be rewarded for not choosing the simpler path, the path of evil.'

I understood. So the care worker will get compensation for the fact that the manager of the nursing home cut her wages to increase his own share of the profits.

That seemed pretty fair.

I still didn't like the concept of punishment though, and I was pretty sure that the care worker would concur. I preferred the idea of a benevolent God. 'So the Almighty is a mean, punishing God?' I asked grumpily.

'Do not speak about the Lord in such a derogatory way,' Jesus said angrily.

For a brief moment, the thought struck me that he really was a bit of a goodie-goodie, a little daddy's boy. Thank God I managed to keep that to myself.

Joshua's eyes were glaring at me angrily. But I just couldn't agree with him. What would become of Kata? She'd most certainly violated the first three commandments about honouring God. And my mother? How was she going to make it into the Kingdom of Heaven? Not if my father had anything to do with it. And what about him? It might not be too bad for Dad, as Svetlana wouldn't be able to break his heart if the world ended.

But suddenly I began to think about Svetlana's child. The world would be ending for her next Tuesday too. Even though I couldn't stand the girl, it just didn't seem very fair. Although she'd be getting into the Kingdom of Heaven – she hadn't sinned – she hadn't really had the chance to live in this world yet. She would never be able to experience the joys that it had to offer: salsa, Robbie Williams concerts, *The Simpsons*, the butterflies that accompany your first kiss, the first night you spend with a man – well, OK, that was not a must...

But it still wasn't fair! Everyone had the right to live their life until the bitter end! Even Svetlana's bloody daughter!

Even Julian Styles.

Even... me.

I was now so ticked off with God and his sonny boy that my eyes actually dared to blaze at Jesus angrily. So we faced one another full of rage by the withered apple tree, which tried hard to be a metaphor for what had become of our developing friendship.

Finally, I broke the silence. 'I think it's unfair that God is not giving people another chance.'

There, I'd said it!

'Are you really daring to rebuke God's plan?' Jesus asked sharply.

'You bet I am!'

'It doesn't suit you to challenge the path of the Lord,' Jesus reprimanded.

'You're such a little daddy's boy!' I replied.

That hit him hard.

I was glad!

'Gabriel was probably right,' Jesus said with a face like thunder.

'About what?' I asked impatiently.

'About you acting on behalf of Satan.'

For a moment I could hardly breathe. Then I burst out laughing. Loudly and hysterically. My anger dissolved into spasmodic laughter.

This clearly annoyed Jesus: 'You are ridiculing me?'

'Yes,' I answered honestly, once I'd managed to calm down a bit. 'If Satan were to send someone to you, then surely it wouldn't be anyone as incompetent as me.'

Jesus didn't know what to say to that.

'Listen,' I said. 'Look at me and listen to your heart. If you really believe that I am of Satan, then wither me like this tree.'

He looked a little tempted.

'But,' I continued, 'if you do not believe it, then give me the chance to prove to you that our world deserves another chance.'

Jesus stared at me, and the longer he stared, the more afraid I became. I'd clearly been too brave – death-defyingly brave. There were probably nicer ways to die than being withered away.

Finally, Jesus opened his mouth. I was almost expecting my death sentence, but he just said: 'The ship for Israel departs tomorrow evening. You have until then.'

I wanted to embrace him again, but as this would probably be misconstrued, I suppressed my desire.

The enormity of my task suddenly dawned on me – the fate of humanity now lay in my hands. I, of all people, was going to try to save the world.

Shame really that I didn't have the foggiest idea about how I was going to do it.

CHAPTER THIRTY-TWO

Jesus and I sat on the pier in silence while I thought about my dilemma. Perhaps I should just show him how many good people there are in the world. Unfortunately, I couldn't think of anyone truly noble. Other than people like Gandhi, Mother Teresa or Martin Luther King. But they were all dead, and Jesus probably knew them all already. He probably played a friendly game of backgammon with them in heaven, or whatever it was he did up there.

Yes, what exactly did people do in heaven all day long? And what would the people do once the Kingdom of Heaven was restored on earth on Tuesday? Pray to God probably. But would that really fill the days? Maybe for an hour a day, or even five? But what about the rest of the time? On the other hand, if you were already so completely happy, and that's what you were supposed to be in this Kingdom of Heaven on earth, then it didn't really matter what you did with your time. Then you could just look at the clouds, smell the flowers and let the grass grow under your feet all day, and you'd still be über-happy. Sounded a bit like being perma-stoned. I wondered whether I should ask Jesus about this, but decided against it.

Perhaps I should just show him who the good people were. But sadly I didn't know anyone of Gandhi's calibre. On the other hand – most people were pretty decent, weren't they? There were no dictators, murderers or call-centre operators in Malente. The last major incident involved a neighbouring village being pillaged during the Middle Ages. But I doubted whether this was enough. Should I tell Jesus that people deserved to carry on living because most of them are neither good nor evil, just average? That didn't seem like a very strong argument against God's plan to divide humanity into good and evil for the rest of time. I let out a heavy sigh.

'Why are you sighing?' Jesus asked me.

'Sigh…' was my sighing answer.

'You don't know how to convince me,' Jesus noted.

'Yes, yes, of course I do,' I answered rather unconvincingly.

'You don't.' He smiled kindly, almost lovingly.

But his smile still made me angry, because I felt found out. I've always detested it when a man I have feelings for uncovers one of my weaknesses. It didn't matter if this man was Jesus or not.

'You're angry at me,' he declared, sounding surprised.

'And you are the master of all things obvious,' I replied, slightly too sharply.

'What's the reason for your anger?' Jesus demanded.

'Well, most people are neither good nor evil, just sort of average,' I explained, 'but that's probably not enough to convince you.'

He didn't say anything and seemed to be deep in thought. He probably didn't want me to be angry at him. Eventually he asked: 'May I make a suggestion?'

I was surprised. My anger actually disappeared for a moment.

'Show me that these people you mention, these ordinary people, have the potential to be good and that they want to make use of it.'

Hmm… nice of him to suggest this. But how was I going to show Jesus that people could make use of their potential? Should I arrange a little general meeting at the Malente town hall and say: 'Listen up, people! Enough with all the adultery and tax evasion. And if I were you, I'd stop saying "damn and blast" quite so much.'

So I let out another heavy sigh.

'May I make another suggestion?' Jesus asked.

I nodded.

'Just show me one person whom you think has the potential to be good.'

He really was being very accommodating – it almost seemed like he really wanted to be convinced by me. As though he really had doubts as to whether this whole thing with the Day of Judgement business a good idea.

So I needed one person to prove this. That was all right. It might actually be possible. But whom should I choose? Kata? Probably not. She would just spend most of her time trying to explain to Jesus that God himself should prove that he had the potential to be good. My father perhaps? Well, he had about as many good things to say about me right now as the Pope did about condom factories. Mum also wasn't a good idea. She was – she'd told me – only together with Jesus's buddy, the Reverend Gabriel, because she was seeking solace. Maybe Svetlana? She was clearly grateful, that Jesus had healed her child. Maybe she was even grateful enough to stop using my father, and I could thereby show Jesus that she had the potential to be good? Should I take a risk with Svetlana? To put the fate of the world in the hands of the woman whom I'd called a vodka-whore?

At that moment I saw my doubtful expression reflected in the water, and two thoughts shot through my head. Why did my hair always look so crap? And what if I was that person?

It was certainly an idea. After all, there was no more average a person than me for miles around.

I turned to Jesus and explained that I would be providing the proof. In great detail, I explained that I already complied with loads of the Ten Commandments and that I would also manage to sort out the rest by tomorrow evening. I would honour my father and mother and I would stop coveting other people's things. Jesus patiently listened to my oration. 'The Ten Commandments are not enough for a good and right-eous life,' he explained calmly.

It seemed like nothing was easy if it had anything to do with God!

'Then what else do I need to do?' I asked. 'I mean, I hope that you're not expecting me to cut off a woman's hand if she grabs a man's private parts during a row?'

Jesus smiled. 'You've been reading Deuteronomy.'

He clearly thought I was rather better-versed in the Bible than I actually was.

'Don't worry,' Jesus explained. 'There are plenty of rules in the Bible that you don't need to follow. You just have to live in the spirit of God.'

'And how would you translate that?'

'You can find out everything that you need to know about a righteous life from my Sermon on the Mount.'

The Sermon on the Mount! Uh-oh! I'd heard of it of course. We'd learned about it during confirmation class, but at that time I was far too preoccupied with my heartache and drawing sketches on my notepad, in which my ex-boyfriend was sought out by the Ten Plagues. I particularly enjoyed having him be guzzled up by locusts. So if you'd asked me now what the Sermon on the Mount was about, I couldn't even have told him if my life or, as in this case, the survival of the world, depended on it.

'You do know about the Sermon on the Mount, don't you?' Jesus asked gently.

I grinned somewhat moronically.

'You don't?'

I grinned even more moronically.

'I thought that you knew the Bible,' Jesus said sternly.

'Frddl.'

It wasn't exactly pleasant to stand in front of Jesus and admit that you don't know the Bible. It's like telling your father that you're on the pill, and have been for two years, despite the fact that you're only sixteen years old. But I forced myself to deliver this brave confession: 'You... you are right. I have no idea what you said there.'

Before Jesus was able to show his disappointment too much, I hastily added: 'But just you wait, by tomorrow evening. I'll live according to its rules, and then you'll see that we human beings have the power and the potential to create a better world for ourselves.'

Jesus smiled at me. He seemed enraptured. Was he actually impressed by my impassioned speech?

Or even by me?

'Is everything OK?' I asked cautiously.

A jolt went through him; he pulled himself together and explained as emphatically as he could: 'I agree to your suggestion.'

'That's good,' I replied, not really knowing whether it was. I so hoped that I hadn't bitten off more than I could chew. I was so scared that I almost prayed to God, but at the last moment I remembered that God and I were not exactly pursuing the same goals right now.

Jesus and I faced each other. We didn't say a word. I would have loved to have spent the evening with him, like yesterday, but that was no longer possible. Far too much had happened. I would never see salsa-Joshua in him again.

With a heavy heart, I bid farewell. I got the impression that he didn't find it easy to part ways with me either. Once I'd got home, I was relieved that my father hadn't put up a 'No dogs or Maries allowed' sign.

I went into the house, saw that the little girl was already asleep on the sofa in the living room, and heard quiet sex noises coming from my father's bedroom. For a brief moment I wished that the Day of Judgement would begin right now.

Kata came out of the loo. Before I could greet her, I heard Dad moaning. He sounded a bit like a wild horse.

'Come into my room – you can't hear the stallion from there,' Kata suggested.

'Then it's a wonderful place,' I answered and disappeared with her into the refuge of silence. But Kata seemed very unsettled.

'Is something wrong?' I asked her.

'I… I'm scared.'

My sister admitting that she was scared? The world really did seem to be going crazy.

'Of what?' I asked.

'I… I'm no longer in any pain.'

'I thought that you didn't have a tumour?'

'Well yes, I do.'

This came as a serious blow to me.

'But now that the pain has gone, it's as though the tumour is gone too. I'm petrified.'

'Because you're hoping that it's gone and you don't want to be disappointed?'

'No, because I'm going to die soon.'

When the tumour was first diagnosed five years ago, the fighting spirit was always visible in Kata's eyes, but now it was just blind fear. And that scared me.

'I… don't want…' she said quietly. She didn't even articulate 'to die'.

I hugged her. And she actually allowed me to.

Lots of questions were darting through my head. If the doctors had found the tumour, then why hadn't Jesus seen it? Or was she just imaging that she had a tumour? But why would she do that? And why had Kata drawn this comic strip that I'd just found on the floor?

Why was Satan suddenly making an appearance in Kata's comic strips? And why did she think that he was superior to her? Was she afraid of ending up in hell? But she didn't believe in a life after death. Should I tell her that it did exist? And talk to her about Jesus? And about what was coming? Or would I be causing her even more anguish by doing so – was she a hot candidate for the eternal inferno after all?

Before I could open my mouth, I felt a tear on my cheek. Kata was crying. It was the first time that I'd seen the adult Kata crying. It almost tore my heart apart. I held her even more tightly and decided not to burden her with the madness that surrounded me. Suddenly, she was the little sister, and I was the big one protecting her.

CHAPTER THIRTY-THREE

Once Kata had gone to bed, I went to my room. It knocked me for six that she was ill again. But it didn't make me cry, because I had high hopes that Jesus could cure her. But for that, I would probably have to convince him that mankind – and Kata included – deserved another chance. So there was even more at stake.

I took my Bible out of my pocket, and while I was lying on the bed looking for the Sermon on the Mount – the Bible was in serious need of an index – I got quite immersed in it. For example, I learned that 'Sheba' wasn't just cat food. And the precise crime that Onan had committed. (There seemed to be more sex and crime in this book than on Channel 5.) When I'd finally found the sermon in Matthew, I was so nervous that I just flicked through the TV channels for a while – I was just too afraid of what kind of demands were going to be placed on me. There was far too much folk music for my liking, so, then I turned the TV off and started to read the words of Jesus. The sermon was a kind of 'Best of', including teachings like the bird parable that he'd made during our first date – it seemed like it was ages ago. I grouped his teachings into the following categories: 1) Can implement them without any problems; 2) Won't be easy to implement; 3) Will be difficult; 4) Will be bloody difficult; and 5) Bloody hell!

There wasn't much in the first and second categories.

The only demand that would not present any great difficultly was not to swear. Watching out for false prophets seemed also to be achievable, and of course I did not cast pearls before swine – although I assumed that this was another one of his parables, which I didn't really understand.

It would be harder for me to live without worrying about food and money. I was so damn good at worrying – if it had been an Olympic discipline I'd probably have won the silver medal, just pipped to the gold by Woody Allen. I was also not to be too attached to my possessions, and unfortunately there were no exception clauses whatsoever about shoes, iPods and Norah Jones CDs. But this was nothing in comparison to what Jesus required with respect to interpersonal relationships – you should give people who have done evil things to you even more. Or as Jesus put it: 'And if any man will sue thee at the law, and take away thy coat, let him have thy cloak also.' That was certainly a rule that would be well-received in tax offices.

But I doubted that I could ever be so selfless. And to turn the other cheek in a fight wasn't something for me either – I wasn't that into masochism. And it was equally problematic when it came to the subject of 'Judge not, that ye be not judged.' That's what Svetlana had accused me of, and I was all too keen to adjudge her to death. Then not even Jesus's parable 'How can you say to your brother, "Or how wilt thou say to thy brother, Let me pull out the mote out of thine eye; and, behold, a beam is in thine own eye?"' could help me get any further. Even though I knew that 'Sven' was carved into the beam in my eye, and I was thereby just as guilty as Svetlana, I was just too angry at her.

The 'Bloody hell' category included demands such as sincerely loving your enemies. I didn't have any enemies other than Svetlana. But how was I supposed to love this woman? Sincerely? And not be two-faced? Was the fate of the world now dependent on my ability to do so?

Then my mobile rang. It was Michi. He was all worked up and finally wanted to know when exactly the world was going to end. When I told him, he was even more frazzled, and when I told him what I'd agreed with Jesus, and that quite a lot depended on me loving Svetlana by tomorrow, he just groaned: 'We're finished…'

Then he gulped. He'd just realised: 'And Julian Styles is going to die a virgin.'

I felt empathy towards him. 'I'm sorry for Julian.'

'Tell me about it.'

I sighed with him in solidarity. This obviously cheered him up a bit and he hemmed and hawed: 'Do you think…'

'What?'

'Well…' he hesitated a while longer, and then flatly said, 'You could… once… with Julian…'

'No!'

'OK,' he said hastily. I almost felt guilty that I'd brushed him off so harshly. But I just wasn't in love with him, and sex without love generally gave me as much pleasure as having my legs waxed.

'Then… then, I hope, for my old friend Julian's sake, that you manage to convince Jesus,' Michi whispered hoarsely. Then he hung up.

I groaned briefly and returned to the Sermon on the Mount. Jesus simply couldn't make a load of demands without providing any advice on how to put this into practice as a normal mortal person.

I flipped through the pages, found something in Matthew 7:12 under the heading 'The Golden Rule': 'Therefore all things whatsoever ye would that men should do to you, do ye even so to them.'

Good, well that was pretty well known, and it sounded a little bit like those signs you find in train toilets: 'Please leave the toilet as you would like to find it.' Every time I read those signs I thought: am I an interior designer?

But now, when I really thought about the words of Jesus, I reached the conclusion that perhaps this was indeed the way to go! If I was nice to Svetlana, then maybe she might be nice to me and change. And then I might actually to be able to love her sincerely. Not an entirely realistic scenario, admittedly, but surely dreaming was allowed.

And maybe, yes maybe, I would be allowed to dream about me and Joshua again some time.

CHAPTER THIRTY-FOUR

Meanwhile...

The Reverend Gabriel was sitting in the moonlight on a bench in the vicarage gardens. The Messiah was resting in the guest room, and in the distance he could hear the gym-body vicar playing his horrendous electric guitar. That he was playing It's the End of the World as We Know It *is not something that Gabriel noticed. It had been a terrible day for him. He had thrown his beloved Silvia out, and even though she repeatedly assured him that she was not of Satan, and shouted angrily that she knew a very good psychiatric ward which she could recommend, he did not believe her. He also didn't believe her when she cried, trying to soften his heart. And most certainly not when she confessed through her tears that she had really come to love him.*

He took his gaze off the moon and stared into the dark garden. He felt lonelier than ever before — he had lost Silvia.

At that moment, the thorny bush in front of him burst into flames.

This encounter was all he needed.

WHY IS MY SON NOT ON HIS WAY TO JERUSALEM?

the burning bush asked. His impressive voice wasn't that loud, but you still felt as though it could pervade the entire world.

All Gabriel wanted to do was flee. But since God was omnipresent, he would probably appear to him everywhere — as a burning palm tree in the Maldives, as a burning fir tree in Norway or a burning bonsai in Japan. There was nowhere to escape to. So Gabriel pulled himself together and thought about how he could best tell the Lord that his Son was currently being led up the garden path by Satan.

'Erm, my Lord, how shall I say this? There is a complication...'

COMPLICATION?

Judging by the tone of his voice, the burning bush did not currently seem to have a high tolerance for complications. And particularly not with respect to the complication that Gabriel was going to have to tell him about.

'Well now, it's not easy to explain,' Gabriel stammered.

THEN EXPLAIN IT IN A COMPLICATED WAY.

the thorn bush suggested.

Gabriel desperately wanted to keep all of this to himself. He knew that the burning bush tended to overreact. You just had to think back to the Egyptian Pharaohs. But Gabriel also knew that he couldn't hide anything from the Almighty. So with a trembling voice he explained what had happened between Jesus and Marie to date, and he didn't skimp on the details:

'...and salsa is a dance in which you move your hips close together...'

The burning bush remained silent and began to look increasingly angry as the oration progressed. At the end of Gabriel's account, he was so angry that he burned as only an angry thorn bush can. Gabriel could hardly stand the fury that the thorn bush was exuding. But he was also quite confused. God was the Omniscient – how come there were things that had escaped him?

He was just about to ask this question when the thorn bush flared up metres into the sky, and his voice sounded angrily:

IF MY SON IS NOT ON HIS WAY TO JERUSALEM BY TOMORROW EVENING, I WILL BE MAKING A PERSONAL APPEARANCE TO THIS MARIE.

CHAPTER THIRTY-FIVE

At least I could still dream about Joshua… We were holding hands, enjoying a lovely hike through the mountains, and when we'd reached the sunny summit, we looked deep into each other's eyes, our lips drew closer, and we would have kissed, had not Svetlana turned up. She was sitting on a stallion, which looked at me and said: 'I am your father.'

Horrified, I woke up. When I'd calmed down again and looked at my mobile, which I had put on silent, I saw that I had fourteen missed calls. They were all from my mother; she hadn't rung me as often as she did last night in the last ten years. I was shocked and worried, so I called her immediately. All I heard at the other end was a choked 'Hello?'

'Has something happened?' I asked clumsily.

At first I heard nothing. Then some gulping. And finally a wailing, 'Gbrllisssttlllycrzzzyy.'

'The rail is totally lazy?'

'Gabriel,' she sobbed.

'Gabriel is totally lazy?'

Why would I care about that?

'Gabriel is totally crazy!'

Well, that made much more sense. I told my mother to calm down, but unfortunately she didn't and carried on wailing. I tried to speak to her as compassionately as I could: 'It's good for you to let your emotions run free.'

'Don't use any of that psychobabble on me,' she snapped.

'Then stop blubbing,' I barked back. I still had to work on this empathy business. But my harsh tones seemed to have an effect. Mum stopped crying. She apologised and then she told me about Gabriel as calmly as she could. She said that she had feelings for him, which was not completely unrelated to the fact that we had made peace and that this had released blockages within her, and that Gabriel had now told her to leave because he thought that she was Satan.

'It's all just an excuse, because he has commitment issues,' she snorted angrily. 'I mean *Satan*. Please! He's about as real as God!'

'Or equally real,' I gulped.

'What?' my mother asked.

'Erm… forget it.'

She started snivelling again. Man, Gabriel really should be happy that I was not able to wither him like Jesus could have. As soon as I had finished my ruinous thought, I was pretty shocked. Not because I felt guilty about thinking such a thing, but because it basically said in the Golden Rule that wishing someone to die was tantamount to killing them directly. Well, this implementation of the Sermon on the Mount had got off to a flying start.

'I'll have a chat with Gabriel,' I offered.

'Would you do that for me?'

'Sure,' I answered. If I was in the midst of saving the world, I may as well have a go with my mother's love life.

Once I'd hung up, I got dressed, went downstairs and met Svetlana in the hallway. It was now or never. Could I bring myself to love her? I looked into her eyes, which were covered in the kind of glittery make-up favoured by transvestites and chorus girls in 'Dancing on Ice' (there was most probably a degree of overlap between groups). I asked myself what I could do with this woman that I would also like done unto me.

'Svetlana, there's a pretty nice café in this backwater town of ours that does a great breakfast. Do you fancy it?' I asked.

'Excuse me?' Svetlana was clearly confused, maybe even suspicious.

'I'm sure it will be a lovely daughter-stepmother morning,' I tried to joke. Svetlana, who clearly found the absurdity of our future family constellation even more amusing than I did, smiled and said. 'Sure.'

Soon after, we were sitting in Malente's smartest café, and the chef was preparing a stupendous omelette with ham, tomatoes and leek right in front of our eyes. Yet I still did not feel any positive feelings towards her, let alone love, even though I was treating Svetlana like I myself would like to have been treated. But food and drink probably wasn't enough. What else would I like? For people to be interested in me. So I tried to show some interest in Svetlana. 'It... it must be hard, to raise a child alone in Belarus.'

'It's hard anywhere,' she replied.

I nodded in agreement and thought about the German zombie mothers with dark circles under their eyes.

'But it was especially hard for me, because I also had to look after my sick father,' Svetlana explained. 'That's why I worked did piece-rate work.'

'In the factory?' I asked, biting into a wonderful chocolate croissant.

'In the brothel,' she answered.

I choked on my wonderful chocolate croissant.

When I'd finished coughing, she quietly said: 'Your father knows. And you may as well know too.'

I would have loved to have ended this conversation right away. But that would probably not have been very good for my Sermon on the Mount mission. So what was I going to do? Show her compassion? I wouldn't have wanted that if I was her. Understanding? More likely.

'OK. That doesn't sound easy...' I stammered. That was all the understanding I had to offer.

'I didn't lie to you. Your father is a wonderful man as far as I'm concerned. No one has ever been as good to me as he is.'

She sounded very level-headed, and genuine. And she'd told me about her dodgy past. A dishonest woman was not likely to do that. I decided to give her what I would most have wanted most in her position – trust.

'It would be lovely if you could make him happy,' I said.

'I will certainly try,' she replied, and it sounded honest.

Then we ate our omelettes. By the end of our breakfast we had reached a reasonable level of understanding. And we respected one another. But I had not managed to love her. Yet I still felt that my efforts deserved to be recognised with a 'nonetheless'.

I wanted to go to see Joshua, to ask him if he shared my assessment (and because I missed him and this was a good excuse to meet with him). But I was met by a very troubled looking Gabriel on the path outside the vicarage.

'Keep away from him!' he called at me from afar, looking a bit like an exorcist in one of those seventies horror movies.

'Good day to you too,' I replied sharply.

'Keep away from him,' he warned again.

'I am not of Satan,' I explained to him as calmly as possible.

'That's precisely what someone in cahoots with Satan would say,' he said angrily, with a logic that was not exactly easy to refute.

'How can I prove to you that I don't have anything to do with Satan?'

'By keeping away from him.'

'I won't and I can't,' I replied.

He looked at me angrily. For a moment, I feared that he would come at me with a crucifix and a holy water gun.

'You have really hurt my mother,' I told him in a much calmer voice.

This silenced Gabriel at first. And I wondered how I could reach out to him, Golden Rule-style. I had tried understanding.

That had helped with Svetlana too. 'I can understand that you are afraid in a situation like this, but my mother is…'

'Hold your tongue!'

'But…'

'Hold your tongue!'

I had trouble suppressing my rage.

How could I calm him down? What would I have wanted in his situation?

'Would you like a schnapps?' I suggested hesitantly.

He looked at me even more angrily.

'So what do you want from me then?'

'For you to become a pillar of salt.'

'You're not really living according to the Sermon on the Mount are you?' I snapped back.

'Don't tell me how to live in your true faith.'

'Well, if you're not…'

'Get lost!'

'Not a chance.'

'Get lost. It's for your own good,' he insisted.

'Surely I should be the best judge of what's good for me or not,' I countered sharply.

'You don't know anything. You're a stupid, naive child!'

'And you are a pig-headed, annoying old man!' I blurted.

'*What* did you call me?'

'I called you a pig-headed, annoying old man, you stubborn old fool!'

We eyeballed each other.

At that moment, I heard a voice behind me saying: 'Marie?'

I turned around and was shocked to see Jesus. He had heard everything, but was not angry with me, just disappointed. I gulped, and didn't know what to say to him, so Gabriel took the chance to speak up.

'My Lord…'

'Please leave us alone,' Jesus requested.

'But…'

'Please.' Jesus spoke calmly, but with enough determination that Gabriel did not object any further. He just glared at me briefly with blazing eyes and toddled off back into the vicarage.

'Shall we go for a little walk?' Jesus asked, and I nodded without saying a word.

We both walked away from the vicarage in silence. Almost automatically, the path led us to our favourite spot by the lake. As we sat down on the pier, Jesus finally broke this oppressive silence and declared, 'It would not seem that you have understood the spirit of my words.'

'I still have until this afternoon,' I countered quietly.

'Will you be able to live according to the Sermon on the Mount by then?' Jesus asked, with a slight glimmer of hope in his eyes.

'Of course,' I answered.

'Really?'

'No.'

Jesus looked at me in surprise. I wondered, whether I should tell him that you couldn't just heed something like the Sermon on the Mount from one day to the next, and that I needed time to implement all of this, so probably something like five to forty years.

'You… can't do it so quickly…' I finally stammered.

'My disciples, except for Judas, were able to do so right after my sermon.'

'Maybe you needed to catch it live?' I argued rather weakly.

'Mary Magdalene also managed to do so, after Peter had told her about the sermon.'

Well, great. Now he was talking about this ex! It's never pleasant to stand in the shadow of his ex-girlfriend, but I surely had to be standing in the biggest ex-girlfriend shadow known to man. What was I going to do now? To save the world? And our friendship? Could I already speak of 'love'? Certainly from my perspective. But what about from his? Well, sometimes he looked at me that way… when he was Joshua… not Jesus. But he probably wasn't going to be doing that again.

Was he? What was it the Golden Rule said? I should do unto others, as I wanted them to do unto me.

At the sight of his beautiful face I only wanted one thing before Joshua went off to Jerusalem – for him to kiss me! What did I have to lose now? So I slowly leant down towards him. I grasped his wonderful, slightly rough face in my hands and moved my lips closer to his.

All that a very surprised Joshua could muster now was: 'Marie…'

I just quietly said: 'Shhh… It's all in the spirit of the sermon.'

Before a very overwhelmed Joshua had the chance to ask why, I kissed him.

Just very lightly.

Like a breath of air.

Our lips touched for what seemed like the blink of an eye.

But during this blink of an eye, I felt as though I was in heaven.

CHAPTER THIRTY-SIX

Meanwhile...

Satan was standing outside the clinic where Kata had scheduled an appointment, as twenty-four hours had passed without her feeling any pain whatsoever. The Prince of Darkness was not roaming around as George Clooney, but Alicia Keys. He knew that he would be closer to Kata's beauty ideal with this slim soul diva. Although he already possessed her soul, he wanted to seem especially alluring to her. She fascinated him greatly. If he was going to win the final battle, perhaps she could sit on the throne next to him, the one he was planning to construct out of the Messiah's bones.

'Hello chocolate face.' Satan's train of thought was suddenly interrupted. Two adolescent skinheads were approaching. Normally, those half-witted skinheads were one of his target groups – and having to deal with such types in hell was another aspect of his job that was making him increasingly depressed – but these skinheads were in the middle of some kind of riot.

'Piss off out of our town, you negro whore!' the larger one of the two threatened.

'Do me a favour and go and bust your head on that wall,' Satan commanded with his soulful female voice, and the skinhead ran – just as he was told – into the nearby brick wall. The other skinhead turned pale.

'And you,' Satan said to him, 'go into the nearest kung fu dojo and tell the grand master he's a chink.'

'Will do.' The skinhead ran off eagerly.

Then Kata stepped out of the clinic. She didn't even register the skinhead lying on the ground. She was far too confused. She was also relieved, but mainly confused. The tumour had gone! As if through a miracle. It was unbelievable. Did that freaky Jesus guy have anything to do with it, or maybe it had been that crazy Clooney? Suddenly, she saw Alicia Keys standing in front of her. Kata rubbed her eyes.

'Hello,' said Alicia Keys.

'Hello…' Kata replied. She had no reason to be rude.

'May I introduce myself? I'm Satan,' Alicia Keys explained.

To prove it, she transformed herself into a being with a blood red face, horns, hooves and a pretty ugly tail, accompanied by terrible sulphur fumes. There were flames blazing around his entire body, which did not burn Satan of course. He only showed himself like this for a short time, before turning himself back into Alicia Keys. The flames disappeared, too. Once the smell of sulphur had dissipated and Kata had found her voice, she bravely said: 'Wow, you have some really good special effects.'

'And I have your soul,' Alicia grinned.

Kata gulped. This was really freaking her out now. Just a short while ago she hadn't even believed that a thing like the soul even existed.

'I sense what you're thinking. That you're going to be the first one to do it. Lots of other people hope that too. You've all just read too many stories in books and seen too many movies, where unrealistic things like that have worked.'

Alicia Keys laughed, while Kata realised that her sister probably was hanging around with Jesus. Maybe he could help her? All she needed to do was to run to Marie quickly and…

But Satan had no plans to let Kata go home.

'I'm going to introduce you to your fellow horsemen now,' Satan explained.

'Horsemen?' Kata had no idea what he was on about. What did he want? To go foxhunting with her?

Satan snapped his fingers, and suddenly Kata was no longer with him in front of the clinic, but at a table outside the Malente ice-cream parlour. The two of them were not alone.

'May I introduce,' Satan said, 'this man who will be the apocalyptic horseman called War…' He pointed at Marie's ex-groom, Sven.

'…and this is the apocalyptic horseman called Famine.' He pointed at a man wearing vestments… and gym clothes.

'And you will be the horseman called Pestilence.'

Kata didn't even understand half of what he was on about. She only knew one thing – she didn't want anything to do with all of this.

'I'm getting out of here,' she said with all the might she could muster.

'I wouldn't do that if I were you,' Alicia Keys smiled.

'If I understand correctly,' Kata countered, 'then you'll only get my soul once I'm dead. So I can do what I like. Like leave. Right now.'

'Yes, but I can kill you whenever I want to,' Satan smiled, conjuring up a fireball from his feminine, perfectly manicured hand.

Kata gulped and answered: 'That must be useful when the cigarette lighter in your car isn't working.'

'And when you're dead, I'll have your soul, and then you will have to bear your tumour pains for all eternity, as a punishment for defying me.'

A terrible fear ran through Kata. Was she going to have this pain forever? The only reason she wasn't completely freaking out yet was because she was still clinging onto the slight hope that she might become the first person to trick Satan into returning her soul.

CHAPTER THIRTY-SEVEN

I was stunned after the kiss. So was Joshua. We stared at the lake for quite a while. We were no longer Marie and the Messiah. We were just two incredibly anxious thirtysomethings.

'Sorry, sorry, that wasn't a very good idea of mine,' I finally stammered.

'A foolish idea,' he confirmed in an unsteady voice.

'The most foolish idea in the whole world,' I added.

'No. That was Peter's idea that he could also walk on water.' This made Joshua smile.

Yes, smile. Only a little, but he smiled. Wasn't he angry with me?

'Aren't you angry with me?'

He hesitated a little before answering: 'No, I'm not.'

He wasn't!

What did that mean? Had he enjoyed the kiss? Did he want more? I certainly wanted more! But should I push my luck and have another go?

It turned out that I wasn't brave enough. First I would carry on staring out over the lake a bit more.

'Sometimes…' Joshua began speaking, before stopping again.

'Sometimes…?'

'Sometimes I ask myself whether there might be another divine plan hidden behind the Day of Judgement, and whether there might not be eternal punishment for the sinners after all.'

'Another plan?' I enquired.

'I don't know which one… but God's ways are wonderful.'

'Whimsical more like…' I mumbled.

'What did you say?'

'Erm… nothing, nothing.'

We both carried on staring out over the lake anxiously. And then – as though the kiss had lifted a veil from me – I suddenly saw a way out of this dilemma. 'Why don't you just walk the earth for a couple of years?'

Jesus looked surprised. 'I should delay the Day of Judgement?'

'Exactly. Then you can show people how to live their lives according to the Sermon on the Mount,' I explained eagerly, 'and save a few more souls.'

This idea also seemed to electrify Joshua. 'That's a wonderful thought.'

And what electrified me was that one of my thoughts had electrified him.

'Well, would you accompany me?' he asked.

He wanted to take me? As a disciple? Deep within me I felt that I would not necessarily be the best disciple.

'Erm… but I wouldn't need to sleep in caves would I?' I asked.

He burst out laughing. 'No, you wouldn't.'

'Then… gladly.'

We smiled at each other. His smile was so wonderful. I would have loved to have cradled his face in my hands again and to have kissed him. But I just managed to restrain myself with all my might.

'Why are you sitting on your hands?' he asked sounding very confused.

'Just because…' I stammered.

We sat in silence again for a while, and suddenly Joshua said: 'I would like to hold your hand.'

'Then… do it,' I told him, my heart beating with excitement.

'You're sitting on your hands.'

'Oh… oh yes…' I stammered and freed my hands.

So we sat holding hands once again on the pier. I was happy. And so was he. It seemed that my suggestion had enabled him to find a good balance, for at this moment he was equally the Messiah and Joshua.

After a few minutes of gloriousness just sitting on the pier, it was time for another one of my popular 'I can destroy any moment no matter how wonderful' performances.

'Don't you think God will mind?' I asked, referring both to the handholding and the new plan to walk the earth again.

'I will pray to him and hope that he will understand,' Joshua replied. He sounded optimistic and determined. I only noticed that he was a little unsure when he loosened his grip on my hand.

'It would be nice if you could leave me alone to say this prayer,' he requested.

'Sure, sure… of course,' I replied, leaving the pier, even though I found it hard to be parted from him.

I went off along the path by the lake. Meanwhile I imagined how my life might change now. Marie from Malente would roam the world with Jesus. That sounded nuts. But wonderful as well. Would Jesus and I kiss again during our travels? Just the idea got me into a right state. I was burning up as I thought about it… or perhaps it was because of the thorn bush that had suddenly caught fire in front of me.

MARIE!

a voice suddenly said. It was impressive, frightening and wonderful all at once. But the main thing was that *it was coming out of the bloody thorn bush!*

I checked the surroundings for loudspeakers and the like.

WE NEED TO TALK.

There were no loudspeakers. It really was the bush speaking.

'Are you who I fear you might be...?' I asked the burning thorn bush, thus speaking to a plant for the first time in my life.

YES, I AM.

CHAPTER THIRTY-EIGHT

'Scotty to bridge.'
'What is it?' asked Kirk.
'I quit!'

YOU ARE KEEPING MY SON FROM COMPLETING HIS TASK.

I didn't know what to reply, or how to speak to God at all for that matter. Instinctively I wanted to ask God for forgiveness, but my voice…

'Ch… r…'… failed me completely.

ANSWER.

'Ch… r…'

YOU DO NOT NEED TO BE AFRAID OF ME.

Not afraid, what a comedian!

DO YOU WANT A DIFFERENT SETTING FOR OUR CONVERSATION?

'Ch… r…' I replied, attempting something of a nod.

YOU ARE REACTING LIKE MOSES DID…

the thorn bush said, sounding amused, something you certainly couldn't tell from the way it looked.

A moment later, the path around me had disappeared, and I was standing in an English country house, like the ones you see in Jane Austen films such as *Sense and Sensibility*. The furniture was from the nineteenth century; there was a delightful smell of black tea and finest orchids in the air, and I was even wearing one of the beige-coloured old English dresses with a corset, which was fortunately not tightly laced, but rather covered my squidgy tummy like a sheet of silk. Through the window, you could see a garden with a lawn. Only English gardeners were able to cut grass quite as precisely as this. Of course I knew that I was no longer in our world. God had simply chosen a setting that I'd always found particularly beautiful in films, and tended to revisit when I was daydreaming. Maybe God had created all of this just for me. Or maybe it was all just part of my own imagination. It actually didn't really matter, as long as he did not reappear to me as a burning thorn bush.

I knocked on a wooden table, which certainly felt damn real. I went through a glass door onto the patio, sat down on an old-fashioned, but extremely comfortable lounger, enjoyed the warmth of the sun on my face and listened to the birds singing. This wonderful late summer's evening at the country house was like balm for my confused soul. The only thing that still seemed a bit creepy was the fact that God knew I'd always wanted to mosey around in a nineteenth-century English country house. Theoretically it was clear to me of course that God knew all our secrets – otherwise he wouldn't have been known as the Omniscient, but rather as the Semi-omniscient – but when I realised this in practice, that he even knew about little things like my fondness for Jane Austen, I was a little ashamed, not least when I recalled that I had once, during my desperate single days, fantasised about an erotic encounter with Mister Darcy.

But you simply couldn't spend too much time feeling guilty or worried in a wonderful garden like this. When I was finally sitting relaxing in the evening sunshine, a voice behind me said: 'How are you feeling?'

A woman of my age came out onto the patio from the house. She looked like Emma Thompson, and she was wearing a stunning, resplendent white dress that flowed down to the ground beautifully. She smiled more sweetly than I'd ever seen anyone smile before.

'I'm feeling much better,' I replied.

'That's wonderful,' Emma said.

'Yes, it is,' I reiterated.

'Would you care for some Darjeeling?'

I actually preferred coffee, latte in particular, but since it didn't really fit into the country house milieu, I answered, 'Yes, I'd love some.'

Emma Thompson took the pot of tea from a three-legged side table that I hadn't seen before now – perhaps it had only just appeared? – and poured the tea into an exquisite white porcelain cup with a red flower pattern. I had a sip, and it tasted surprisingly like latte. In fact, the best latte that I'd ever had.

'I think this is how you prefer your tea,' Emma Thompson said with a smile. It was such a wonderful, friendly, even loving smile, so I couldn't help but smile back.

'Is this heaven?' I asked.

'No, I created this especially for you.'

'It must be very convenient to be God,' I said when I saw the beautiful garden.

'Yes it is,' Emma/God laughed.

'Are you always a woman?' I was not afraid to ask questions in this wonderful setting.

'I could show you my true face, but I'd better not.'

'Why not?'

'Because you would go insane upon seeing it.'

'That's a good reason,' I replied. Now I was starting to feel slightly afraid again. So I decided not to ask any more of the questions I'd always wanted answered. What was there before God created the universe? Did paradise really exist? What the heck was God thinking when he invented periods?

And tumours?

Instead I took another sip of the Darjeeling/latte and looked at the exceedingly carefully cut lawn.

'I haven't spoken to anyone like this in more than two thousand years,' Emma/God explained.

Whether or not I wanted it to, this certainly fed my ego. I looked up again and asked: 'Did you invite Moses for tea back then as well?'

'No, after all those years in the desert all he wanted to do was eat leavened bread again,' Emma/God replied, taking a little sip of tea. Then she finally got to the point. 'You are keeping my son from completing his task.'

'Yes.' I admitted. What was the point of denying it?

'You love him.'

'Yes.' I couldn't much deny that either.

'In a way that you are not supposed to?'

'Hmm…' I mumbled evasively. Of course I knew that my feelings for Joshua were not normal, but they did feel genuine. Then how could they be wrong?

'Please leave him alone,' Emma/God asked gently, taking another sip of her tea.

'No, I won't do that,' I blurted out.

Emma/God put the cup down and looked at me mildly surprised. Though not as surprised as I was having dared to contradict God. That had probably never been good for anyone.

'You don't want to let go of him,' she said.

'No.' It was too late now to eat my words now.

'You doubt my divine plan?' Emma/God was now no longer smiling.

'Yes…' I replied, my voice shaking. I'd really got myself into a big hole. So I may as well keep digging. I just couldn't understand the need for the lake of fire or the Great Flood (as a little girl I had imagined three penguin friends – Pengy, Pongo and Manfred – waddling onto the Ark, only to hear Noah say that only two of them could come. Pengy and Pongo waddled up the ramp of the ship more quickly, and Manfred had to stay behind, disappointed by his friends for the rest of his life. (Although the rest of this little penguin's life wasn't all that long, as it had already started to rain).

'You doubt my goodness?' Emma/God demanded to know.

'It's just hard to see whether you are the benevolent or the punitive God,' I answered bravely.

'I am the benevolent God,' he answered emphatically.

I was not convinced. All I could think was: 'Tell that to Manfred the penguin.'

'But,' Emma/God continued, 'I am also the punitive God.'

This divine logic was, like so many other divine logics, completely incomprehensible to me. And it was probably written all over my face.

'You people are my children, and like children you grow and change perpetually,' she explained. 'You are no longer as you were in paradise. Or during the Great Flood. And like children you need to be brought up, and as you get older that needs to occur in a different way.'

'Oh I see…' It was slowly becoming clear to me. Humanity was an innocent baby in the Garden of Eden with Adam and Eve, and then a wild pubescent teenager at the time of Sodom and Gomorrah. God had also been a loving parent, sometimes kind but also stern. 'If you mess around like that again, there'll be no TV.'

And what was it Jesus said in this regard? The precise etiquette for the house of God was there for all to read in the Bible. God was a consistent mother (or father or whatever) with clear instructions.

Thinking about it, she was actually quite a patient parent. At the end of the day she only really banged her fist on the table every couple of thousand years, and otherwise permitted plenty of freedoms to develop, make mistakes and correct them, only to go on and make some more mistakes. So, if you believed the words of these parenting experts, she was actually an archetypal mother.

But although it all made a bit more sense now, I wondered why she needed to make with the punitive threats. Of course, there were lots of people who did not follow selfish impulses, because they were afraid of being punished for them in the afterlife – in that sense it worked. But did it really have to be an eternal hell – wasn't a TV ban enough?

And there was another thing I didn't understand. 'Did it have to be the cross?'

'Excuse me?' Emma/God sounded surprised.

'Crucifixion is an agonising way to die – would a sleeping potion not have been enough?'

Now that I knew Joshua, his suffering moved me even more than it had just a few days ago in the church.

'Does a loving father… a loving mother… do that?' I asked accusingly.

'It was not me. It was the people who nailed him to the cross,' Emma/God corrected me gently.

'But why did you allow it to happen?' I was not letting go now.

'Because I gave you people a free will.'

So we'd got to the question of all questions, that I'd already asked myself aged fourteen when I had my first taste of heartache. Why did God give people a free will to do such incredibly stupid things with?

'Because…' Emma/God declared – it seemed that she had read my thoughts or at least guessed what I was thinking – 'because I love you.'

I looked into her eyes and she seemed to be telling the truth.

'Or would you like to live without a free will, Marie?'

This made me think of people in North Korea, Scientologists and other apathetic zombies without a will of their own.

'No…' I answered.

'You see,' Emma/God smiled benignly. She really did seem to love us. Perhaps she had created humanity because she missed not having someone to love. Yes, perhaps God had been living in a perfectly ordered universe that was not yet inhabited and was not all messed up. Like a couple living in a massive house with an as-yet empty nursery who long for a child so that the house might be filled with laughter, shouting and chewing gum squashed into the carpets. For a moment I felt sorry for God, who had once been alone in the universe and must have felt incredibly lonely.

'You are the first person who's ever shown me compassion,' she said smiling sweetly. She took my hand – which felt very warm and human – and added, 'The same compassion that you have for my son.'

She seemed to be the first potential mother-in-law who liked me.

'But…' Emma/God continued, '…if you stay with him, my son will be unhappy.'

'W… why?' I asked, fearing the answer.

'Because he will have to turn away from me,' Emma/God explained, thoughtfully stirring her tea. The thought seemed to make her sad. This one person, whom she loved more than all the others. She certainly didn't want to lose him.

'And if he turns away from me…' she began saying wistfully.

'…it would endlessly hurt Joshua and tear his heart apart,' I added, finishing this sad thought.

'You are a wise human child,' she said earnestly.

'So you are commanding me to stay away from him?'

'No, I'm not.'

'No?' I asked.

'You have a free will. It's your decision.'

At that moment, the garden, the country house, the porcelain, all of it, just disappeared. But, above all, Emma Thompson had disappeared as well. I found myself standing in my own clothes by the lake in Malente, in front of the thorn bush, which was no longer burning and looked completely unscathed.

I thought about the decision with which I was faced. If I were to stay with Joshua, it would crush him to go against God. If I left him, my silly, childish dream of loving Joshua would come to an end.

So I had a choice between two pretty evil evils! Great thing, free will.

CHAPTER THIRTY-NINE

I stood before the innocent-looking thorn bush, boiling with frustration and shouted: 'This is all just not fair of you!'

'Are you talking to some undergrowth, Marie?' a surprised Joshua asked from behind me. I froze on the spot. As I didn't turn around to face him, he walked around me, looked at my stunned face and asked: 'I thought that you'd have been home by now?'

What was I going to do now? Tell him about my tea for two with God? I decided to try to win some time by saying something trivial. 'No, I'm not at home.'

Joshua nodded. He could see that for himself.

We remained silent for a while, and then the thought struck me that maybe God had also invited his son for tea to discuss these relationship problems. Whatever it was, she/he/it/ whatever was probably more than capable of having two conversations at the same time. So I carefully asked: 'And… have you spoken to God?

'Yes, I have,' Joshua replied, and my heart almost stood still with excitement. Perhaps he already knew that I was going to have to make a decision, and might therefore be making it for me? But then again, I probably didn't want that after all, as I would surely not be able to stand it if Joshua ended it.

'What… what did he say to you?' I asked nervously.

'Nothing,' Jesus replied, sounding a little disappointed. It seemed that he had hoped for more too.

'Nothing?' I could hardly believe it.

'God only speaks to people very rarely,' Joshua explained.

'Damn coward!' I blurted out.

'What?' Jesus appeared mildly surprised about my criticism of God, who really did seem to be leaving it entirely up to my own free will to break Joshua's heart.

'Erm. I mean… not you,' I hastily explained.

Joshua looked around, but there was no one to be seen anywhere, not on the path, nor in the bushes, nor in the trees.

'So whom do you mean then?' Jesus asked sounding confused.

'Erm… … the… … the… the tree!' I stammered, as I didn't want to tell him that I was shouting at God either, and especially not about what it was about.

'The tree?' Joshua was completely confused now.

It was one of those conversations in which you want to press the rewind button.

'The tree… is erm… a coward, because it doesn't offer its fruits to God,' I explained, a little relieved that I'd managed to save myself with this explanation that both sounded reasonably believable and biblical.

'But that's a fir tree…' Joshua said looking puzzled, 'it doesn't bear fruit.'

'Nevertheless!' I insisted, for lack of better excuses.

Perhaps I would have been even more affected by my idiotic ramblings had not my anger at God got the upper hand again. After all, it was he who had got me into this situation in the first place. One thing was sure, I would not be accepting another tea/latte from this woman.

'Why do you look so angry all of a sudden?' Joshua asked.

If I were to tell him the truth now, I thought, he would probably become angry with his God as well, for the first time in his life. But if Joshua were to be angry with God, he would suffer and… and… and… Even just the thought of seeing Joshua suffer made my anger disappear and turn to sorrow.

'Marie, what is it…?' Joshua was confused. No wonder

really. I currently had greater mood swings than a woman going through the menopause.

The question was: what would hurt Joshua more? Conflict with God? Or living without me? That wasn't really a difficult question to answer. Joshua would never be able to live without God; being his son was the essence of his life, his destiny. He could certainly live without me – like all other men before him.

As hard as it was – perhaps even for him – my free will had at that moment made the only decision possible. I had to be the woman to break up with Jesus.

'I… I don't think it's a good idea if I stay with you,' I said, trying to find the right words.

Joshua looked confused.

'You need to go your way and I need to go mine,' I continued.

'You don't want to stay with me?' Jesus asked in disbelief.

'No.'

Joshua just couldn't understand what I was getting at. No wonder – he didn't have as much experience of being dumped as I did.

'We… are not compatible,' I said honestly, yet still using one of the most popular break-up phrases.

'Why not?' Joshua asked. He was a little bit slow on the uptake.

That just made him even more lovable. And this whole thing even harder for me.

Should I use the age difference? I was in my mid-thirties. Bodily he was a little over thirty as well, but in actual fact he was more than 2,000 years old. Or should I claim that I wasn't worthy of him? After all, he could turn water into wine. My special talent was having no special talent.

'It's… it's not you… it's me.' I spared him the details and noticed that I used another classic break-up phrase.

If I carried on like this I might even end up saying: 'We can still be friends.'

'I… I… don't understand,' Joshua replied.

'Look,' I tried to argue, without mentioning God, because I didn't want to turn his wrath on him, 'even if you cancel the Day of Judgement, and travel around the world trying to convert people, we would both be living together platonically, like you did with Mary Magdalene, and to be honest, that's not really for me.'

I decided that it was better to keep it to myself that Kata had always called Plato 'a complete idiot'.

'It will be different from how it was with Mary Magdalene,' Joshua countered.

'Yes?' I was completely flabbergasted now.

'I finally want to experience love.'

It took a while before I could even begin to process this sentence. Joshua was serious about this. That… was… unbelievable… I felt hot. I felt cold. I felt hot again. Now I'd started getting the hot flushes of a menopausal woman as well.

'I think,' Joshua explained, 'that I deserve to experience human intimacy, like other people do.'

My kiss had unleashed a whole load of suppressed desires that had been pent up through all his deprivation. All the protective barriers that he had built up during his role as the Messiah were now down, and his feelings were revealed. He was now entirely human.

And if anyone deserved love, then it was him, after all that he'd been through.

All right, perhaps not necessarily with me…

'I am not worthy of your love…' I said.

'Every person…'

'Now please don't go and compare me with the Pope,' I interrupted.

'Every person, who bears within them a love like you do, is special.'

After he'd uttered this sentence my hot flushes became even more intense.

His hand was now touching my cheek, and that feeling was almost as heavenly as our kiss.

'I have a desire that I also felt with Mary Magdalene...'

'And what desire is that?' I asked, a little cooler. Some time I would really have to teach him to stop constantly talking about his ex.

'It's my desire to...' he hesitated, 'I'd wanted to confess to Mary Magdalene, but then she said those words that stopped me from doing so...'

Then he remained silent. The memory was painful.

But I was far too eager to find out what Mary Magdalene had said to him. But what was even more interesting was: 'What is your desire?'

'One day...' It was really taking a great deal of will to express this desire, and his fear of being rejected by me as well was very evident.

'One day?' I asked encouragingly, trying not to show my excitement. I felt that this must be something extraordinary.

'...to start a family.'

My heart skipped a beat. That was something extraordinarily extraordinary. A family... Perhaps with two little daughters... Like I'd always dreamed of.

For a nanosecond I envisioned us in our amazing converted tour bus, like you normally only see in American road trip movies, travelling around the world from Australia to the Grand Canyon. Joshua was preaching the word of God, I taught our two daughters Mareike and Maja – and repeatedly forbid them, in case they took after their father, to turn water into Coke.

During this nanosecond, I was happier than I'd ever been

225

before in real life. But of course I could never realise this fantasy. My eyes filled with tears.

'Marie? Did I say something wrong?' Joshua asked, in a sad, almost despondent voice.

'No… no… you didn't say anything wrong…'

Quite the contrary.

He breathed a sigh of relief. I, on the other hand, was about to start bawling my eyes out. He wanted to give me a hug to comfort me. But I couldn't allow this to happen. Because then I would definitely stay with him. Forever. Regardless of what God wanted.

So I pushed Joshua away.

'Marie?' He couldn't understand anything anymore. I was hurting him, but he didn't want to let go of me. He reached for my hand again, so I had to tell him something that would push him away from me for good, something – and then the words came to me that might be able to do it, and were actually truthful as well: 'Joshua… I… I don't believe in God enough.'

Joshua was in shock. The woman with whom he wanted to start a family was not a suitable candidate.

I could not shoulder his pain, especially as my own was so great. So I just whispered quietly: 'We can still be friends.'

Then I ran off in despair. Over my shoulder I could still see him looking at me, confused and sad. But he was no longer running after me. He no longer wanted to follow a woman who did not believe in God enough.

I quickly rushed home without stopping, because I knew that I would start bawling my eyes out. I had done the right thing, that was true, but why did it have to feel so rotten doing the right thing?

No sooner had I opened the door than Dad greeted me in the hallway and smiled at me for the first time in days. 'I'm so happy that you are trying to find a way to be friends with Svetlana.'

At first I thought: 'It didn't do anything for me,' but then I realised that that wasn't true. Thanks to the Golden Rule I had, or at least it seemed as though I had, regained my father. He tried to give me a hug, as awkwardly as only fathers trying to hug their adult daughters can do, and I let him. Once he'd let go, he said: 'Your sister left in mad rush.'

'What?' I couldn't believe it. 'Did... did she say where she was going?'

'She mumbled something about Jerusalem.'

I immediately grabbed my mobile and called Kata, to find out what was going on. But it went straight to voicemail.

She wasn't allowed to leave! Jesus still had to cure her tumour, and he would do so, even though I'd dumped him. He wasn't your typical miffed ex-boyfriend. He was Jesus for Christ's sake!'

'She... she left something for you in your room,' Dad explained.

'A parting gift...' I feared.

He nodded and I ran up into my room. There I found another one of her comic strips:

Once I'd read that I did end up bawling my eyes out.

CHAPTER FORTY

Meanwhile...

Satan, still in the form of Alicia Keys, approached a Learjet on the runway of a nearby military airport with his three Horsemen of the Apocalypse in tow. It was supposed to take them to Jerusalem and belonged to an Austrian bodybuilder who had a great deal to thank Satan for.

As they climbed the gangway with their light baggage, Kata desperately fought for her soul by drawing Satan's attention to the futility of the whole apocalyptic horseshow: 'But we're definitely going to lose the final battle. God is stronger than you, isn't he?'

'We will not lose,' Satan countered.

'But it says in the Bible that we will lose against Jesus and that our live bodies will be cast into the lake of fire,' the gym-body vicar added anxiously, causing Sven to start chewing his fingernails.

'That's not going to happen,' Satan explained sternly, keen to go up the last steps of the gangway.

'But perhaps you are one of God's tools, just like we horsemen are?' Kata was not letting loose. Satan's feminine forehead started creasing. This woman who fascinated him so had hit a nerve. He had been harbouring this doubt for quite a while himself, or rather, since his time as a serpent in the Garden of Eden. Even then, during that whole apple business, Satan had not been able to rid himself of the feeling that he was just being used by the Lord up there in heaven.

'You're just playing into God's hands with everything that you're doing,' Kata said.

Satan stood still. This beautiful artist was right. He was preparing everything as planned, and if he carried on like that, he would also lose, as planned.

'That's probably true,' he conceded after pondering the matter for a while.

Kata could hardly believe it. She had actually sown seeds of doubt in Satan's mind.

'We're not going to Jerusalem,' he announced.

Kata's hopes were rising. Could it really be so simple?

'And we're not going to commence the final battle next Tuesday.'

Kata was inwardly jubilant. It was this simple! She had put a stop to Satan's plans. But in the midst of her jubilation, he announced: 'We are going to commence the battle against Good today! In Malente!'

And Kata thought: things are not going quite as hoped.

'You'll get your horses right away!' Satan declared.

'Horses?' Kata asked. She'd already hated horses when her classmates still papered their walls with pony magazine cuttings.

'You're not called the Pedestrians of the Apocalypse,' Satan joked. Pretty poorly in Kata's opinion. 'I made you the second most powerful horseman,' he explained to her.

That was something that made the gym-body vicar mightily jealous.

'Only the second most powerful? Am I not your favourite?' Kata snarled.

'Yes, you are. But the place of the most powerful horseman has already been assigned. I don't have any choice about that. It's someone who's been roaming the earth since the beginning of time,' he explained in a voice that made Kata shudder.

'I want to introduce you to this being,' he said and pointed at Marie, who, to Kata's great surprise, stepped out of the Learjet onto the gangway.

'This is my horseman called Death,' Satan declared.

'That's my sister,' Kata replied, completely stunned.

Satan just grinned. 'Death likes to take on the form of the person whom he intends to take next.'

CHAPTER FORTY-ONE

I lay there on my bed for ages, bawling my eyes out – somewhere between half and three quarters of an eternity. If I wasn't crying because of Joshua; it was because of Kata, and when it wasn't about Kata, it was about Joshua. It was a bawling carousel from hell. As far as I was concerned, this silly old world may as well go under immediately. And I'd stopped caring whether I would end up in heaven or would spend the rest of my days burning in the lake of fire. The main thing was for this to come to an end.

'Marie?' a deep voice said.

The Reverend Gabriel was standing in the doorway. I needed him like the *Titanic* needed a second iceberg.

'Your father let me in,' he explained. Then he asked: 'Are you crying?'

'No, I'm watering the plants,' I replied.

I realised that Gabriel's presence did entail something good. I didn't want to cry in front of him and thus found the strength to stop.

'Is it because of Jesus?' Gabriel asked, sitting down on my bed, even though I hadn't asked him to. 'He told me that you ended things with him.'

Had Joshua told him to come and see me? Maybe he refused to accept me breaking up with him and he wanted to fight for me again? They say there are men who regard women who play hard to get as a challenge.

'He's going to set off for Jerusalem this afternoon,' Gabriel said, dashing my hopes.

So as not to start wailing again, I asked him what he wanted.

'To apologise to you,' Gabriel replied. 'You are not of Satan. Otherwise you would not have let Jesus move on. I'm sorry.'

'It's fine,' I said. I was far too jaded to be angry with him.

'And I also wronged your mother.' Gabriel was very remorseful now. 'Do you think you might be able to put in a good word for me with her?'

'I think that might require a barrage of words actually.'

Gabriel nodded in agreement. Then he hummed and hawed a bit, before finally saying: 'There's something else you both should know.'

'And what's that?'

'I'm an angel.'

'That's not very modest of you.'

'I mean, I am a real angel,' he clarified. 'The Archangel Gabriel, who is become flesh.'

Just a few days ago, I might have responded to this by saying something like 'zip-a-dee-doo-dah'. But now nothing could shock me. And thinking about it, it certainly did explain quite a few things – Gabriel's scars on his back, why Jesus slept over at his place and why he claimed to have announced his birth to Mary.

'Should you not be fighting with the heavenly host in Jerusalem side by side with Jesus?' I asked.

'Well yes. Although I'm a human being now, it would be my duty.'

'But…?'

'I defied it. I want to be with Silvia and speak on her behalf when she steps before God.'

To my surprise, he explained to me that he had asked God to make him a human for my mother's sake, and that he had then spent all those years hoping for a sign of love from her. I was touched to hear this. It was so romantic of him, so amazing – yet also completely foolish. But then most romantic actions are.

I caught myself feeling envious of my mother, for the fact that Gabriel had turned his once winged back on God for love.

I spoke to my mum on the phone and convinced her to meet up with Gabriel. I asked him to keep the story about his origins to himself until the end of the world. She would probably not believe him until then and would think that he was winding her up.

Gabriel agreed and apologised to my mother for his behaviour, without telling her about his secret. Afterwards the two of them sat side by side on my old bed for a while without saying a word, like a couple of nervous teenagers. Far too long, I thought after a while. In times like these you didn't have any more time to waste. So I blurted out: 'Go on, kiss!'

Both of them laughed nervously. Then my mother plucked up the courage to give Gabriel a kiss. He was a bit flustered at first – after all, I was still standing in the room – but my mother pressed her lips so tightly onto his that he couldn't do anything but kiss her back. For a long time. Far too long, I thought after a while, especially as they seemed to have forgotten about me and started fondling each other. It occurred to me that this was a good moment to escape, so I turned to the door to leave, but there was Dad. Watching his wife caressing another man.

'Silvia?' he asked in surprise.

The two of them stopped kissing and looked at him guiltily. There are moments in which I really wished I was Speedy Gonzales, the fastest mouse in all of Mexico.

I was expecting my Dad to go on a major rampage. After all, he'd been pining for my mother for the last twenty years. But he did nothing of the sort. Instead he smiled and said: 'It seems as though we have both found happiness.'

Mum smiled back. 'Yes, it would seem so.'

Strange. Until two days ago, I had still secretly hoped that my parents would get back together. But now I was overjoyed that they no longer argued and were happy for one another. Yes, it seemed as though I might be growing up. Just in time for the end of the world.

My father invited us round to his place for a hearty meal of cabbage, potatoes and sausages, and even bought us ice creams in town for dessert. Mum and Gabriel looked at each other lovingly. So did Svetlana and Dad. But I wasn't looking at my potatoes particularly lovingly.

I was sitting alone between two happy couples – basically a singleton's nightmare – and I missed Joshua so much. There were still a few days to go until next Tuesday, and I would spend them feeling lovesick. Great.

Svetlana's little girl came running into the kitchen because Dad was getting the chips that he had specially made for her out of the oven. She had a new friend in tow called Lulu, one of those seven-year-olds who likes to wear lipgloss. They both sat down at the table and successfully fought off any of Svetlana's attempts to put even a tiny amount of vegetables on their plates. I saw these two little girls and immediately thought about Maja and Mareike, the two daughters I had always longed for, and I finally realised what a wonderful, extraordinary man Joshua really was. Not because of his miracle healing, and not because of his special kind of aqua jogging. No, he was the first man who had wanted to start a family with me and with whom I could actually imagine doing so. When I was with Marc it was always me who longed for a family, whilst he was about as interested in children as he was in monogamy. And when I was with Sven, he was the one who was always secretly hoping for a family, whilst I always made sure to take my pill. But now it turned out that the wrongest of all men whom I could have fallen in love with was in fact the right one – *the* one.

But I had pushed this extraordinary, wonderful man away, because God had commanded me to do so. Well, not commanded as such, rather more advised me to do so. He had left the decision up to my own free will. And with it I'd decided against my actual will.

Lilliana and her lipgloss friend burst out laughing as my Dad squeezed ketchup all over himself trying to put some on their plate. Their laughter was only moderately sweet – to be honest, it sounded like baby hyenas finding an antelope with a broken leg. But I thought about Maja and Mareike's laughter – that would probably have been much more charming.

Why hadn't I fought for our love?

Just because it was unrealistic?

And God had something against it?

What kind of silly arguments were those if you were really in love?

Gabriel hadn't cared about the divine order had he? I watched him as he enjoyed my mother putting her hand on his lap in a way that wasn't really suitable in company. If Gabriel could be this happy having not followed his destiny, then maybe Joshua could too? If he really had feelings for me – I had no doubt about that, he was incapable of lying – he would be able to cope with the conflict with God as well. And he'd have to! You couldn't spend your life being a little daddy's boy (mummy's boy, whatever) could you?

I looked at the clock. Joshua would be making his way down to Hamburg any moment now to take the ship to Jerusalem. Maybe he was already there, singing psalms with the punters and prostitutes?

I certainly wouldn't ever know if I carried on staring at my potatoes.

And I certainly wouldn't ever start a family.

Of course I knew that the chances of that were about 1 in 234 bajillion. But I had to try. If God had something against it, then he simply shouldn't have given me a free will! Or not have invented this damn thing called love.

I jumped up from the table, explained to my Dad that my departure had nothing to do with his culinary skills – although his cooking did have the potential to trigger mass panic – ran out of the house and then along the path by the lake towards the vicarage. I ran like Harry in *When Harry Met Sally*. But unfortunately I was knackered after four hundred metres. And after seven hundred metres I was gasping for air. Shortly after that I started getting a stitch. How the devil did people in those romantic comedies always manage to run through half of New York? Sure, they did have a director to catapult them through the city in just a few scenes, so they probably only spent about forty seconds actually running. They also tended not to wear high heels, as I was right now. When they were, they took them off as they were running, without breaking their legs, and then carried on running through the metropolis without stepping on glass shards or in dog shit.

But I wasn't in a film. The path was full of dog shit, glass shards and condoms (the school kids called this path the 'Way of Life') so I couldn't take my shoes off. Sometimes reality was pretty damn annoying.

Plagued by a stitch, I dragged myself along the edge of the lake and up to the vicarage. When I stepped onto the gravelled path I saw Joshua coming out with his luggage. In spite of the pain, I rang up to him gasping, spluttering, sweating and hoping that he wouldn't see the sweat patches under my arms.

'Marie, you look like you've been wandering through the Sinai desert,' he said, looking surprised to see me.

I didn't respond to that. I was just really happy that he hadn't departed yet. But he didn't look the slightest bit pleased to see me standing in front of him. Quite the contrary.

'Please get out of my way,' he said.

'I…'

'You don't believe in God,' he cut me off.

'I never said that,' I countered, trying to contextualise my statement. 'I said that I don't believe in God enough.'

'Not enough is not enough,' he replied sharply and walked past me. He left me standing. Just like that.

No one was allowed to just leave me standing like that! Not even him!

Angrily I called after him. 'Don't be such a sour puss! Let's talk to each other like grownups.'

Joshua turned to me and replied: 'I have no idea how a cat can be sour?'

'It's a metaphor,' I said impatiently.

'And I'm being ironic,' Joshua countered.

Oh great. It would happen to be now that he finally understood what irony is!

We glared at each other angrily, as only people with feelings for each other can do. We seemed to be miles away from reconciliation, let alone starting a family. Time for the Golden Rule. What would I have wanted in Joshua's position? A rational explanation!

'I believe in you,' I began and adopted a gentler tone, 'and I think that most of what you said in your Sermon on the Mount is pretty good…'

He was now of a milder disposition. He was no longer frowning.

'…even if I still haven't fully understood that thing about pearls and swine…'

'It means that…' Joshua launched into an explanation.

'It doesn't bloody well matter!' I interrupted him stroppily.

He kept quiet and I got the impression that he didn't care that much about the swine either.

'Through you,' I explained to him more calmly, 'I have made peace with my mother, my father and even with the woman whom I called a vodka-whore...'

'Vodka-whore?'

'Also doesn't matter,' I said. 'And I almost think that I've become a bit more mature, more grown-up. I'm sure no one would have bet a cent on that three days ago, me included... But there is one thing that I just can't get my head around. That's the whole God-punishment-heal thing ... You see, I'm more in favour of anti-authoritarian upbringing.'

'Anti-authoritarian upbringing?' Joshua asked looking puzzled. 'Marie, you sound like the Demoniac of Gadara.'

I had no idea who this demoniac was, and assumed that it was best never to have met him. But Joshua was right, I had to be clearer, and speak in a way that he would understand.

'So what does it say in the Bible?' I asked. 'Carry no fear in your hearts. Live without fear of punishment and the fires in hell. Do good unto those around you, because it is your free will, be it only for your own will, for your own lives will thus become richer and greater.'

Joshua said nothing at first. Then he replied: 'It... it doesn't say that in the Bible.'

'Well it should!' I had finally made my point crystal-clear.

This clearly made him think. So I added: 'Well the way I see you, you don't seem like the kind of man who could punish people!'

He almost nodded.

'You're so different,' I urged him, 'a man who can teach... a man who can heal... a man who can inspire... a man...'

'…who's a damn good kisser,' is what I wanted to say, but my voice failed me thinking about all these memories.

'You're right,' he replied. 'Fear should not govern man, but love.'

When he said the word 'love', he gave it a fluid meaning. With 'lo' he seemed to be referring to charity and virtue. Once he'd reached 've' his mind had already started thinking about us.

He looked at me like he had before our kiss. That wonderful kiss. I couldn't stop myself… My lips drew closer to his again… And this time his drew closer as well… They came closer… And closer… Ever closer…

Until we heard a neighing sound.

This neighing was so loud and screeching that it sounded otherworldly. It sounded incredibly evil. It came from above, from the heavens. Our heads recoiled, our faces strained upward, and we caught sight of four horses that were breaking out of the skies, burning like flares. On these flaming steeds that were charging down to earth were beings that I was not able to identify from afar. But I knew instinctively that these horsemen were more terrifying than the animals.

'The Horsemen of the Apocalypse,' Joshua stated. He masked his surprise with a clear, strong voice.

My heart shrunk into a small knot through fear.

'I need to go there,' Joshua declared.

And I'm so scared I need to have a wee, I added in my thoughts.

CHAPTER FORTY-TWO

Meanwhile...

The first horseman to land in Malente's town centre on his blazing steed was the man called War. Satan had accorded Sven with two supernatural powers, one of which was not burning his bum on the fiery horse – all the others had this too – and the other was to release all the suppressed hatred in people through his mere presence. Sven alone bore enough suppressed hatred within himself, particularly towards women. He had always been nice to them – to his mother, to the female doctors at the hospital where he worked as a nurse, to his fiancée Marie… And what had he got in return? His mother felt that the agony of labour had not been worth it, the doctors disparagingly referred to him as 'Sister Sven', and Marie had reached new levels on the open scale of humiliation. But now, thanks to Satan, Sven could finally give free rein to his hatred. Within seconds, Malente's town centre was transformed into a no-go area. Innocent shoppers became beings who foamed at the mouth and wanted to split each other's heads open. A mother hit her husband where it hurts because he had refused to have the snip, despite already fathering four children. A plump woman clawed her friend's face because she couldn't stand the fact that she could eat anything she liked without her figure suffering. Two Jehovah's Witnesses forced their way into people's houses at knife-point, and the Turkish owner of Malente's best kebab shop went after a neo-Nazi with his electric kebab knife. 'That… that's really not very tolerant of you…' the skinhead stammered.

The second horseman landed in the middle of this warzone. As a child, the gym-body vicar Dennis had been really fat. The other children had called him things like 'Jabba the Hut', 'Road Block' or 'Please don't squash me'. When he got older, he started exercising like mad, and only ate carrots and drank energy drinks that tasted more artificial than a polyester shirt, the cuffs which he used to nibble on because of all his insecurities. In the end Dennis had become nice and slim, but he still felt this hunger, which he never satiated through fear of ending up looking like he did before. But now, as the horseman Famine, he suddenly saw that everyone felt a longing in their lives that they were unable to satiate. Some of them longed for love, others for money, sex or a full head of hair. Dennis was now able to bring all these personal insatiable desires that everyone suppressed within themselves to the surface. A man in his mid-fifties called his wife, whom he'd been married to for thirty-five years an old trout, and started pestering twenty-year-olds wearing boob tubes. Single women stole babies from buggies, a completely exhausted single mother did not object, the local Weight Watchers group ransacked sweet shops, and primary school children raided mobile phone shops, whilst several men stole from clothes stores to try on women's clothes. One honest citizen, who had thus far suppressed his tendencies for pyromania, delighted in how flammable listed timber-framed buildings seemed to be.

Above the inferno, the third Horseman of the Apocalypse was circling on a blazing steed. It was Pestilence. Whilst Sven and Dennis were revelling in their newfound powers, Kata was still battling with herself, but the temptation to give in to her dark side was growing stronger. As her horse circled above the hospital, she could no longer resist. She flew down and headed straight for the top floor. The flames caused the brickwork to burst asunder. The patients looked aghast and afraid, but Kata, who was now standing in the hospital hallway with her horse, only had eyes for the doctors, whose profession she so hated. Most of them had not cared the slightest about her suffering, so she took revenge with her new powers – she could bring out any illnesses that were lurking within a person's body, and make them appear much sooner than they would have. The senior consultant got a combination of diabetes and Parkinson's, so it would certainly not be a pleasure for her to inject her insulin. The emergency response physician began suffering from a compulsive eating disorder and also developed a wide spectrum of food allergies. And the young SHO received a double whammy of dementia and incontinence, so that every time he needed to go to the loo, he couldn't remember where the toilet was.

Any thoughts of tricking Satan were long gone – she was now intoxicated by her powers.

The only horseman who retained a dignified distance and calmly sat on his steed like a vulture circling the skies of Malente was Death. He was still in the form of Marie, waiting for her to become the first casualty of the Day of Judgement.

CHAPTER FORTY-THREE

Joshua rushed towards the town centre, from where black smoke was now rising. I could hardly keep up with him. Bloody shoes.

Despite the three apocalyptic horsemen and the burning town centre, I could only think of one thing as I looked at Joshua's determined striding – the kiss we missed. I was incredibly sad that this magical moment had been interrupted. But then again I did feel blissfully happy, because Joshua really had wanted to kiss me again, and then my heart sank, because I feared that it was all too late for us now that the Day of Judgement seemed to be jumping the gun.

'What's going on with Day of Judgement?' I asked Joshua, gasping for air. 'I thought we had until next Tuesday? And we're actually in Malente right now, not Jerusalem.'

'Never underestimate Satan's power and guile,' Joshua replied earnestly.

'Erm…' I'd suddenly had a worrying thought. 'What actually happens if he wins the final battle?'

'Then,' Jesus declared, 'evil will prevail for all of eternity.'

I trembled as I pictured how murderers, sadists and investment bankers would take hold of the sceptre. They would torture, torment and exploit the good people, and as no one was allowed to die, this would carry on for all of eternity. The lake of fire was a spa in comparison.

The town centre looked like one of those warzones you see on the news that makes you want to see what's cooking on *Come Dine With Me*. Houses were on fire, the crowds were busy ransacking the shops, people ran through the streets covered in blood, and a Turk was chasing a skinhead with an electric carving knife – admittedly you didn't see the latter all too often on the Ten O'Clock News. Before I had time to think about whether I had actually seen the 'Skinhead gets sliced up' story on the news, Jesus approached an injured man sitting in the gutter who had a cut under his eye, couldn't see and was babbling on to himself that 'She'd never told me that she thought I was no good in bed…'

Joshua sat down next to him, and the man jumped with fear, as though he might get hit again. But Joshua said to him: 'Fear thou not.'

Then he spat on the ground, made a little paste with his saliva and rubbed it under the man's eye. Then he drizzled a little water from a bottle he had in his bag on the spot, and washed the paste away; the cut had disappeared and the man could see again. But not only that. Joshua's mere presence meant that the people in his vicinity forgot all about their anger and unbridled greed. The evil thoughts gave way to inner peace. The ransacking ceased, as did acts of violence. A woman gave a mother her buggy back, although she didn't look that overjoyed about it. I was not that close to finding my own inner peace in this disturbing inferno, especially since it had just struck me that my parents had planned to go and eat an ice cream in the town with Gabriel, Svetlana and the children. I wanted to ask Joshua to help me find them, but he was just in the middle of saving a traffic warden from a group of drivers who had stuffed their parking tickets (all 200 of them) down her throat, thus realising a widespread motorists' fantasy.

It was clear to me that Joshua could not desist from helping these people who were in danger just to look for my family, who might have been all right. With a bit of luck they were

244

still sitting at home digesting Dad's indigestible food. So, with aching feet, I ran towards the ice cream parlour – past burning houses, men in women's clothes and children beating up a mobile phone salesperson. The siren of an ambulance was sounding, and I was happy that there would be a doctor on site to help Joshua. But when I looked at the vehicle, I noticed that it was swerving all over the place… towards me! I was petrified with fear. The vehicle came ever closer, but I couldn't move, even though my brain was screaming at my legs: 'Oi, you stumpy little stems, move it!' But my mortal fear had blocked the connection between my brain and the stumpy stems.

'Scotty, are we going to make it?'
'It'll be tight.'
'How tight.'
'Tighter than Uhura's skirt.'
'That's pretty damn tight!'

I could already see the driver through the windscreen, his face red and bulging, frantically scratching all over as though plagued by a full-body allergy. Was there such a thing? And what had caused it? Perhaps the bananas that were being greedily consumed at lightning speed. Was I even visible through these swollen eyes? And if so, had the driver, who was very busy with all the eating, even noticed me? What terrible thing had caused this manic behaviour?

In only a few seconds this vehicle would run me down. It was no real comfort to me that I'd at least have immediate access to medical assistance.

Then I heard that terrible screeching of the blazing apocalyptic horses of hell above me. I looked up, saw the horsemen that were now gathering in the sky, and managed to catch a brief glimpse of their faces. For a moment, I thought I recognised them... no, surely not!

Just the thought that my eyes had not deceived me sent such shockwaves running through my body that the connection between my brain and legs was restored. The latter now heard my brain's command: 'Run! Or else cellulite will be the least of your problems!' My leg muscles tightened, preparing to bolt; the vehicle was only a few metres away now, and instead of breaking, the driver was chomping on a bag of hazelnuts, resulting in facial swelling. I ran, as far as I could, which was less than two metres. The vehicle now completely lost control and hit a lamppost, not more than a foot away from me.

I got up, which was painful, as I had grazes on my legs. As soon as I'd recovered from my initial shock, I looked into the vehicle. The driver was unscathed, at least by the accident. Other than that, the allergic boils and the manic scratching meant that not even the Elephant Man would have wanted to be seen in public with him.

I hoped that Joshua would reach the driver soon, and hobbled off towards the ice cream parlour. I had to know whether my family – and yes, Svetlana and her daughter now somehow belonged to it – were in danger. I avoided a woman who was stamping on her husband's private parts yelling: 'You'll be sterile in a minute!'

I was pleased that the most aggressive people didn't seem to be interested in me – they were far too busy with their own battles. It was a minor miracle that no one had died yet, and probably only a matter of time. Then a man in his mid-fifties stood right in front of me and said: 'I'm most keen on twenty-year-olds...'

'Well then you're quite obviously too late with me,' I answered, trying to get past him. But he blocked my way.

'...but I can't ensnare those.'

'Ensnare?'

'But you're pretty pert too,' he ascertained and drool began flowing out of the corner of his mouth.

'Nothing like you then,' I replied, making a renewed attempt to get past him. But again he blocked my path.

'I like the chubby ones too,' he explained and took hold of me. I didn't know what made me more angry – this guy putting his hands on me or that he'd called me 'chubby'.

I kicked him in the shin. He cried out in pain and I ran off as quickly as my tortured feet and flayed legs would carry me. Fortunately that old codger was pretty slow, and so our pursuit race through the blazing high street was probably one of the slowest in the history of disaster zones. In the end, the man was apprehended by two Jehovah's Witnesses, who wanted to talk to him at length about God, and no longer accepted 'No, thank you' as an answer.

I carried on running towards the ice-cream parlour, where the two little girls were fighting each other outside in the pile of sand, scratching and biting, because Lilliana desperately wanted her friend's lipgloss. This didn't bother mummy Svetlana as she was far too busy going at men at random with a broken Pellegrino bottle – she probably regarded each one as a potential punter – whilst my father was trying to strangle my mother screaming, 'I was miserable for twenty years because of you!' I was just about to try and separate them when I saw Gabriel standing on the roof of the four-storey building opposite. He was a person, but something had brought out an insatiable longing within him to fly again, even though he was lacking wings. I didn't know where to intervene first; the brawling children, the crazed Svetlana, my strangling Dad or the potential grease spot. Then Joshua arrived and made the decision for me. He convinced Gabriel with calm words to step away from the guttering on the roof, assuaged my father's and Svetlana's anger by placing his hand on them and managed to get the two girls to share the lipgloss in a sisterly way: 'Lay not up for yourselves treasures on this earth… For where your treasure is, there will your heart be also.'

As he said that, his eyes were filled with love for the people. And I suddenly realised what Mary Magdalene must have said to him. It must have been…

'You really do take ages!'

No, those were not the words.

'Can you please call the heavenly host of yours so that we can get going?'

Of course she hadn't said that either.

I turned around, and at the table I saw a woman happily slurping on her espresso, looking at Joshua sneeringly. She looked like Alicia Keys, the one that Kata was so keen on. Kata? Had it really been her up there… No, it couldn't… it simply could not be!

'We haven't seen each other in ages, Jesus,' said the soul diva, who almost certainly was not a soul diva.

'The last time we met was in the Judean Desert, when you were trying to seduce me,' Joshua said to the woman.

'You were a pretty hard nut to crack,' Alicia grinned and, with a bang, transformed into a horrible red creature with horns and hooves that you might see in a puppet show created by Stephen King.

'Scotty?'

'Yes, Captain?'

'I'm quitting too.'

'What do you think about us both going into organic farming?'

'An excellent idea, Scotty. An excellent idea.'

My entirely body was shaking, my nose was filled with a pungent stench of sulphur, and the smoke stung my eyes, but Joshua didn't even bat an eyelid. Satan gestured for him to sit down at his table. But Joshua stood still, and just signalled to Gabriel to keep us all out of the way. My family, Svetlana and the children hastily followed the vicar, but I stood still. Gabriel ran towards me, touched my arm and wanted to drag me away, but I just said: 'I will not leave his side.'

Gabriel smiled proudly. 'I did you wrong.'

Then he led the others away as quickly as possible. But it didn't bother the blood-red Beelzebub. He was probably confident of the fact that he would get them in the end. He turned to Joshua and explained. 'It's time for you to fight. The war has begun.'

To illustrate his point he gestured at the high street, happily bringing the cup of espresso to his mouth with his hideous tail.

'I will not fight,' Jesus replied.

'You, you do not want enter into the final battle?' Perplexed, Satan put his espresso down.

'No,' Joshua said calmly but firmly.

'Are you doing another one of your "turn the other cheek" moves?' Satan tried to keep his countenance – there he'd been, hoping for a battle, and Joshua was refusing.

'I would call it something else, but your statement is correct,' Joshua confirmed.

Satan was unnerved. Maybe, I anxiously hoped, this would throw him off his tracks so much that he would call an end to this whole thing… where there was no opponent, there was no possibility of waging a war, was there?

But then Satan laughed maliciously, as only a King of Hell can laugh: 'If that's so, my dear Jesus, I will just have to destroy you without you putting up a fight.'

Oh dear, this 'turn the other' cheek thing didn't really seem to be working!

'*Come to me!*' Satan called into the sky, and the four horsemen sped down to us on their blazing horses. Now, as they approached, I recognised their faces... and one of the horsemen was the new vicar?

The next one was... Sven?

And then there was... *Kata*?

And the fourth horseman looked like me.

I didn't even bother asking myself why this might be. I'd run out of questions.

The horsemen scooted down from the sky towards the town centre, and their intentions were clear – they wanted to destroy Jesus.

The horsemen landed right in front of our feet. The horses snorted, and hellish fire came blazing out of their nostrils. In combination with the remaining smell of sulphur in the air following Satan's transformation, this created quite an unbearable stench. Sven and the new vicar were clearly eagerly anticipating the forthcoming slaughter; they were drunk with power. The one who looked like me, on the other hand, had cold, empty eyes, and since I knew the names of the four Horsemen of the Apocalypse and was able to draw some logical conclusions I sensed that this must be Death. The fact that Death looked very like me was, beyond any shadow of a doubt, a bad omen.

Yet my fear of dying was completely eclipsed by my sympathy for Kata. She sat on her blazing steed without scorching her bum. Her eyes were filled with sadness as she looked at me, whispering in a broken voice: 'He threatened me with having to suffer this tumour for all eternity... I'm not strong enough, to disobey... or to trick him... Forgive... me...'

There was nothing to forgive. I understood her. I was not

exactly easy to live according to the Sermon on the Mount if you were healthy, but if you were sick and a tumour was devouring your own body, you'd probably gladly sell your soul to the devil.

'I wouldn't be that strong either,' I said to Kata, and a very slight, hardly discernible sad smile crossed her mouth. She was grateful that I wasn't condemning her.

Satan stood between us. 'I hope that I'm not disturbing your sisterly chitter-chatter too much by ordering you to destroy Jesus now.'

'We'd be delighted to,' Sven said to Joshua.

'It's your own fault.' The gym-body vicar smiled at Joshua sadistically. 'If you'd given me as much power as Satan, I would never have changed sides. But you always left me alone. Even when the lifeguard at the swimming pool told me that I was an eyesore in front of that group of Year 9 girls.'

Joshua didn't answer. His whole posture and determined expression showed no fear. That's probably how he stood in front of Pontius Pilate too.

While all the other horsemen focused on him, Death only had eyes for me. This was the kind of attention I could happily have done without.

Dennis and Sven now gave their supernatural powers free rein. I couldn't quite understand what they were doing, but they stretched their arms out towards Joshua and he briefly cried aloud, his whole body cramping up. Sometimes I saw wrath blazing in his eyes, hatred even, then desire, but he always managed to keep these feelings in check. This was something that certainly displeased Satan. His smug smile had disappeared. He then turned to Kata and shouted: 'Help them!'

My sister wanted to resist, but as she'd already said herself, she was too weak, and the fear of the eternal tumour caused her to direct her horse closer to Joshua. Suddenly all the old

252

wounds on his hands and feet started to bleed again. I didn't know what was more terrible – to see Joshua suffer, or watch Kata, as Pestilence, extending the pain she had suffered to another person. It was this pain that she so feared to suffer for all eternity. I had to stop her, for Joshua's sake, but also for hers. I stepped in between the horsemen and Joshua, who could hardly stand up and only just managed to stop himself from screaming out in pain with the last of his willpower.

'If you want Jesus,' I said to the horsemen, 'then you'll have to kill me first.'

I had some remaining hope that Sven and Kata still had enough feelings for me that they'd let us go. Joshua made a weak hand gesture – he could no longer speak, his inner battle was too terrible – but the gesture was clear. He wanted me to flee. He did not want me to sacrifice myself for him. But I stood still.

Kata manoeuvred her steed back a few steps – she did not want to punish me with terrible diseases. Her love for me at this moment was greater than her fear.

'Fight!' Satan commanded her.

She just shook her head. In the end he didn't have that much power over her. For her love for me was stronger than her fear. In her own way she'd therefore managed to trick Satan after all.

This was certainly not to his liking. He pointed at Sven with his curly tail. He was no longer able to defy Satan's power, and didn't want to for that matter. His hatred had eaten him up a long time ago. 'OK,' he said to me, 'killing you will fit into my plans very nicely.'

When Kata heard this, her whole body started shaking. Joshua was also suffering, but he was powerless. Thanks to the horsemen he was fighting his inner demons, which reside in every human being. And a cold smile was stretched across the face of the one who looked like me. I knew that I was going to die now. I had no fear. Only anger. At God. Because Kata was suffering. And Joshua too. And because they would suffer even more if I were to die now.

So I angrily shouted into the sky: '*Eli, Eli, patika sabati!*'

And I got this answer

THAT MEANS, MY GOD, MY GOD, MY MEATBALL IS INFERTILE.

The scenery all around me suddenly froze, as though someone had taken a still frame. Everyone had stopped moving and stood like statues. The satanic beast had an angry look on his face, Jesus was bent double with pain, the fire that was flicking out of the nostrils of the horses was hanging in the air, frozen in time, and even Kata was no longer shaking. Nobody did a thing – no one was shouting because of pain, greed or aggression. Suddenly, everything was peaceful.

Very calm.

The only thing that could still be heard were the sizzling flames of the burning thorn bush, which had appeared next to me out of nothing.

'*Eli, eli, intesti, sabalili!*' I shouted at him accusingly, hoping to have found the right words this time.

AND THAT MEANS: MY GOD, MY GOD, MY BOWELS ARE DOING HEAVY LABOUR.

'You know exactly what I mean!' I yelled, wishing that I could spray a whole cylinder of foam extinguisher on his leaves.

FORGIVE ME,

the bush answered, and immediately turned into Emma Thompson, who instead of wearing an eighteenth century dress was just wearing some H&M stuff. God didn't seem the type of woman who was into expensive designer labels.

'I did not forsake you. I do not forsake anyone,' Emma/God replied.

'Yeah, I can see that from looking at your son,' I countered, trembling with rage.

Emma/God looked compassionately, even pityingly at Joshua, who was standing there as if frozen, his face distorted with pain. Then she said: 'My son does not want the Day of Judgement.'

'If you want to blame me for instigating this, then please go ahead! I'm actually proud of myself!'

'The blame? Well, you are responsible for it,' Emma/God stated in a calm tone of voice.

'You can turn me into a pillar of salt if you want; you seem to enjoy doing that,' I scolded.

'And why would I do that?'

The question surprised me and took a little steam out of me: 'Because… because I messed it all up…'

'Yes, you have.'

'But?'

'You did it out of love.'

Her wonderful, benevolent smile really did dissipate my anger.

'Yes, I did…' I confirmed.

Her smile became even more benevolent, more wonderful, and then Emma/God said to me: 'How could I punish you for that? There is nothing that could make me more proud.'

I stood there, completely dumbfounded. Emma/God turned around and where she looked, the world healed. The frozen people stopped bleeding, flames and smoke dispersed, and the charred houses were as new again, as were the ambulance and the lamppost. Even the paramedic looked like a completely normal person again. Emma/God looked at Satan and the blazing steeds, and they vanished into thin air. And so did Death, which greatly relieved me. Kata, Sven and the gym-body vicar were now sitting at a table at the ice cream parlour in a very civilised manner, and the high street looked just like a normal high street again, if you disregarded the fact that all the people still looked as though they were frozen, including Joshua. Emma/God stroked his hair with her hand, and then he disappeared.

'Will I ever see him again?' I asked fearfully.

'That depends on him,' Emma/God answered, and I felt that she wanted to disappear now too.

'I have one more thing to ask.'

'Ask.'

'Why tumours?'

'Or periods?' Emma/God smiled.

I nodded.

'Without birth and death there is no life.'

I added, 'Well yes, but can't you make it a bit more pleasant…?' but she'd already gone.

A moment later, the high street was once again full of life, as though nothing had ever happened. People were no longer marauding through the streets. They were shopping, and no longer smashing the shop windows. Everyone seemed to have entirely forgotten about what had happened. Almost everyone. The former human Horsemen of the Apocalypse looked at me guilt-ridden and full of shame. I couldn't have cared less about Sven and the vicar, but not…

'Kata…'

I approached her, but she got up and ran away. She couldn't bear to look at me. I wanted to run after her, but Gabriel, who

257

had approached me, stopped me. 'Give her some time. She needs to process all of this.'

I nodded. The retired angel was right. He also recalled what had happened and presented the theory that all those who had been touched by the supernatural would never forget about it.

'But… why did God cancel the Day of Judgement?'

'There are just two explanations for that,' Gabriel answered. 'Either this was always planned as a trial by God, as with Abraham and Job…'

'Abraham and Job?' I asked.

'In the end, Abraham was not forced to sacrifice his son, even though he thought that it was God's will. But it turned out just to be a test. And Job, who underwent all this suffering that God had bestowed upon him, was also tested by the Almighty. In the end he was cured of his illness and allowed to have a family once again.'

'I'm missing the connection…' I said sounding confused.

'Maybe,' Gabriel replied, 'the Day of Judgement and this prophecy of the Book of Revelation were just a chimera, and never meant seriously, just to find out what potential humanity has. And on this occasion, the chosen one for this test was not Abraham, not Job, but you, Marie.'

I still didn't really get it.

'Your love convinced God of the people.'

I took a deep breath, and Gabriel started grinning: 'You, like a biblical character… who'd have thought it?'

His theory, that everything – the Day of Judgement, my encounter with Joshua, tea time with God – had just been a test for humanity with me as an exemplary representative, made me feel very anxious. So I asked: 'And… what's the other possible explanation.'

'You were just damn lucky.'

Yet I wasn't feeling particularly lucky, if luck is really all it was, because Joshua wasn't with me. Would he ever even want to see me again? I said goodbye to Gabriel and went to our favourite spot by the lake, not feeling particularly hopeful. But then something incredible happened – Joshua was sitting on the pier, looking out onto the water, with the sun shining down on it peacefully. I was endlessly happy to see him. I sat down beside him and let my feet dangle down over the water next to his. After we'd been sitting there in silence for a while, he said: 'I have spoken to God.'

I could have asked whether Gabriel's theory was correct and I really was a quasi-biblical crash test dummy, but there was another thing that was much more important to me: 'Is he allowing us…' I began, only to stop talking again, because I was far too afraid of hearing the answer. I would have loved to suggest to Joshua not to say a word and to spend the next centuries just sitting next to me on the pier.

'He is leaving our future up to our own free will,' Joshua explained.

'You… you… you… me?

'Yes, you and me, if that's what we want.'

'You… you… you… ?' I now asked Joshua about his free will.

'Yes.'

It was simply unbelievable.

He grabbed my hand. Just as his fingers touched mine, he said: 'I will become mortal like Gabriel.'

'Mortal?' I asked sounding puzzled.

'I will return to earth as a mortal human being and live my life until my earthly death.'

He was really prepared to give up everything for me, even his immortality. That was seriously romantic. The greatest thing that a man had ever wanted to do for me.

But I still didn't like the sound of it.

'Is that dying bit really necessary…?' I demanded, and pulled my hand away again.

'Yes, that's the only way I can age,' Joshua explained. 'Imagine if you were seventy-nine and I was still as old as I am now…'

'Then I'd have a younger man. What's wrong with that?'

'But that's the only way we can live a normal life, have children and start a family.'

'A family…' I sighed longingly.

'And I will provide for them as a carpenter.'

I didn't know whether a carpenter's wages would be enough for a family; that probably depended quite a lot on the state of the building sector, but I could work as well of course. And if it was his free will to become mortal, then who was I to deny him that?

At that very moment a conker hit me on the head. It came from the direction of the lake. To be precise, it came from a pedalo that Svetlana's little girl and her friend were riding in. The girls were now both wearing lipgloss, and laughing hysterically. I really had a hard time thinking they were cute. But Joshua smiled at them, and that reminded me of the inferno again, and how he'd helped these little girls and how that had made me realise what Mary Magdalene must have said to him back then.

Deeply saddened, I looked at Joshua.

'What's the matter with you?' he asked, and for the first time ever, I thought I heard a hint of fear in his otherwise strong voice.

Quietly I whispered: 'Our free will needs to decide against us…'

'Now you sound even more muddled than the Demoniac of Gadara,' Joshua said, trembling slightly. It was terrible to see him tremble.

'What did Mary Magdalene say to you about why you were not allowed to live out your love?' I asked.

He remained silent for a while, stopped trembling and finally answered wistfully, 'Because my love needs to belong to everyone.'

'And that's why you're never allowed to die,' I whispered, so quietly that my voice was almost scarcely audible. 'And you can't stay with me.'

He didn't even reply to that. Because I was right. Or rather, Mary Magdalene was right.

It is never nice when you realise that the ex was smarter than you.

Joshua no longer fought for a shared future with him as a carpenter. His free will followed his destiny. And he decided against us.

And my free will fell into line with his.

Sometimes it is just no fun agreeing on things.

We sat there silently, gazing out onto the lake one last time. I fought back my tears, which were ready to flow. I succeeded with most of them, but the odd cheeky, annoying, stupid tear did come out of my eye and trickled down my face.

Joshua touched my cheek with his hand and gently and tenderly kissed my tear away.

I stopped crying.

With that kiss he had taken away my sorrow. Just like he's taken away little Lilliana's epilepsy.

Jesus stroked my cheek and said: 'I love you.'

Then he vanished into thin air – this amazing summery air.

And I was left alone on the pier.

No man had ever left me quite so wonderfully.

CHAPTER FORTY-FOUR

Meanwhile...

Emma Thompson and George Clooney sat on the bench by the lake and fed the ducks. Every time that one of them ate one of Clooney's poisoned bits of bread, Emma brought the animal back to life, which greatly frustrated Clooney. But it annoyed him even more that he had clearly only been a variable in God's test.

'So,' Clooney finally asked, as he noticed that he was even losing the battle for the ducks, 'the Day of Judgement is no longer going to occur?'

'Humanity has grown up,' Emma answered.

'But it's far from perfect.'

'Well, are any grown-ups?' Emma smiled.

Clooney was not able to smile as well. He'd been so focused on the final battle his whole existence. His raison d'être had suddenly disappeared. This is how it must feel to be unemployed and willing to sell your soul for a new life.

'You will get what you hoped for most of all,' Emma said, trying to cheer him up.

'A free will?' Satan hardly dared to hope.

'Yes, you can now travel to that lonely desert island, like you always wanted.'

Clooney smiled with relief. He was now able to live alone and no longer needed to bother with annoying sinners. God had just handed him his very own personal Kingdom of Heaven.

'Can I...?' he began.

'No, you can't take the artist with you.'

Clooney bit his lip for a short while, before he shrugged his shoulders and said: 'You can't have it all', and went on his way without even saying thank you. He would be flying to the South Seas with the Learjet that belonged to the Governor of California.

While Satan disappeared, Jesus was walking along the path by the lake and sat down next to Emma Thompson on the bench.

'And you, my Son, are you coming back to be with me in the Kingdom of Heaven?'

'No,' Joshua answered emphatically.

'You're staying with Marie?' Emma was surprised, but not angry. Jesus could do what he liked with his free will.

'I will not be doing that either. But thanks to her, I know what I have to do.'

'And what's that going to be?' Emma was really rather intrigued now.

'I will travel the world.'

'And will you ever see Marie again?'

'Yes, I will,' Jesus said wistfully. 'I will come back here every now and again, without her knowing, to see whether she is all right… and her children… and her grandchildren.'

'And her great-grandchildren?' Emma asked with a smile.

'And their children,' Jesus smiled back.

CHAPTER FORTY-FIVE

I stood on the pier for quite a while, staring out onto the water, filled with inner peace. I didn't feel any heartache. Joshua's loving kiss really had made sure that I no longer needed to suffer, and that I would be free to fall in love again with someone in this life. It was not until the sun had set that I picked myself up and headed home. Once I'd got half way, that mundane but urgent 'I need to pee' feeling really came to the forefront of my mind. As I had a rather ambivalent attitude towards bushes these days, I went to Michi's video store. He obviously wanted to know what had happened, and I told him, through the toilet door, that next Tuesday was no longer the appointed date for the end of the world.

'That's fantastic!' Michi cheered full of relief.

But there was still that thing of him being in love with me that stood between us. So, once I'd washed my hands and came to join him at the counter, I asked: 'So what's Julian Styles going to do with this newly won time?'

'Good old Julian,' Michi replied, 'has realised that life can come to an end at any moment.'

'And?'

'He therefore no longer wants to pine for a love that will never be, and intends to sign up to every available online dating site. Except maybe s-and-m.com.'

'Julian is a pretty smart guy,' I declared.

'I never said anything else,' Michi replied, grinning. I was just happy that we were able to continue our platonic friendship.

When I got home, Kata was sitting in the garden under a nice, shaded tree, drawing in the last of the day's daylight. I sat down next to her. She looked sad and said: 'I am no heroine.'

'You are to me,' I replied.

'I followed him.'

'Not all the way…'

'I should have resisted him completely… but I'm not as strong on my own as I had always thought, otherwise I might have managed it…'

Kata seemed very fragile now.

'…but I don't want to be on my own any more, I need someone…'

My sister needed me. Just like I needed her.

'Are you going to stay around in Malente a while?' I wanted to know.

'Why are you asking?'

'It's better if I stay with you, until you feel better again,' I explained.

'The entire hundred years?' she asked gloomily.

'As long as it takes,' I grinned.

Then she hugged me.

'You're crushing me,' I groaned.

'Yes. That's my intention!'

Then I hugged her back. After all the madness, it was nice to feel something resembling peace in her arms again.

'Scotty?'

'Yes, Captain?'

'I love our organic farm.'

'So do I, Captain. So do I.'

When Kata and I had finally finished hugging each other, she showed me her sketchpad with her latest comic strip.

'It says "The End" on it,' I said in a surprised tone.

'Well it's the last strip that I'm doing for my "Sisters" series,' Kata explained.

'The last one?'

'I'm someone else now,' she smiled. 'And so are you.'

Kata was right. I had made peace with my parents and had even found the courage to speak up against God and confront Satan. I'd discovered I was capable of all sorts of things.

I was no longer a M.O.N.S.T.E.R.

And all just because I'd fallen in love.

Special thanks go to Ulrike Beck, who always believed in the project, Marcus Gärtner, Marcus Hertneck and Michael Töteberg, the best agents in this and any other universe.

BIOGRAPHICAL
NOTE

David Safier was born in 1966 and is one of the most well-known and successful German scriptwriters. After training as a journalist, he turned to writing scripts in 1996, landing a number of hit TV series, including *Berlin, Berlin*, for which he won the 2003 Grimme Prize and an International Emmy. He lives and works in Bremen. His novels *Lousy Karma* and *Apocalypse Next Tuesday* were on the German bestseller lists for months.

HESPERUS PRESS

Under our three imprints, Hesperus Press publishes over 300 books by many of the greatest figures in worldwide literary history, as well as contemporary and debut authors well worth discovering.

HESPERUS CLASSICS

handpicks the best of worldwide and translated literature, introducing forgotten and neglected books to new generations.

HESPERUS NOVA

showcases quality contemporary fiction and non-fiction designed to entertain and inspire.

HESPERUS MINOR

rediscovers well-loved children's books from the past – these are books which will bring back fond memories for adults, which they will want to share with their children and loved ones.

To find out more visit www.hesperuspress.com
@HesperusPress